X

THE
KENNEDY
CONNECTION

ALSO BY R. G. BELSKY

Loverboy
Playing Dead

THE
KENNEDY
CONNECTION

A Gil Malloy Novel

R. G. BELSKY

ATRIA PAPERBACK

New York London Toronto Sydney New Delhi

ATRIA PAPERBACK
A Division of Simon & Schuster, Inc.
1230 Avenue of the Americas
New York, NY 10020

First Atria Paperback edition August 2014

ATRIA PAPERBACK and colophon are trademarks of Simon & Schuster, Inc.

For information about special discounts for bulk purchases, please
contact Simon & Schuster Special Sales at 1-866-506-1949 or
business@simonandschuster.com.

The Simon & Schuster Speakers Bureau can bring authors to your
live event. For more information or to book an event, contact the
Simon & Schuster Speakers Bureau at 1-866-248-3049 or
visit our website at www.simonspeakers.com.

Manufactured in the United States of America

10 9 8 7 6 5 4 3 2 1

Library of Congress Cataloging-in-Publication Data

Belsky, Richard.
    The Kennedy connection : a Gil Malloy novel / R. G. Belsky.
        pages cm
1. Journalists—Fiction. 2. Kennedy, John F. (John Fitzgerald), 1917–1963—
Assassination—Fiction. 3. Oswald, Lee Harvey—Family—Fiction.
4. Assassins—Fiction. 5. Murder—Investigation—Fiction. I. Title.
  PS3552.E53385K36 2014
  813'.54—dc23
                                                    2013047387

ISBN 978-1-4767-6232-6
ISBN 978-1-4767-6233-3 (ebook)

PROLOGUE

The most important thing a journalist has is his integrity.

An old newspaperman taught me that. He said it was the one constant, inviolate truth to remember about this business. More important than all the scoops, the bylines, or the number of press awards you won. "If you ever compromise your integrity, Malloy," he told me, "you are lost." I believed that then, and I believe it now.

There's something else that I have learned. Integrity is an absolute value. You can't lose a little bit of your integrity any more than you can be a little bit pregnant. You're either all in or all out on the integrity issue. And once you've crossed over that irrevocable moral line, you can never go back. No matter how hard you try.

I think about all of this a lot these days. Mostly late at night when I lie awake, replaying all of the events that got me to where I am.

And trying to make some sort of sense out of the incongruity of it all.

The most important thing a journalist has is his integrity.

I lost my integrity somewhere along the way.

And yet I am still a journalist.

So what does that say about me?

PART ONE

THE MAGIC BULLET

We've come to know it as the "magic bullet" theory.

The magic bullet enters the President's back, headed downward at an angle of 17 degrees.

It then moves upwards in order to leave Kennedy's body from the front of his neck—wound number two—where it waits 1.6 seconds, presumably in midair, where it turns right, then left, right, then left and continues into Connally's body at the rear of his right armpit—wound number three.

The bullet then heads downward at an angle of 27 degrees, shattering Connally's fifth rib and exiting from the right side of his chest—wound number four.

The bullet then turns right and re-enters Connally's body at his right wrist—wound number five.

Shattering the radius bone, the bullet then exits Connally's wrist—wound number six—makes a dramatic U-turn and buries itself into Connally's left thigh—wound number seven—from which it later falls out and is found in almost pristine condition on a stretcher in a corridor of Parkland Hospital.

That's some bullet.

—From the movie *JFK*

Death is the great equalizer.

—William Shakespeare, *Hamlet*

CHAPTER 1

MET NIKKI REYNOLDS for lunch on a summer afternoon in New York City.

We were sitting at an outdoor table of a restaurant called Gotham City, on Park Avenue South in the East 20s. The pasta she ordered cost $33. My hamburger was $26.50. The prices weren't on the menu, though. It was the kind of place where if you had to ask the price, you didn't belong there. Me, I didn't care how much the lunch cost. Nikki Reynolds was paying.

Reynolds was a New York literary agent. In another lifetime, when I'd needed a literary agent, she'd been mine. But I hadn't heard from her in a long time. So I was surprised when she called me up out of the blue and invited me to lunch.

"I suppose you're wondering why I wanted to talk to you today," she said.

"Why?" I asked.

I always like to ask the tough questions first.

"I have an author with a new book—a nonfiction blockbuster about the John F. Kennedy assassination—that's going to make big news," she told me. "It's very timely too, coming right after all the attention everyone paid to the fiftieth anniversary of the JFK killing."

"Timely," I said.

"The basic concept of the book is that more than a half century later, we still haven't solved the greatest crime in our history. It's called *The Kennedy Connection*. Catchy title, huh?"

"Catchy," I agreed.

"The book will reveal shocking new information about what really happened that day in Dallas and afterward."

"Wait a minute, let me guess," I said. "Lee Harvey Oswald didn't really do it, JFK really isn't dead, and both of them are living secretly somewhere right now with Jim Morrison and Elvis."

Reynolds sighed. "You know, everyone told me, 'Don't take this to Gil Malloy. He's a smart-ass, he's an arrogant, sarcastic son of a bitch—hell, he's pretty much of an all-around pain in the ass.' I keep trying to defend you, Gil. But that's getting harder and harder to do."

"Some days I guess I just wake up kind of cranky," I shrugged.

Nikki Reynolds was somewhere in her fifties, but plastic surgery and Botox had taken about ten years of that off of her face. Blond, pixie hair and a tight, trim body from lots of workouts at the health club. She was wearing a navy blue pin-striped pantsuit, a pink silk blouse open at the collar, and oversized sunglasses that probably cost more than the meal we were eating. The Manhattan power broker look. She looked like she belonged at Gotham City.

I had on blue jeans, a white T-shirt that I'd washed specially for the occasion, and a New York Mets baseball cap. No one else in the restaurant was wearing blue jeans. Or a T-shirt or a baseball cap. When I'd walked in, someone at one of the tables had mistaken me for a busboy. I had a feeling—call it a crazy hunch—that I might be a tad underdressed for this place.

"Who's the author?" I asked.

"Lee Harvey Oswald."

I smiled. "Right."

"No, I'm serious."

"Lee Harvey Oswald is alive and a client of yours?"

"Lee Harvey Oswald Jr."

"He had a son?"

"Yes."

I thought about that for a second.

"I don't remember anything about Lee Harvey Oswald having a son. Didn't he have a baby daughter or something with that Russian woman he married?"

"Oswald had two daughters with Marina, whom he married while he was living in the Soviet Union. One of them there before he returned to the U.S. Another baby girl that Marina gave birth to just a few weeks before the assassination. There's never been any mention of a son. Until now."

"I don't understand . . ."

"Lee Harvey Oswald had an affair. In New Orleans where he lived in the months before he went to Dallas."

"So you're saying ol' Lee Harvey was as much of a horndog as JFK, huh?" I laughed.

"The mother was a twenty-one-year-old girl who died less than a year after the assassination. The baby boy wound up being adopted. For much of his life he's been haunted by uncertainty over what his infamous father did or didn't do on that day in Dallas where Kennedy was killed. He finally decided to try to find out the truth. That's why he's written this book."

I took a bite of my hamburger. It was okay but nothing special. At these prices? Actually, I've had better at McDonald's.

"I'm sure you have a lot of questions," Reynolds said.

"Just one, really."

"Go ahead."

"Why me?"

"You're a newspaper reporter. I want to get some advance publicity, build up some word of mouth before the book comes out. I figured if you wrote a story now—"

"Nikki, there's lots of newspaper reporters in this town. You could have picked any of them to talk to about all of this. Why me?"

Nikki Reynolds put her fork down and pushed her still almost full plate of pasta away. She didn't seem to like it any more than I did my hamburger. Maybe we could both stop at a McDonald's later for a snack.

"I think I know the answer," I said. "I'm the only reporter in town gullible enough to fall for something like this. Maybe you wanted to go to some other reporter. Someone with a better track record than me. But, in the end, you figured Gil Malloy—whom you haven't talked to, haven't taken phone calls from, and couldn't even be bothered to return messages from in a very long time— was your best choice. Because he's easy. He doesn't ask a lot of questions or dig very deep or spend too much time making sure a story is true. Hell, you can buy him off with a lunch."

"C'mon, Gil . . ."

"The only problem with your plan is that the same reason you figured I might go for it . . . well, that's why I couldn't be of any help to you, even if I wanted to. No one is going to believe me if I start talking about someone claiming to be Lee Harvey Oswald's secret son and solving the Kennedy assassination. People—people at my own newspaper—would say, 'What's next? He's going to claim he saw Elvis at a shopping mall? Or reveal those flying saucers and little green men that the government is really hiding at Area 51?' Hey, I'm damaged goods, Nikki. You should know that better than anyone."

There was a long, uncomfortable silence between us. I sat there waiting, watching people go by on the street and listening to the sounds of the city. Horns honking. Car doors slamming. A radio turned up somewhere to a rap station. It was the middle of summer, and a lot of New Yorkers had already fled to the Hamptons, the mountains, or the Jersey Shore. In another few weeks, the city would be empty, which was fine with me. I remembered sitting at a restaurant just like this one a long time ago with Nikki Reynolds. Listening to her tell me how she was going to make me rich and famous. I'd believed her. That was before I found out that fame and fortune aren't all they're cracked up to be, as Bob Dylan once said.

"I'm sorry I never returned your phone calls after . . . well, you know," she said finally.

"Don't worry about it. Lots of people didn't return my phone calls. Everyone wanted to keep their distance from me."

"But I'm here now."

"And bought me this lunch," I pointed out.

"This could be a big story for you."

"I'm already working on a story."

"We're talking about John F. Kennedy's murder here."

"Mine's a murder story too."

"Bigger than JFK?"

"Big enough."

"What's the story?"

"The murder of Victor Reyes."

"Who's that?"

"A kid who belonged to a gang in the South Bronx."

"Who killed him?"

"Probably someone from another gang."

"Are you telling me that chasing after some cheap gangbang

murder in the Bronx is more important to you than maybe finding out the truth about the assassination of John F. Kennedy? The biggest unsolved crime of our lifetime. Maybe of all time. How can you even compare a murder of that magnitude to the killing of this Vincent Reyes?"

"Victor."

"Excuse me."

"His name was Victor Reyes, not Vincent."

"Who the hell cares?"

"Everyone matters," I said, quoting something I'd read in a book once. Not because I really believed it, but because I couldn't think of any way to explain my decision to someone like Nikki Reynolds.

She wrote down Lee Harvey Oswald Jr.'s address and phone number on a piece of paper and handed it across the table to me. I looked down at the paper, shrugged, and stuck it in the pocket of my jeans.

"I really need your help on this," Reynolds said.

"Have you checked out this guy's story about being Lee Harvey Oswald's illegitimate son?" I asked.

"Of course, I have."

"And?"

"Well, it's not easy to find out about records from fifty years ago, but I'm pursuing it vigorously."

I shook my head.

"Who's the publisher that bought this book?"

"We don't have a publisher yet."

"Has he written the damn book?"

"He's working on it . . ."

"So you have a guy who may or may not be Lee Harvey Oswald Jr., who may or may not have a book, and—even if he finishes this supposed book—you don't have a publisher at the moment. And now you're asking me to put whatever few shreds are left of my professional reputation on the line to promote this for you. Does that pretty much sum up the situation here, or have I left anything out?"

She reached over and put her hand on top of mine. She looked me straight in the eye.

Earnest. Sincere. Pleading, almost desperate.

"Do it as a favor for me," Nikki Reynolds said. "Do it as a favor to me for old times' sake."

It was a helluva performance. She was always very good at getting people to do what she wanted. Except I'd seen it all before.

"I gotta tell you, Nikki," I said, "the old times weren't that great."

CHAPTER 2

T HE *New York Daily News*, the newspaper where I work, is located at the lower end of Manhattan, close to where the Staten Island Ferry docks. That's about as far south as you can go in Manhattan without falling into the water. It's only four miles away from Times Square, but it feels like four million.

When I was growing up, I used to dream about working at the *Daily News* one day. It all seemed so romantic and so glamorous and so right back then. The *News* office in those days was on 42nd Street in the heart of Manhattan. The building was the same one they used for the *Daily Planet* in the Superman movies. In fact, a lot of people used to think that the *Daily Planet* and Metropolis from the old TV show and the comic books were based on the *Daily News* in New York. I would watch Clark Kent on the screen and imagine it was me fighting for truth, justice, and the American way. I didn't have superpowers like he did, but I was a helluva reporter. And a helluva reporter could accomplish anything. Overcome any obstacle. Right any wrong. I really believed that once.

By the time I got to the *Daily News*, the legendary 42nd Street office was already gone, a victim of the realities of the Manhattan real estate market during the mid-'90s. But the dream was still alive and kicking for me. In my senior year at NYU, I wangled an internship to work at the *News*. I was supposed to be there only ten hours a week, while at the same time attending regular classes. I worked sixty–seventy hours a week. Needless to say, I didn't spend much time in class that last year.

After NYU, I got a full-time job as a reporter at the *News*. I started out at the bottom, of course. Running around to press conferences and meetings and crime scenes, then calling the details in to a rewrite man in the *News* office. Eventually, I was transferred to the Bronx borough office. I was given the education beat there. The borough staffs covered local community news, which was the least desirable place to work. And of all the boroughs the *Daily News* covered, the Bronx was considered the worst office to be assigned. Plus, the education beat in a borough was by far the least desirable assignment any reporter could have. I didn't care. I still thought I was Superman. I thought I could do anything. And that was pretty much what I did. I broke a big education story about corruption in a Bronx school board fund that got several people indicted and later sent to jail. I did a series on best and worst teachers in the borough that won me and the paper all sorts of awards. I exposed overcrowding in the classroom, shortages of textbooks and other equipment, and unhealthy conditions in school cafeterias on my beat. I also wrote about the exceptional students who were able to rise above all this and somehow achieve an education in a school system out of control.

Many of my stories were making the front of the paper. Sometimes even the front page. I was a rising star. It was only a matter of time until I'd get promoted out of the Bronx into the main newsroom in Manhattan. Six months, a year tops, I figured.

And then 9/11 changed everything. I was headed for a press conference in the Bronx about reading scores when the first plane hit the North Tower of the World Trade Center on that unimaginable morning of September 11, 2001. I turned around and raced to get to the scene. By the time both towers went down, I had filed reams of copy to the city desk, trying to capture the horror and the devastation and the enormity of the losses that terrible day. I was so close that I was literally covered in ashes and debris from the towers. I stayed there all day, then the next day, and the weeks after covering the grim search for bodies and for answers. I hardly changed clothes, I didn't shave most days, I even slept at Ground Zero a lot of the time. It was the biggest story of my life, and I didn't want to let go—not even for a few hours. I would win awards for my coverage. I would get promoted at the *News.* I would get more money from the paper. But I wasn't thinking about any of these things when I spent all those days and nights in lower Manhattan. I was just thinking about covering the story.

More big stories followed in the years after that. I got an exclusive interview with the mistress of a disgraced politician. I broke the news of a terrorist plot against the New York City subway system that was foiled by the NYPD and Homeland Security officials. I did a series of articles revealing how millions of taxpayer dollars were being wasted on personal use and pet projects by the City Council.

Eventually, the *Daily News* gave me my own column. It would run up front in the paper three days a week. My own column. Just like Jimmy Breslin once had in the *News.* Or Pete Hamill. Now it was Gil Malloy. I was really on my way to the top now. Hell, I was probably already there.

And then, just as easily as everything went right for me, it all fell apart extraordinarily quickly.

It wasn't supposed to have happened that way. In fact, the story that led to my downfall was supposed to be my biggest triumph. My shining moment as a reporter. The story that would define me as a journalist. And, in the end, I guess that's exactly what it did. Just not in the way I had anticipated.

It was a massive investigative series that ran in the *News* about prostitution in New York City. I wanted to do an in-depth look at the problem of prostitution and its impact on everyone involved, as well as the people around them. I talked to madams, prostitutes, johns, and law enforcement officials. I took a look at the trade from the streetwalkers near Times Square to the high-end hookers who worked out of expensive escort agencies. The governor of New York had been forced to resign after being linked with a high-priced hooker. I thought it was a great peg for a series on prostitution and all of its aspects on the New York scene. My editors thought so too.

The highlight of the series was a young woman who called herself Houston. Houston got her name from the street in downtown Manhattan where she'd first plied her trade. By the time I did my series, she was working on call for high rollers at hotels and expensive apartments around Manhattan. She had become quite a legend in the world of call girls. Men clamored for her services, and she truly seemed to enjoy her work. One of her specialties was the Houston Hello. She named it after the famous Brentwood Hello that the women in the O. J. Simpson case used to call a blow job. She also offered the Houston Hero Sandwich—her and another girl—and the Houston Honeymoon Special, which provided a bridal night fantasy beyond any man's wildest expectations. But there was a dark side to Houston too. She'd been attacked by clients, once almost fatally; beaten up by pimps; extorted for money and sex by cops; and battled drug and alcohol. Houston put a face on prostitution for the first time—she made us understand the people who were involved in this industry and the complexity of the issue of women who sell their bodies for a living. I didn't say that last part. The *Daily News* editorial board did when they submitted my series for a Pulitzer Prize.

Everyone wanted a piece of Houston. She became a tabloid sensation. Other newspapers searched for her. TV stations too. Network shows like *Dateline* and *60 Minutes*—and even *Oprah*—were desperate for an interview. Book publishers threw big-money offers at me to write about her story. There was even talk of a movie deal. That was when I first met Nikki Reynolds. She pursued me relentlessly after the series came out. Took me to lunch at "21," for drinks at Elaine's, and then eventually back to her penthouse apartment on Central Park West where we made love through the night. I remember lying in her bed early the next morning, watching the sun come up over Central Park outside her window, and thinking about how perfect everything in my life had turned out to be. This series had put me on the fast track of journalism. It had made me a star. It had given me everything I'd ever wanted—or at least everything I thought I wanted back then.

But in the end, the series was too good. Houston was too good. She became a monster I could no longer control. That's when the whole story began to fall apart. And my life along with it.

Because there was no Houston.

Or, if there was, I hadn't been able find her either, just like all the other news organizations now looking for her.

Everyone I'd talked to while I was working on my series had stories about Houston. She was a legend in the world of call girls and hookers and escort agencies that I was writing about. The more stories I heard about her, the more I knew she had to be the linchpin of my series. But I never could actually track her down. I talked to a lot of people who had met her, or at least claimed they had. And, I guess, after a while she became real to me too. I collected so many anecdotes and experiences from other prostitutes that were similar to the stories I'd heard about Houston. Some of them related stuff they'd heard about Houston to me. But I never found the ultimate prize. My white whale.

And so I took the anecdotes and incidents and quotes I had about Houston—along with stuff from the other women—and put them all into Houston's mouth. I didn't just write about Houston. I wrote about talking to her. I turned Houston into a real person. I created a fictional character, or at least one I wasn't sure really existed.

Maybe things had just moved too quickly and too easily for me. Maybe I thought things would always be that easy. Maybe I was so cocky and arrogant I thought I could do anything I wanted, that I was impervious to failure and was somehow above the rules other journalists needed to follow.

At first, when the questions about my story and about Houston started, I was able to deflect them all by claiming she was a confidential source and I had promised not to reveal her real identity or location to anyone, in return for allowing me to tell her story. Wrapping myself in journalistic principles like this to cover up my own lack of journalistic principles was something I was not proud of. But at that point I was just desperately hoping that the Houston controversy would go away.

It took a while for the truth to come out. But things began to unravel when the rival *New York Post* did a Page Six item speculating that the story could be a hoax because no one except me had found any evidence that Houston existed. A few of the local TV stations picked up on that. Then the *New York Times* did a long piece raising serious and sobering questions about my investigation, my answers to questions about it, and the facts—or lack of facts—about Houston. After the *Times* article was published, the Pulitzer committee announced it was dropping my series from consideration because of "troubling issues and inconsistencies" that had arisen following its submission.

For a while, my editors at the *Daily News* believed my denials that anything was wrong. Or at least they claimed to. They publicly stood by my story despite the growing skepticism from other media. But when they eventually demanded that I produce Houston for them as proof of the credibility of my investigation, the story quickly fell apart. I finally told them the truth. The paper tried to make the best of it in an announcement saying what I had practiced was a kind of "new journalism" in which I created a fictional character to tell a story that had been supported by other facts. But no matter how much you tried to sugarcoat it, there was no getting around what I had done. I had fiddled with the facts. I had made up an interview that never happened. I had crossed over that crucial line of integrity that no journalist can ever cross and survive. I had betrayed the public trust. I had screwed up, big time.

The next day the headline in the *New York Post* gleefully proclaimed: HOUSTON, WE HAVE A PROBLEM!

———

The *Daily News* could have fired me, should have fired me. But they didn't. I've never known exactly why, but I assume it had something to do with the paper's own internal damage control efforts. Firing me would have been admitting wrongdoing—or at least editorial malfeasance—on their part. Or maybe they just felt compassion for me, feared I'd jump off of the Brooklyn Bridge or something if I lost my job. For whatever reason, I still worked at the *News*.

Not as a columnist anymore, though. No, far from it.

I was the low man on the totem pole in the newsroom now. Right down there where I started as an intern. Busted back to being a reporter, I had a desk in a far corner away from the city desk and hubbub of the newsroom. I rarely got much to do. When I did get an assignment, it was to interview a *Daily News* contest winner, or write a public service item about the importance of regular cancer checkups or the benefits of flossing daily. Once in a while, if I was lucky, I'd get to write some soft feature or fluff interview piece for the Sunday paper.

I hated it, but I didn't know what else to do. No other newspaper or media outlet would hire me now. And so I showed up for work every day, did my job, and hoped that someday I could accomplish something worthwhile enough to make people forget about what had happened and let me be a real reporter again. Except I knew, deep down in my heart, that it never could happen. No matter what I did for the rest of my career, I would always be defined by that one moment of weakness when I crossed over the line and surrendered my integrity as a journalist.

And there was absolutely nothing I could do to change that perception of me.

It was like the story of Sisyphus, a character in mythology sentenced by the gods to forever push a heavy rock up a hill, only to see it roll back down to the bottom each time. The gods felt that being forced to do this work without ever being able to accomplish anything was the worst punishment possible. Sisyphus's only satisfaction could come from the simple act of pushing the rock up the hill each time. The journey up the hill became his only reward, even if he was destined never to change his fate.

Was that what I was doing now?

Working every day in a futile effort to change my life back to the way it had once been.

The rock was at the bottom of the hill for me, and all I knew how to do was keep pushing it back to the top.

———

I walked over to the reporters' assignment board behind the city desk. Marilyn Staley, the city editor, looked up at me.

"Hey, Malloy, what are you doing here?" she asked.

"I work here, remember."

"You're supposed to be at a doctor's appointment now."

"I'm headed there soon," I said.

I looked up at the assignment board behind her. It listed all the stories for the next day's paper and the reporters who were assigned to them. My name wasn't on the list.

"I could cover one of those stories," I blurted out.

"They're already covered."

"Maybe I could help—"

"Go to your doctor's appointment."

"The appointment's only an hour," I said hopefully. "I could start when I get back . . ."

Staley shook her head. "Go to the doctor, Malloy."

"What do you want me to be—a reporter or a patient?" I asked.

"I just want you to get your goddamned life together."

"It's going to take me a lot longer than an hour to do that," I said.

CHAPTER 3

S O HOW ARE you doing, Mr. Malloy?" Dr. Barbara Landis asked.

"I'm doing fine."

"Excellent."

"Damn straight it is."

"Have you had any more episodes?" she asked.

"Such as?"

"Blackouts?"

"No."

"Dizziness?"

"No."

"Loss of memory or lack of ability to concentrate?"

"Uh . . . I don't remember."

Dr. Landis smiled, but not like she thought it was funny.

"You seem to enjoy using humor to deflect issues you don't want to deal with, Mr. Malloy. Jokes are a defense for you. By being funny, you don't have to deal with the realities of your life. Realities like a panic attack."

A few months earlier, I'd suffered a panic attack in the middle of the *Daily News* city room. A full-fledged, really scary event that freaked out everyone at the paper, including me. All I remember is feeling light-headed as I stood up from the chair at my desk, then gasping for breath and suddenly seeing the room start to spin around me. They told me later I'd passed out a few seconds afterward, falling to the floor and opening up a gash on my head as I hit the edge of my desk on the way down. I woke up in a hospital with no memory of any of it. The doctors did a lot of tests on me but could find nothing physically wrong. Eventually, they diagnosed it as a panic attack, probably brought on by all the psychological stress I'd been under because of the Houston thing. They recommended professional counseling to deal with my problems, which is how I wound up with Dr. Barbara Landis. The paper didn't ask me to go to Dr. Landis, they told me.

I'd been seeing her for several weeks now. I'd missed a couple of appointments, claiming that I was too busy with stories to show up. She interpreted this, probably accurately, as a hostile act on my part. Maybe because I spent most of the time in the sessions I did attend complaining the paper never gave me good stories to do anymore and how bored I was there. So, as excuses go, mine was a pretty lame one. Damn, I couldn't even lie well anymore.

Landis was a distinguished-looking woman with gray hair, probably in her fifties. She always wore a business suit of some bland color—like gray or beige—and sat perfectly still and erect in her chair as she talked to me. She had an old-fashioned three-ring notebook and a fountain pen that she used to take notes continuously during the sessions. The notebook annoyed me. So did the fountain pen. Hell, the business suits did too. Everything about her was just so precise and so perfect that it pissed the hell out of me. Maybe if I'd met her in a different setting—at a party, in a bar, working on a story—we would have hit it off better. But sitting in her office and feeling the walls close in around me . . . well, let's just say she wasn't my idea of the perfect shrink. But then I probably wasn't her idea of the perfect patient.

"How are things at the paper?" she asked me now.

"Peachy."

"Peachy," she repeated.

"Sure. They don't expect anything from me anymore, I sure as hell don't expect to give them anything—and I'm still getting paid. So everyone's happy. Like I said, it's just peachy."

She wrote that in her notebook.

"How is your personal life going?" she asked.

"It isn't."

"Meaning?"

"I have no personal life."

"Don't you have some friends?"

"Most of them keep their distance from me these days. Not too many people want to admit to being my friend after . . . well, after everything that happened."

"Do you have any hobbies?"

"Well, I watch a lot of TV."

"Romantic interests?"

"Huh?"

"Are you seeing anyone?"

"I haven't gotten laid in a long time, if that's what you're asking."

"How do you feel about that?"

"Horny."

She wrote that down too. Damn this woman and her damn notebook.

"Have you talked to your wife?"

"My ex-wife."

"Okay, your ex-wife. Have you been in contact with her?"

"I talked to Susan awhile back, about two months ago."

"How did that conversation go?"

"I asked her if she wanted to get back together. I said I still loved her. She said she'd just gotten engaged to someone else. Someone she loved now. Someone who didn't come with as much emotional baggage. I kinda got the feeling she wasn't as broken up about our divorce as I was. I told her that. I also told her a few other things that, in retrospect, were probably unfortunate choices on my part. I believe, at one point, I called her a bitch. She told me to go to hell. So, in answer to your question, no, the conversation with my ex-wife Susan did not go very well."

Landis paged through her notes. "And you say this happened approximately two months ago?"

"I guess."

"That's about the same time you collapsed in the newsroom."

"Okay."

"You realize, of course, that the two events could be connected."

"Are you saying that I was so upset about Susan getting remarried that it could have brought on my panic attack that day in the newsroom?"

"I think it is very possible."

"You may be right," I said.

"I believe we are making some real progress here today, don't you?" Dr. Landis said.

"Absolutely," I said.

———

Except I was lying to her.

The first panic attack had not come after I had the conversation with my ex-wife.

I'd been having them for weeks before—smaller ones, but just as scary—only no one else had ever seen them. I didn't even want to admit to myself that they had happened. But sitting in my apartment late at night and switching with the remote between cable news channels and old reruns on TV Land because I couldn't sleep, I'd started gasping for breath, gotten dizzy, and felt I was going to faint or pass out or something worse. Eventually, the feeling would pass and I'd pretend that nothing ever happened. Until that day in the newsroom.

And I remember exactly what I was thinking about when it happened.

It wasn't Susan.

It was Carrie Bratten.

Carrie Bratten was the new hotshot reporter at the *Daily News*. She was twenty five years old, pretty, very bright, very talented, and even more ambitious. I hated her. Looking at her running around the newsroom, reveling in her front-page stories and exclusives—well, it was just too much for me to handle. She was everything I wanted to be, everything I once was—but couldn't be anymore. And every time I saw her and all of her success, it reminded me of that all over again.

That morning, I'd found out about a Ground Zero follow-up story. One of the survivors, someone I'd written a number of stories about in the past, had been suffering from kidney failure and urgently needed a transplant to stay alive. The normal waiting time for a new kidney was at least three months, and doctors said there was no way he could last that long without a transplant. But then a cop, one of the cops who had been there at the doomed World Trade Center in 2001, donated his own kidney to save the man. "I couldn't save many lives on 9/11," the cop said in explaining his reasoning for the decision. "That's haunted me for years. This time I can at least save one life of one of those people who were down there. That's why I want to do this." It was a great story. The kind of story that sent the adrenaline flowing through me in a way I hadn't experienced in a long, long time.

The editors at the *Daily News* liked the story too.

They were excited when I told them about it.

It was the perfect story.

Except for one thing.

I didn't get to work it.

Carrie Bratten did.

"Carrie's the star reporter here now, not you," Marilyn Staley explained to me that day. "You should know better than anyone how that works. This is a big story. She's our top reporter. Ergo, she gets the story, not you."

I got very agitated. I complained about how unfair it was. I screamed at her. I threatened to quit if I didn't get to do the story. Which, in retrospect, was probably the worst thing I could have done. Staley did not yell back at me. She just looked at me sadly until I was finished with my tirade.

"Look, Gil," she said, "I think everyone here has been fair and kind and compassionate to you to allow you to stay here after what happened. You know that as well as I do. And if you do your job and keep your head down, maybe, just maybe, you will survive here. You can have a life here, a career here as a reporter. Just not the reporter you once were. If that's not enough for you, if you cause any more scenes like this, well then . . . we'll just part ways right now. I don't think any other major newspaper or media outlet would touch you after what you did on the Houston story. It's your choice. Think about it."

I went back to my desk and did just that.

It was shortly after that that I suffered the first full-blown panic attack that had landed me in Dr. Landis's office.

———

Sitting there now, watching her take notes on everything I was saying and writing it all down in her notebook, I knew what I had to do.

Say anything, do anything so this woman will give a good report on me to the *Daily News* people who'd sent me here. I had to
play the game. No matter how much I wanted to grab that notebook out of her hands, rip it up into little pieces, and storm out of
her office. I needed her to tell the *Daily News* that I was making
progress. I needed her to tell them there was hope for me. I needed
her to save my job.

Because I realized what was at stake here.

I had no wife. I had no real friends to rely on anymore. I had no
family—my mother and father were dead, and I was an only child.
I had no real interest in anything else these days. The job was all I
had. Without that, I had nothing.

Which is why, I suppose, I cared so much about Victor Reyes.

"I'm actually working on a story right now," I said to Landis.

"So they did give you an assignment?"

"Nah, this is a story I've been working on my own."

"What's it about?"

"The unsolved murder of a man named Victor Reyes."

"Will the paper publish this story when you're finished writing it?"

"Maybe. Maybe not."

"Why wouldn't they?"

"Actually, it's not really that good a story."

"So why are you doing it?"

"Because I'm a reporter. No matter what anybody else thinks
of me, I'm still a reporter."

She wrote that down too.

"Tell me about this Victor Reyes story," Landis said.

CHAPTER 4

'D FIRST HEARD about Victor Reyes from a homicide detective named Roberto Santiago.

Santiago worked on the Priority Murders Squad, an elite division of the NYPD that focused on major, high-profile homicides in the city. I met Santiago long before that, though. Down at Ground Zero. He'd been one of the cops who toiled there day and night in those horrible weeks and months after 9/11. Just like me. And, like a lot of us did down there in the fall of 2001, we formed a strong bond, Santiago and I. Later, he helped me out on police stories as I rose to prominence at the *News* and he rose in the ranks of the police department. I even sought his help when I was trying to track down the infamous Houston. I never heard from him after the story fell apart, and I assumed he'd given up on me just like so many other people had.

So I was surprised to get a phone call from him in the middle of the night.

"I've got a story for you, Malloy," he said, without apologizing for the late hour.

"I don't really do stories anymore," I said, yawning into the phone.

"I'm at Lincoln Hospital in the Bronx," Santiago told me.

I looked at the clock on the table next to my bed. The dial said it was 3 a.m.

"Can this wait until morning?"

"If you grab a cab, you can be here in less than thirty minutes. Not much traffic out there at this hour. I'll be waiting for you in the emergency room."

I groaned. I thought about just hanging up the phone and going back to sleep. But I didn't. Maybe it was because I was curious about why he wanted to see me after all this time. Maybe I felt I owed him something. Or maybe, just maybe, I still had that old reporter's instinct and wanted to find out what the story was that was so damn important to Santiago.

———

A half hour later, I was in the Lincoln Hospital emergency room with Roberto Santiago. He was standing over the body of a man on a stretcher.

"Who is he?" I asked.

"Victor Reyes."

"Is that supposed to mean something?"

"I grew up with him."

I nodded sympathetically, even though I still had no idea what I was doing here.

"We used to run in a gang together," Santiago said. "I got out of the gang life. He didn't. Then he got shot. The bullet hit his spinal cord and paralyzed him. He's been in a wheelchair ever since."

I looked down at the body of Victor Reyes on the stretcher.

"How old was he?" I asked.

"Thirty-four."

"And how did he die?"

"A heart attack."

"A heart attack," I repeated, still confused about why I was there.

"His mother found him struggling to breathe. She called 911. But he was already dead by the time they got him here to the hospital. The doctors say it was a massive coronary."

"Detective Santiago," I said, "I am very sorry for the loss of your friend. And I'm sure that the late Mr. Reyes was a very fine person who will be greatly missed. But why the hell exactly am I here?"

"I want you to write the story."

"What story?"

"I'm going to catch the person that killed him."

"Wait a minute, you work on the Priority Murders Squad."

"You don't think the death of Victor Reyes is a priority murder?"

"It's not even a murder," I pointed out.

"Actually it is," Santiago said.

———

"When Victor Reyes was just nineteen years old, he was shot from a passing car as he came out of his apartment house," Santiago told me. "No specific motive, although it appears to have been gang related."

I took notes as he talked.

"The bullet first shattered two of his ribs."

"That's not good," I said.

"It ruptured his spleen."

"Worse."

"And the bullet lodged in Reyes's spinal cord, leaving him unable to walk or feel any sensation whatever below his waist."

"The worst."

"The assailant inside the car was described as—"

"Let me guess . . . a young male Hispanic."

Santiago gave me a dirty look.

"What?" I said. "You think he's going to be Irish in that neighborhood?"

"The doctors I talked to tonight said it was the gunshot that killed him. The bullet did it. The same bullet. That damn bullet."

"Wait a minute—I thought he died of a heart attack."

"He did. But contributing factors to the heart attack, doctors say, were bronchial pneumonia, paraplegia, and coronary atherosclerosis. All of these things were brought on by his being in a wheelchair for so many years."

I nodded.

"At some point, probably within the last few hours of his life, the remains of the bullet that had been in his spine all this time—there was no way to take it out without causing more damage—became dislodged and traveled through the bloodstream to his heart. In his weakened condition, that proved fatal."

"Are you saying that if he hadn't been shot fifteen years ago, he wouldn't have had the heart attack now?"

"That's what the doctors told me."

"Interesting."

"So technically, whoever shot him back then is guilty of murder."

"And you're going to try to solve a murder that happened fifteen years ago, except no one even knew it was a murder until now."

"Yes."

"That's the story you want me to write?"

"Not a bad story, huh?"

———

I needed some coffee. We found a vending machine that still had some coffee available. It wasn't great, but at that hour of the morning, the bar for acceptable coffee is set pretty low for me. We found seats in the empty cafeteria and sat there drinking our coffee and talking about Victor Reyes.

"When I was growing up, my mother died," Santiago told me. "My father was never around much. Camille Reyes, Victor's mother, sort of became a surrogate parent for me."

"And that's how you and her son Victor became so close?"

Santiago nodded. "I was older than him, but we ran together through most of our teenage years."

"Define ran."

"We belonged to the same gang."

"I find it hard to picture you as a gang member."

"Everyone ran in a gang in my neighborhood. You either were a part of a gang or you became the victim of a gang. It was a matter of survival."

"How did you manage to get out of that life?"

"I got lucky," Santiago said. "I met a cop who was a good guy. He saw something in me that no one else ever had. Including myself. He told me I was wasting my life and got me to finish school. When I did, he encouraged me to join the police. Helped me get into the Police Academy. If I hadn't been lucky enough to meet that police officer, I probably wouldn't be here today."

"And Victor Reyes?"

"He wasn't so lucky."

Santiago took a sip of his coffee.

"Victor's mother has taken care of him for fifteen years. She's fed him, taken him to the park in his wheelchair—hell, she even had to help him go the bathroom. Now that he's dead, the most important thing in the world to her is that we find whoever did this to her son. She wants justice for Victor. So do I."

"You can't make this personal," I told him.

"It is personal."

"The first rule for a police officer—for a journalist too—is to never let any case or any story to become personal."

"The job never gets personal for you?"

I sighed. "It's not a hard-and-fast rule . . . okay, it's not even a rule at all . . . actually, no one ever really follows it."

There was something else I wanted to ask Santiago.

"Why me? Why did you ask me to come here tonight?"

"I want people to know about Victor Reyes. I don't want him to have died for no reason. To have his life forgotten about by everyone except me and his mother. That's why I called you. I want someone to tell people his story, to make his life, and his death, matter. I decided someone in the press could help make that happen. And you're the best press I know."

"Not if you talk to a lot of people these days."

"I heard about all that. I don't know exactly what you did or didn't do. What I do know is the guy I met at Ground Zero. We shared a lot down there, we talked about a lot of things. Life and death was a big topic. I remember we talked about how the victims—from the rich investment bankers to the busboys from Windows on the World on top of the tower—all died together that day. How death doesn't differentiate between rich and poor, famous and not so famous. How, in death, no loss is greater or less than the other."

"Death is the great equalizer," I said.

"That's why I want you to write this story. You're the one person I hoped would understand. Who could help me make sure that Victor Reyes's life—and his death—mattered."

"You've got no witnesses?"

"No."

"No real motive?"

"Not yet."

"No clues?"

"Right."

"Probably no forensic evidence worth anything after all this time?"

"Nope."

"What exactly do you have to help you solve this case?"

Santiago shrugged.

"You don't have a damn thing."

He smiled sadly. "Malloy, that is an excellent summation of this case at the moment."

———

I'd like to say that I was so moved by Detective Roberto Santiago's emotional plea and his compassion for Victor Reyes and his quest for justice for his dead boyhood friend from the Bronx that I threw myself into the story right after our meeting that night at the hospital.

But that wasn't what I did.

Instead, I did nothing.

I'd gotten pretty good at doing nothing.

I just slipped back into my normal routine of feeling sorry for myself and the mess I'd made of my own career and my own life.

The truth was I pretty much forgot about that conversation at the hospital with Santiago. Almost. Oh, it was there in the back of my mind, and every once in a while I would think about doing something about the Victor Reyes story. I figured I owed it to Santiago for everything we had shared during those days after 9/11. But I never did anything about it. Nothing at all.

Until it was too late. After I found out Santiago was dead.

It wasn't a big story in the *Daily News* or anywhere else. He didn't die in the line of duty or as a hero or anything like that. He was killed by a drunk driver. It was one of those senseless things— just being in the wrong place at the wrong time—that make you wonder if fate is laughing at us somewhere as we earnestly go about our lives.

Santiago had finished up his shift at about eleven one evening, and he was crossing the street to his parked car. Another car ran a red light and plowed right into him in the middle of the intersection. He died instantly.

The driver of the car was a drunk who fled the scene when he realized what he had done. But a witness got his license plate number. The cops picked him up at a bar an hour later. His blood alcohol level was nearly 0.20, drunk enough so that he could barely stand up. But not drunk enough to stop him from getting behind the wheel of a car. After hitting and killing Santiago, he'd driven to the bar and kept on drinking.

The pointlessness of it was what bothered me the most, I suppose.

Roberto Santiago was a cop who put his life on the line every day when he went to work. He'd been in shootouts, hostage situations, run into burning buildings, and done all sorts of other heroic—and dangerous—things in the line of duty. He'd survived that all. And then, on his way home from work at the end of his shift, Santiago gets run down by a damn drunk driver in the street.

The wrong place at the wrong time.

It seemed so unfair.

But life, as I had found out, was often that way.

CHAPTER 5

JUST BECAUSE I could no longer work on big stories didn't mean I couldn't read them.

A few days after my lunch with Nikki Reynolds, I sat in a coffee shop on Water Street at eight o'clock, sipping my second cup of coffee and reading the front-page story in that morning's *Daily News*.

The first thing I saw, of course, was the byline. By Carrie Bratten. My personal nemesis at the paper. The front-page headline said BEAUTY SLAIN IN UNION SQUARE PARK. There was a huge picture of an attractive blond woman.

The story itself got a two-page spread on pages four and five inside, including pictures from the scene and a map of the Union Square area where the woman's body had been found.

The victim's name was Shawn Kennedy, and she had been shot to death. Her body had been found by a dog walker in the park early the previous morning. She was dressed in designer jeans, a pink tank top, and sandals. There was a gold chain around her neck and what looked like a very expensive bracelet and ring on her right hand. An expensive-looking watch was on her left wrist. Whatever the motive for her murder, it sure hadn't been robbery.

This one had a personal feel to it. Her purse was still with her. The ID and money and credit cards inside all seemed untouched.

Shawn Kennedy was a photographer who did a lot of fashion and celebrity shoots in Manhattan. She'd worked for *People*, *Us Weekly*, *InStyle*, many of the big publications. She lived in a converted loft on St. Mark's Place, a few blocks south of the park.

Police found a witness who saw her in a bar in the Union Square neighborhood the evening before. The witness was the bartender. He said she'd been alone, had a couple of drinks at the bar, and then left. He said he'd chatted with her in between customers and that she'd told him she was waiting for someone. When he looked back at the bar and she was gone, he assumed her date had shown up. Or she'd given up on him and just gone home.

The bartender was considered a potential suspect at first. Especially after cops discovered he had an arrest record for drug possession and robbery. His name was Kevin Gallagher, and cops brought him to the East 21st Street station house for formal questioning. But it went nowhere. Even the cops who took him in seemed to know he wasn't the guy who did it. Gallagher stuck to his story about having a casual conversation in the bar with the woman, and they couldn't budge him from it. Probably because he was telling the truth. His criminal record for robbery didn't fit in. Nothing had been taken from the Kennedy woman, even though she was carrying money and wearing expensive jewelry. Besides, Gallagher wound up having an alibi. He'd been working at the bar until closing time at two in the morning. The owner said he never took a break all night. The ME's report estimated that Kennedy had died sometime before midnight.

Bratten's story went on for nearly forty inches. It was filled with all sorts of details—the same kind of details I would have used—

about the crime. The color of the victim's purse. A description of the jewelry. The exact position of the body when it was found. A vivid picture of the scene in Union Square Park around her: The grassy expanse in the middle of the park. The trees that had hidden her body until daylight when the dog walker discovered her. The type of dog he was walking (a black-and-tan miniature dachshund). Even the fact that a coin had fallen out of the victim's purse—possibly in a struggle with the assailant—and been found lying next to the body. The coin was a Kennedy half-dollar. Bratten noted the tragic juxtaposition of the Kennedy coin next to the dead woman of the same name.

All in all, it was a helluva job of reporting by Carrie Bratten.

Which pissed me off even more than the fact that she was doing the story instead of me. I wanted to find something wrong with it. I wanted to believe that I could have done a better job on the story if someone had just given me the chance. But I couldn't find any real flaws in her work. She was as good as I was. Or at least as good as I used to be. That pissed me off even more.

I took another refill on my coffee and reread the article from beginning to end. That's when it hit me.

A Kennedy half-dollar had fallen out of the victim's purse and been found near the body. The victim's last name was Kennedy. That was just a bizarre coincidence, of course. A tragic twist of fate, as Bratten described it in her story. Except for one thing. A few days before, Nikki Reynolds had talked to me about a book she was trying to promote about the John F. Kennedy assassination.

Another coincidence?

Probably.

But I'd always been taught as a reporter never to trust in coincidence.

"There are no coincidences," an old newspaperman had taught me when I was starting out as a cub reporter. "There's always a reason for everything. Coincidence should be your last option for an explanation—after you've tried everything else and still can't explain an event or a series of them. You go to the facts, the facts never lie. That's what being a reporter is all about. If the facts fail you and all you're left with is the coincidence explanation, then maybe it really is a coincidence. But let me tell you something, son, that hasn't happened to me very often. Coincidences are the easy answer, the simple way to wrap up a story. But they often lead you into the wrong direction, away from the truth. Go after the facts if you want to find out the truth."

I finished my coffee, put the paper under my arm, and walked to the *Daily News* building a block away.

CHAPTER 6

How many Kennedy half-dollars are there in circulation at the moment?" I asked Carrie Bratten.

"What?"

"A ballpark figure is fine."

"I have no idea." Bratten shrugged.

She looked annoyed that I'd even come over to her desk in the *Daily News* city room to talk to her. That was okay with me. Lots of people got annoyed when I talked to them these days. I wasn't very popular in the city room anymore. That bothered me at first. But I was getting used to it.

Bratten was blond and cute and kind of sexy, I suppose, but in a pretty obvious way. She wore short skirts, high heels, and low-cut blouses and sweaters, which attracted a lot of attention in the newsroom and out on the streets as she chased down stories.

Some female reporters play down their looks and their sexuality because they want to be taken seriously. Not Carrie Bratten. It was pretty clear she would do anything for a story. And I mean anything. Of course, I didn't have any direct evidence that she'd actually slept with some of her sources to break exclusives, but that was the kind of ambitious, hard-driving, do-whatever-it-takes journalist she was.

I'd heard her father was some kind of big-shot plastic surgeon or something from Boston, and she had that spoiled, rich-girl aura about her. Maybe if we'd met under different circumstances I might have been at least a little bit attracted to her. But not here. Not now. Now Carrie Bratten just pissed me off every time I saw her or her damn byline.

"When the Kennedy half-dollar first came out after JFK's assassination, it was incredibly popular," I said. "They made nearly three hundred million of them in 1964. But, as the years went by, they didn't turn them out nearly as much. At some point, people pretty much stopped using half-dollars altogether. Did you know that most cash register drawers in stores don't even have a spot to put half-dollars these days? Slot machines in Vegas and Atlantic City used to take them, but now they're pretty much all computer driven with tickets instead of coins. The number of Kennedy half-dollars has declined dramatically over the years since JFK's assassination. Last year, there were only a million or so of them. They're not easy to find."

"When did you become such an expert on Kennedy half-dollars?" she asked.

"I'm not. I looked up all this information. Just like you could have done."

"Why bother?"

"I was curious. Maybe you should have been more curious about it too."

Her eyes narrowed. She tried to keep the bored/annoyed look on her face. But I could tell I'd struck a nerve. She suddenly could see where I was headed with this.

"What's your point?" she asked with more bravado than I knew she was feeling at that moment.

"Your murder victim's name was Shawn Kennedy."

"So?"

"There was a Kennedy half-dollar found next to her body."

"A coincidence."

"Probably."

"You said there were still a million Kennedy half-dollars out there . . ."

"Right."

"No reason one of them couldn't have wound up in the victim's purse, then fell out in the struggle with the killer."

"No reason at all."

"Like I said, just a coincidence with the name."

"Except there were three hundred million Kennedy half-dollars in circulation in 1964, and there are only a million now."

"Meaning what?"

"Meaning it would have been a lot less of a coincidence back in 1964 than it is now."

She nodded. Grudgingly. I'd made my point.

"What am I supposed to do with this information?"

"I have no idea."

"Then why make such a big deal out of telling me?"

"I always figure that it's better to know stuff about a story than not know about it. That's the way I always work as a reporter. That's the way good reporters work. They ask questions. They check out details. They try to make sure they get the whole story. Of course, I'm not sure if that matters to you, Carrie."

I walked back to my desk, feeling satisfied—and, truth be told, a bit ebullient—over what I had just done.

The truth is the Kennedy half-dollar found next to the Kennedy woman's body probably did mean nothing. But I'd planted a seed of doubt in her mind. I'd seen something that she missed. Plus, I'd pissed her off.

All in all, it was a win for Gil Malloy.

I sure as hell didn't have many of them these days.

So I tried to savor the good feeling of this one for as long as I could.

Which turned out to be about five minutes.

———

Marilyn Staley sent me an email saying she wanted to see me in her office right away. That could mean a lot of things. None of them good.

"How are you doing, Marilyn?" I asked when I sat down in a chair in front of her desk.

"Fuck you, Malloy."

"Interesting response. Not exactly an answer to my question, but . . ."

"What the hell do you think you're doing?"

"Topic?"

"Carrie Bratten."

"Oh."

"Carrie says you tried to steal her story. You told her you could do it better than her. She said you were confrontational, condescending, and downright rude to her."

"I'm not sure you can be confrontational and condescending at the same time," I pointed out.

"Let me tell you something, Malloy. Carrie Bratten is a very bright, very talented, very highly thought of reporter on this paper."

"She's also a snitch. She really came to you and whined all this crap about me? Well, that settles it, I'm not giving her any more reporting tips."

I stood up to leave. There wasn't much more to say. Just before I got to the door, though, I turned around and looked at Staley.

"I can still be a good reporter, Marilyn," I said.

"That ship sailed a long time ago."

"If I just got a good story to work on . . ."

"Like I said, those days are over for you."

"I'm not giving up. I'm still a reporter. No matter what you think about me now. Look, I know I deserve a lot of what happened to me. But I can't dig myself out of this hole I'm in by writing about lottery contest winners or bridal showers or new animals at the Bronx Zoo. I'm just looking for another chance. Another chance to prove myself. Another chance to be a real journalist again."

"It would take a miracle for that to happen," Staley said.

CHAPTER 7

WHEN I BEGAN working on the Victor Reyes case a few weeks earlier, I needed a starting point. So I went to see Reyes's mother. It seemed like as good a place as any.

She lived in a really bad section of the Bronx, a neighborhood of abandoned buildings, boarded-up stores, and street corners owned by drug dealers, pimps, and gangs.

Her apartment was small and inexpensively furnished, but neat and taken care of—almost as if it were a sanctuary from the nightmarish streets outside. Camille Reyes was about sixty. She had gray hair and a face that looked as if she'd once been pretty but was now worn out after years of struggle.

I sat in her living room and talked to her about her son.

"Why do you want to write about Victor?" she asked me right off.

"He's a good story," I said.

"And you really think that the readers of your newspaper will care about some poor kid from the Bronx who died?"

I didn't say anything.

"The police didn't care," she said. "On the night Victor was shot, the police were here for a very short time. They asked a couple of questions and then I barely heard from them again. My son wasn't an important case to them. He was just a kid from a bad neighborhood who nobody really cared about very much. Not the police. Not you people in the press. No one."

"Well, we're going to try to do better by your son this time," I said.

"The only one who ever cared was Roberto."

"Roberto was a close friend of mine," I said, exaggerating our relationship a bit to try to get her on my side.

"And now he and Victor are both dead."

She picked up a picture of her son from a table next to her and looked at it. It was a picture of Victor as a young man before the shooting. He was standing, not in a wheelchair. I wondered if that's how she wanted to remember him.

"Victor was trying to turn his life around just before he was shot," she said. "He was taking night courses to get a high school diploma; he got a job; he promised me he was going to quit the gang life. He was very excited about all of this."

I wrote down everything she was saying in my notebook.

"The job was especially important to him. It was the first real job he ever had. He was working as a busboy at Fernando's, a restaurant in a much nicer Bronx neighborhood than this. Victor liked it there. He talked about how maybe he'd even like to own his own restaurant one day. I thought it was a crazy dream, but Victor had a lot of dreams back then. He seemed so happy. And I was so proud of him."

"And the dream died after he was shot?"

She nodded. "His life was over at nineteen. He couldn't work; he couldn't have a relationship with a woman; he couldn't have a normal life anymore. That heart attack he had wasn't what killed him. It was that bullet fifteen years ago. It just took him a long time to die."

She looked down at the picture in her hand again and started to cry. I waited until she stopped and pulled herself together before continuing.

"What do you remember about the night Victor was shot?" I finally asked softly.

"It was about eight p.m.," she said, her eyes still glistening with tears. "Victor told me he was going out. A few minutes later, I heard a gunshot. I ran outside and Victor was lying there on the street. I held him in my arms until the ambulance came."

"Did he say anything to you?"

"He asked me why he couldn't feel his legs."

She began to cry some more. I waited again.

"Did he see anyone inside the vehicle who shot him?"

She shook her head.

"I heard there was a description put out for a young Hispanic man in a car as the shooter."

"Victor said he never saw anybody," she said.

———

Fernando's restaurant went out of business a couple of years ago. But I was able to track down an old staff employee roster and found the names of some of the people who worked there. One of them, a guy named Miguel Pascal, owned another restaurant in the Bronx now.

"Do you remember Victor Reyes?" I asked Pascal.

"Sure, we worked together at Fernando's when I was just starting out. He was a busboy, I was a waiter. Then he got shot."

Pascal was going about his business in the kitchen of his restaurant as we talked—checking out orders, tasting menu dishes being prepared, and supervising the kitchen help.

"Reyes just died," I told him. "He had a heart attack. Apparently brought on by being in a wheelchair all these years."

"Sorry to hear that."

"I'm trying to find out who shot him."

Pascal shook his head. "It sure took someone long enough to give a damn about that."

"Better late than never." I shrugged.

Pascal took a sip now from a pot of soup cooking on the stove in front of him. He made a face and told the cook it needed more seasoning. Then he turned back toward me.

"The police suspected at the time it was a gang shooting," I said. "Maybe Reyes was shot because he was a member of a rival gang."

"Not anymore he wasn't."

"Excuse me?"

"Victor quit the gang life. He told me so."

"When did he tell you that?"

"A day or two before the shooting."

"Did he say why?"

"As a matter of fact, he did. He wanted to join the police force. He had a friend or a brother or somebody who had gone to the Police Academy and changed his life around. Victor wanted to do the same thing."

"Did he say who this person on the police force was?"

"No, he never gave a name to me."

That was okay.

I knew who it was.

Roberto Santiago.

Victor Reyes had wanted to turn his life around just like his friend Roberto Santiago had by becoming a police officer and leaving the gang life behind.

But someone had shot him first.

CHAPTER 8

THE NEXT THING I did was go talk to Roberto Santiago's widow. There had been no official record of any follow-up police investigation with the Reyes shooting. Just the long-ago original one from fifteen years ago. That wasn't altogether surprising. Santiago had admitted this was personal to him. So he might not have wanted to do it officially or even tell his superiors what he was doing. Still, even if he was doing it off duty, he must have talked to someone about it. He talked about it with me. Maybe he talked about it with someone else too.

His wife seemed like the most likely person he would have confided in about anything he discovered.

Miranda Santiago was an attractive dark-haired, olive-skinned woman in her thirties. We sat in the living room of her house on Staten Island, which was filled with pictures of her husband. Dressed in his official blues for a formal event. Wearing casual stuff around the house and the neighborhood. The worst pictures of all—the hardest to look at—were the ones of him and his children. A boy twelve years old, a girl who was eight, and another boy just a year old.

"It's still so difficult for me to accept," Mrs. Santiago said to me. "When you're a policeman's wife, you know what comes with the territory. Every day, when you say goodbye to your husband before he goes to work, it could be the last time you'll ever see him. Roberto's life was on the line every day with that job. He knew that, and I did too. And maybe if he'd been killed chasing down a murderer or stopping a bank robbery or trying to rescue someone from a fire . . . well, maybe that would have been easier to accept. But this . . . this is too senseless. A drunk driver. A damn drunk driver. And Roberto wasn't even on the job when it happened. He was crossing the street on his way home to me and his children, and then . . . he was just gone."

I let her talk like that for a while. Because I'd seen it before. The anger over the randomness of it all. The sadness and the grief over the loss of someone you loved so much. And, most of all, the realization that the person was now gone forever from your life. Finally, I brought up Victor Reyes.

"The person Roberto grew up with in the Bronx," she said sadly.

"Yes."

"He died a few months ago."

"Roberto told me he was going to try and find the person who shot him fifteen years ago. Did he ever talk to you about this, Mrs. Santiago?"

She shook her head.

"Not really. Not the specifics. Just that his boyhood friend had died. We never talked about his cases. That was Roberto's rule. He said he saw too much violence and ugliness as a police officer. He didn't wanted to relive it when he was home. He just wanted to enjoy time with his family. I understood that, so I never asked him about the cases he was working on. Once in a while he'd mention something in passing about things that had happened on the job. Like you. He told me about you."

"Roberto talked about me?"

"Yes."

"Probably because we spent so much time together down at Ground Zero after 9/11."

"No, not that. That was something he never talked about. The collapse of those towers. I think that affected him far more than I could ever imagine, but he never really opened up to me about it."

"So how did you know about me?"

"He told me he met with you at a hospital after Reyes died. That he asked you to write a story about him. He desperately didn't want Victor to have died unnoticed like he did. He wanted Victor to be remembered in some way, to matter to the world. That's what he said. And that's why he reached out to you."

She looked at me now with sad eyes. I looked away. I couldn't hold her stare.

"But you never wrote that story," she said.

"No, not then."

"Why not?"

"I don't know. I guess I was busy . . . no, that's not true. I'm not really that busy with anything as a reporter these days. I'm not sure why I didn't write the story at the time, Mrs. Santiago. I guess it didn't seem like something that important to me."

"Roberto was disappointed he never heard from you after that. He said he remembered you as a good man. A man he trusted to do the right thing. I think it hurt him very badly when you didn't come through for him."

"I'm doing the story now," I pointed out.

"For Roberto?"

I nodded. "For myself too."

She smiled. "I think Roberto would have liked that."

———

Santiago had kept a small office at the back of the house. His wife let me look through it when I asked if he kept any files or records of his cases at home. She said it was just the way he'd left it on that last day when he went off to work. She hadn't had the strength to deal with it—or with any of his personal stuff in the house—since his death.

There was a desk with some paperwork on top, a filing cabinet, some bookshelves, and a bulletin board with maybe two dozen pictures on it. Some were of him with his family. Others showed him at the precinct and on the job over the years. I recognized a couple of them that had been taken at Ground Zero a decade earlier. I looked at these the most closely. I found myself in one of them, standing with Santiago and other rescue workers near the ruins of the fallen towers. I stared at the picture for a long time, thinking about all the things that had happened to me—and Santiago too—since that day. Then I started looking through the room.

The papers on his desk were mostly bills, financial paperwork, and other personal stuff. I realized that some of the bills were now past due and had gone unpaid since Santiago died. I wondered if I should point it out to Mrs. Santiago. If maybe her husband had always handled all the finances, and now it was something she would have to learn to deal with. Instead, I simply pushed them aside. I was intruding enough already in this family's personal grief. It was none of my business.

The filing cabinet was more helpful. The drawers were filled with case files. Like a lot of cops, Santiago kept his own record of cases he had worked on in the event he ever needed to refer to them if there were any questions about his actions from the department or anyone else. I figured I'd find the official police file on the Reyes case from fifteen years ago somewhere there. I was right.

I spotted it quickly, along with more recent notations he'd made about the case, on top of most of the other files. Which made sense since he'd been working on that file the most recently. I sat at Roberto Santiago's desk and paged through what was there.

The papers were in chronological order. They began with the shooting of Victor Reyes. The original police report said that a 911 call had been received at 8:11 p.m. reporting a shooting in the South Bronx. The call was from a woman who identified herself as the mother of the youth who had been shot. The EMS dispatcher who took the call was quoted as saying the woman had been "extremely emotional and almost hysterical" so it took several minutes to ascertain the exact details and the location of the shooting.

Whether for that reason or because it was just a bad night of mayhem in the Bronx, the paramedics didn't arrive at the scene of the shooting until thirty-eight minutes later. Reyes was taken to Lincoln Hospital—the same hospital where he would die a decade and a half later—for treatment.

The first police officer had arrived on the scene shortly after the ambulance. Probably took that long for the same reason the ambulance did. There were a lot of shootings and violence in the Bronx on a summer night, and one more Hispanic kid shot in a bad neighborhood wasn't exactly a priority crime.

The officer, a young patrolman named Gary Nowak, in his rookie year on the job, interviewed people in the neighborhood who might have witnessed the shooting but reported that no one he spoke to had seen anything. Nowak cordoned off the crime scene and waited until detectives arrived. The two detectives who responded were named Brad Lawton and James Garcetti. They conducted their own survey of the area, talked to neighbors too, and interviewed Camille Reyes. There was no indication of any follow-up interviews with Mrs. Reyes. Which must have been

what she meant when she said cops spent very little time investigating the case. That was probably true. But it wasn't Lawton or
Garcetti or Nowak's fault. That was just the way it was. Same as
the way the *Daily News* ran a one-paragraph short about a killing
in the Bronx and splashed the news of the murder of a pretty
Upper East Side coed or a wealthy stockbroker all over the front
page.

At some point, an all points bulletin was put out for a young
Hispanic in a beaten-up old car, possibly green, as a suspect in the
shooting. The suspect was identified as Bobby Ortiz, who had a
long rap sheet for gang activity in the Bronx.

More recently in Santiago's file, I found a copy of the hospital
report from the night Reyes died, listing the extent of his injuries
from the shooting, then a summary of his medical history over the
years and the cause of death. It was officially listed as a heart attack. But there was additional material from medical personnel
detailing—just as Santiago had done that night at the hospital—
how the bullet had dislodged from Reyes's spine and traveled to
his heart, bringing on the heart attack that killed him. Santiago
had written in large letters at the bottom of the medical report:
"CAUSE OF DEATH: MURDER!"

Trying to find evidence for a shooting that happened fifteen
years earlier is difficult. But Santiago had pursued the one solid
piece of evidence he had: the bullet. Santiago had retrieved the
bullet after the autopsy and logged it in as official evidence before
Reyes was buried. Amazingly, it had somehow remained virtually
intact after all this time. He had it run through the police lab,
where it was identified as having been fired from a .38 revolver.
The weapon, though, had never been found.

There were also more details about the gang affiliations of

Reyes and Bobby Ortiz. Reyes had belonged to a gang in his neighborhood loosely connected to the infamous Bloods, but the Bloods were not a major gang presence in that area of the Bronx then. Ortiz belonged to the Latin Kings, the dominant gang at the time. So it wasn't that much of a leap to theorize that Ortiz had shot Reyes over some sort of gang rivalry or dispute. Even if Reyes really had been trying to escape the gang life.

The files gave no indication that Santiago had tried to find out what happened to Ortiz or that he had even reached out to the three original cops on the case, Nowak, Lawton, and Garcetti. That surprised me a bit at first, because I knew these were obvious moves for any investigator to make, and Santiago had been a top-flight homicide detective. But then I realized why he hadn't done any of these things.

He never had a chance.

Santiago had simply run out of time. The last entry was dated the day before he had been hit and killed crossing the street.

I thought again about how much easier this all would have been if I'd started the story right after I saw him that night in the hospital. I could have worked with Santiago on the story, and then maybe things would have worked out differently. But it was too late to change that now. Too late to change a lot of things.

CHAPTER 9

James Garcetti was still a detective working out of the Bronx. I met him in a bar one day on East Tremont a few blocks from his precinct. He was probably in his fifties, but he looked a lot older. Gray haired, maybe forty pounds overweight, with a big paunch and a florid drinker's face.

It wasn't even noon yet, but he was already working on a beer and a shot. I had the feeling it wasn't his first.

"I've been on this damn job for twenty-nine years, seven months," he said. "Five months to go until I get my thirty years in. That's all I want. Then I'm outta here. I'm taking my pension and getting out of this city and never looking back."

I nodded and took a sip of the beer I'd ordered to make Garcetti feel more comfortable talking to me.

"Do you remember the Victor Reyes case?" I asked him.

"Who's that?"

"A kid that got shot outside of his house about fifteen years ago."

Garcetti took a swig of his shot. "Some Hispanic kid dies in the Bronx fifteen years ago and you expect me to remember it?"

"Actually, he didn't die fifteen years ago. That's when he got shot. He died a few months ago from the wound."

Garcetti shrugged.

"Nothing, huh?" I asked him.

"Like I said, I've seen so many murders and shootings and all sorts of other crap on the streets over the years . . . well, after a while, you tend to forget a lot of the specifics. They all just blend together into one big pile of shit. You know what I mean?"

He drank some of his beer.

"Does the name Bobby Ortiz mean anything to you?" I asked.

"Nope."

"He was a suspect in the shooting."

"We catch him?"

"No."

"We probably had too many other cases to worry about. More shootings. Robberies. Drug dealers. In a place like this, you aren't supposed to waste too much time over one crappy case. You do what you can and you move on. There's only so much time you can spend on a case like this kid you mentioned . . . what was his name again?"

"Victor Reyes."

"If there was an arrest to make on Reyes, I'm sure we would have made it. If not, well . . . there're a lot of Victor Reyeses out there."

I told him about Roberto Santiago.

"Did you know Santiago?" I asked.

"Never met him. Heard about what happened to him, though. A damn shame."

"He never approached you about this case?"

"No, why would he?"

"Same reason I'm here now."

"Never heard from him."

"You're sure about that?"

"Hey, I remember cops. Just not all the victims and the perps."

He ordered another round for himself. Beer with a shot chaser.

"Your partner fifteen years ago, when Reyes got shot, was Brad Lawton, right?"

"That would be about the time we were teamed up together, I guess."

"How long were you and Lawton partners?"

"A year or two."

"What happened?"

"Brad moved up. He was very successful, very ambitious. Me, I never had ambition."

"Are you still in touch with him?"

"Brad?" He laughed. "Oh, I run into him from time to time over the years. Funerals, retirement parties, that sort of thing. He's very polite and asks me how I'm doing and all of that. But no, we're not really in touch anymore. I was a pretty good cop back then—the drinking came later. Our careers—our lives—just sort of went off in separate directions, I guess you might say."

He stared down at the shot glass in front of him, then took a big drink to empty it. He signaled the bartender for another.

"You better be careful," I told him. "Don't you go on duty soon?"

"I am on duty," Garcetti said.

————

Gary Nowak, the first patrolman on the scene of the Reyes shooting, was no longer on the force.

He'd left the NYPD about six months after it happened. Overall, he'd spent barely a year on the force. I'd run into a lot of young cops like that when I was working the police beat. They had all these grandiose ideas about what being a policeman would be like, and then—when they were confronted with the grim day-to-day reality of the job—they decided it wasn't for them. I was disappointed when I found out about Nowak, though. It made him a lot harder to track down.

The last known address I could find turned out to be a dead end. Neighbors told me he'd moved a long time ago, and one said he'd talked about leaving New York City. Because he hadn't been on the force long enough to qualify for a pension or other benefits, there was no active file on him in the police department records bureau. I put in a request with Public Information to try to find an address, and they said it might take a while to get back to me with whatever they could find out.

———

Brad Lawton, Garcetti's partner, who had been the third cop at the scene of the Reyes shooting, was a lot easier to find. All I had to do was go to police headquarters. He was a deputy police commissioner now.

"I remember the Reyes shooting," Lawton said to me as we sat in his office at One Police Plaza in downtown Manhattan.

"Really? I figured since it was so long ago . . ."

"I remember them all. All the murders, all the victims, all the violence. Sometimes I wish I didn't. But they're all there somewhere inside me—the names, the faces, everything—whether I like it or not. Yep, I remember everything I've seen out there."

Lawton was a distinguished-looking, impeccably dressed guy in his late forties. I'd read up on him before I got there. He'd worked his way up from street cop to detective to precinct commander to deputy commissioner. It was an impressive résumé. He was a very high-profile cop too, doing a lot of newspaper interviews and appearing on TV and radio talk shows; he'd even written a book about fighting crime in urban areas such as New York

City in the twenty-first century. His name sometimes appeared on Page Six of the *New York Post* or one of the other gossip columns for parties or events or openings he attended. Lawton was definitely a cop on the way up. The exact opposite of his old partner, James Garcetti.

I told him about Santiago and his involvement with the Reyes case.

"Fifteen years is a long time to go back and try to find a murderer," he said when I was finished.

"I understand. But that's what Santiago was trying to do. Did he ever come and talk to you about the case?"

Lawton shook his head.

"Your partner, James Garcetti, never heard from him either?"

"Uh-huh."

"Santiago would have wanted to talk about it with the two detectives on the case sooner or later," I said. "But he was probably doing this on his personal time, before or after his shift. Working on the case for a few hours a day here and there. He probably thought he had plenty of time. He had no idea just how little time he really had left. I guess none of us can ever be sure of that."

Lawton looked at me sadly. The death of a cop always was traumatic for other cops. Because they realized how easily and unexpectedly the same thing could happen to them too.

"If there's anything I can do to help . . ." Lawton finally said.

I told him about Bobby Ortiz, the suspect from fifteen years ago.

"I'll make sure we check Ortiz out," Lawton said. "See if we can track him down, if he's still alive. Then maybe we could find out some answers from him about what happened to Reyes."

"That's great. But why wouldn't someone have done that right away, fifteen years ago?"

Lawton sighed. "Are we off the record here, Malloy?

"Sure."

"Then you know the real reason for that as well as I do."

I nodded. "Because no one cared enough about Victor Reyes to make the effort."

"I was only on that case when it began. I'm listed on the file because we were the first investigating detectives on the scene that night. But the case quickly got shuffled off to the gangs squad. They were supposed to be the ones who prioritized going after these kinds of street shootings. But I imagine Reyes wasn't really a priority for anyone."

I appreciated Lawton's honesty. He seemed like he'd been a pretty good street cop. Someone who really did care. Sadly, that was rare in the cops I'd met, probably because so many of them had become cynical and defensive about all the problems they'd found trying to enforce the law in treacherous parts of the city.

I thanked Lawton for his help and asked him to keep in touch with me if he found out anything more about Ortiz or the shooting.

He promised he would.

There was something else bothering him though. I could tell that. He finally brought it up as he walked me to the door of his office.

"You said you saw Jimmy Garcetti, my old partner?" he asked.

"Right. Yesterday morning in the Bronx."

"How's he doing?"

"Counting the days until he retires."

"He was doing that when we were on the street together. No, I mean how is he . . . well, how is Jimmy really doing?"

"Do you mean his drinking?"

"Yes."

"Well, we met in a bar. It wasn't even noon. He was already getting pretty drunk. And he seemed to be on a first-name basis with the bartender."

Lawton smiled sadly.

"I've run into Jimmy a few times over the years. It's always been uncomfortable. We were very close when we were on the street together. Hell, you have to be close to your partner. But then . . . then we went our separate ways. I've offered to help Jimmy with his drinking problem a few times, but he just got angry and defensive. I guess there's only so much you can do to help people who've lost their way like that. No one else can help them until they're willing and ready to help themselves."

He was right, of course.

I knew this from experience.

Hell, there were probably lots of people who said the same thing about me.

———

"Why is this story so important to you?" Dr. Landis asked me after I had told her about it that day in her office.

I shrugged. "Roberto Santiago was a friend of mine."

"All right."

"I don't have that many friends anymore. And even though most of my old friends avoid me these days and want nothing to do with me, Santiago . . . well, he came to me when he needed something. Something important. He still trusted me. He believed in me. That meant a lot to me."

"And you feel that you let him down?"

"I suppose that's right."

"So maybe you're trying to make it right by finishing this

story—doing what he asked you to do—in his memory now that he's dead?"

I nodded.

"I think you're looking for some kind of a magic bullet," Landis said to me.

"A magic bullet?"

"Yes."

"You mean like the bullet that killed Victor Reyes fifteen years later?"

She smiled. "In a sense. In medicine, 'magic bullet' refers to a miracle cure—a panacea for everything that ails you—that will make everything all right for you again. I think you believe this story about the bullet that killed this young man after all this time could be a sort of magic bullet for you too. That's why you care so much about the story. But the problem, Mr. Malloy, is that the magic bullet doesn't exist. It's pretty much a myth. In medicine. And in life too."

It was the first thing she had said, during all of our sessions together, that I completely agreed with. Because I knew she was dead on the money about this one. There could be no "magic bullet" for me.

Nikki Reynolds had been right when I told her about Reyes in the restaurant, of course. No one cared about a story like Victor Reyes. Hell, I wouldn't have cared about Reyes myself when I was Gil Malloy, star reporter. But now he was the most important thing in the world to me. Because I needed to do a real story again.

If I could just do this one thing right.

It wouldn't make any difference to the rest of the world or change my career in any meaningful way or undo any of the wrong that I had done.

It was too late for that.

But it would mean something to me.

And so I decided I would put every bit of my journalistic abilities and all of my energy and all of my heart into doing this one story right.

The rock was at the bottom of the hill . . .

CHAPTER 10

CARRIE BRATTEN WALKED over to my desk in the newsroom and stood there in front of me, looking a bit uncomfortable.

"You might be right," she said.

"About what?"

"The Kennedy half-dollar."

"It does mean something?"

"I checked with a police source of mine in the department. I asked him if a Kennedy half-dollar had ever been found at any other crime scenes. He just got back to me. Said they'd found the body of a homeless guy a few days ago down on the Bowery. The guy had been stabbed to death. He had a Kennedy half-dollar in his hand."

I sat there stunned. Despite all my bravado with Carrie earlier, I sure wasn't expecting this.

"No one thought much about it at the time until it happened with the Kennedy woman too," she said.

"But now the cops think it might be the same killer?"

She nodded. "And, if so, the Kennedy half-dollar could be his trademark."

"Jesus, a serial killer?"

"Maybe."

"Any indications of any more murder victims with Kennedy half-dollars?"

"I asked my source. He said no, not at the moment. The police are going through records of recent homicides now."

"Do you have enough to write a story?"

"Not yet. It's just speculation at the moment. The source said he'd get back to me as soon as they found anything concrete between the two murders."

"It doesn't make much sense, does it?" I said. "If it turns out to be true, the victims don't fit the traditional serial killer pattern. A successful fashion and celebrity photographer in an upscale neighborhood and a homeless guy on the Bowery. One's a man, the other's a woman. One was shot to death, one was stabbed. The only possible connection between the two is the Kennedy half-dollar."

"Serial killers—if that's what this is—generally go after the same kind of victims. Young women, children, or whatever. This doesn't seem to fit any kind of serial killer pattern."

"Unless the victims aren't the motives in this case."

"What do you mean?"

"A serial killer who targets attractive young women does it for sexual needs. Schoolteachers or nurses . . . well, the killer is maybe acting out some kind of unresolved trauma from the past. Whoever killed Shawn Kennedy and this homeless guy had a motive too. But it could be a completely different motive from the victim itself, some other reason for murdering them and leaving the Kennedy half-dollar clue that the cops aren't seeing."

"Any idea what that could be? Or what the Kennedy half-dollar connection is about?"

"No," I said. "Of course not. No idea at all."

I took out the address and phone number Nikki Reynolds had given me for Lee Harvey Oswald Jr., who was writing a book about the injustice he believed had been done to his father after the assassination of John F. Kennedy a half century earlier.

I was grasping at straws here. I knew that. But I also knew I needed to check it out. The connection between the Kennedy half-dollars at the two crime scenes was too intriguing to pass up. I had no idea what one thing might have to do with the other, of course. But I learned a long time ago that the best way for a reporter to get answers for things he didn't know was to ask questions.

Maybe Lee Harvey Oswald Jr.—if that really was his name— would have some answers for me.

The address was in Washington Heights, at the northern tip of Manhattan, a long trip from the *Daily News*. I decided to call instead of going all the way up there. I dialed his telephone number, listened as it rang a few times and then went to an answering machine. "Hi, this is Lee," a male voice said. "I'm not home right now. Leave a message at the beep, and I'll get back to you."

"Hey, Lee," I said, "my name is Gil Malloy, and I'm a reporter with the *New York Daily News*. Nikki Reynolds, your agent, gave me this number. I'd like to talk to you about your book. It sounds fascinating, and I want to do a story about it for the Sunday *Daily News*. Call me back as soon as you can."

I left my direct extension at the paper, my cell phone number, and my email address in the newsroom.

I thought about what to do next. I had a couple of choices. I could sit there and wait for Oswald to call back. I could go back to work on the Reyes case. Or I could head up to Washington Heights and knock on Oswald's door.

I walked to the subway station and caught an uptown train to Washington Heights. Just because he didn't answer the phone didn't mean he wasn't home. Or around the neighborhood somewhere. Besides, I always preferred the face-to-face interview to the phone interview anyway.

He lived in a six-story walk-up a few blocks from the George Washington Bridge. I found his name on one of the mailboxes in the lobby: Lee Harvey Oswald Jr. Just like that, for all the world to see. I pressed the buzzer. No one answered.

There was a deli across the street with a bench in front. It was hot out. The temperature was climbing into the nineties. I walked into the deli, bought a cold soda, and sat down on the bench to watch the apartment building. Every once in a while someone went in or out. Each time I approached men and asked if they were Lee Harvey Oswald. If they weren't, or if it was a woman, I asked if they knew Oswald.

No one did. That might mean he hadn't lived in the building very long. Or that he was quiet and kept to himself. Or that it just wasn't a very friendly or neighborly building. One man said he'd seen the name on the mailbox and wondered who would call himself Lee Harvey Oswald Jr. But most of the tenants didn't seem very interested in the tenant's infamous name. Hell, why should they be? The JFK assassination had been a half century ago. Now it was just a part of history.

After I waited for an hour or so, I walked back to the subway and took the train back to the *News*. Sitting on that bench in the hot sun had been uncomfortable. By the time I got onto the subway train, I was drenched in sweat. It was nearly noon and I'd wasted half the day. And I had nothing to show for it. Worse yet, I had absolutely no idea what I was looking for in the first place. Yep, it was a complete waste of time. No question about it.

But what the hell, I had plenty of time on my hands these days. It wasn't like I had anything else important to do in my life. The subway was air-conditioned. When I first got on, it felt like a relief from the heat outside. But now, as we rolled underneath the streets of Manhattan, I felt trapped, like the walls of the car were closing in around me. I wanted to get out of there. For just a second, I started to gasp for breath. I felt dizzy. I was afraid I might have a full-blown panic attack and pass out or something right there on the train. But then the moment passed and I made it back to the *Daily News* okay.

CHAPTER 11

MARILYN STALEY HAD told me I'd need a miracle to ever get on a big story again.

The miracle came in a plain brown paper envelope.

It was addressed simply to me. Gil Malloy. Reporter. *New York Daily News.*

You get lots of mail like that when you're a reporter. People who think they've got a great story to tell you. Most of the time they don't. But you never know, you can never be sure. So you open them all.

This one had a single piece of paper inside along with a sealed envelope. I unfolded the paper and read the words on it.

Everyone made such a big deal out of the 50th anniversary of the assassination of President John F. Kennedy. JFK's words from a half century ago were repeated over and over on the air and in print.

"Ask not what your country can do for you, ask what you can do for your country," blah, blah, blah.

Well, for my country, to commemorate John F. Kennedy's death, I am going to blow the living shit out of Kennedy International Airport.

But first some preliminaries . . .

I opened the envelope. There were two newspaper clippings inside. One was Carrie Bratten's story about Shawn Kennedy. The other was a short metro brief about the homeless man found stabbed to death on the Bowery.

There was something else in the envelope too.

It fell out after I read the note and the two newspaper clips.

A Kennedy half-dollar.

———

It had been awhile since I sat in on a top-level editors' meeting at the *News*. But I was in one now. In fact, I was the main topic of conversation. Staley was there. And Bratten. Plus assorted other assistant city editors and managing editors. Most of them I knew but hadn't had much to do with in a long time. A couple of them were new faces to me, editors who had been hired since I crashed and burned on the Houston story. All they probably knew about me was what they'd heard from other people in the newsroom, which couldn't be good.

Staley had the letter I'd gotten on the desk in front of her. She stared down at it, read the words one more time, and then looked up at me.

"Have you notified the police about this yet?" she asked.

"I thought I should show you guys first."

"We need to let the police know about this immediately."

"Absolutely," I told her.

No one said anything for a few seconds.

"And then I'll write the story," I said.

More silence from around the room.

"I am going to write a story about this, right?"

"Well, let's talk about that," Staley said.

I sighed. "You're not going to tell me you're letting Carrie Bratten write this, are you? This is my story. Not hers. The letter came to me."

"No one's suggesting that Carrie write the story," Staley said.

"So what's to talk about, then?"

"Whether or not there will be a story."

"How can we not write a story about this? It's blockbuster stuff. We've got a crazy guy—apparently set off for some reason by all the JFK fiftieth anniversary stuff that happened—threatening to kill more people and blow up Kennedy Airport. This is a huge story. It will get picked up everywhere, all the other papers in town, TV newscasts, the national cable networks . . ."

"If it's true," someone said.

The lightbulb suddenly went off in my head. I knew what this meeting was all about now. I understood what was going on here. I knew what they were concerned about and why they wanted to talk about it with me.

"Given your track record and journalistic reputation in the light of everything that happened, I'm sure you understand why we have to be absolutely certain that the letter is legitimate and that you are telling us the complete truth about how you managed to get it," Staley said.

"You think I made up the letter?" I asked.

"We never said that."

"That I sent it to myself just to get back onto a big story and onto the front page again? Do you really think I'd do something like that? That I'd stoop that low?"

Staley looked at me sadly. So did everyone else in the room. That's when I realized how far I'd really fallen.

"Are you telling us the truth—the entire truth—about everything?" Staley asked me now.

There were a lot of things I could have said at that moment. But I didn't. Because I knew there was only one right answer for me.

"Yes, I am telling you the truth."

"The entire truth?"

"The entire truth."

"How can we be sure of that?"

"You're just going to have to trust me, Marilyn," I said. "All of you are just going to have to trust me again."

———

Sitting at my desk after the meeting in Staley's office, I looked through the file containing all the notes I'd made about the Reyes story. The Reyes case had been my salvation—a pure story, a real story where I could find the truth and see justice done and make things right somehow for Victor Reyes and Roberto Santiago in death. If I could do that, I told myself, I could somehow crawl back over that line I had crossed, undo the damage I had done, and restore my integrity.

I thought about Roberto Santiago. About Camille Reyes. About Miranda Santiago and the three children she now had to raise without a father. "Roberto said you were a good man," Miranda Santiago had told me. "A man he trusted to do the right thing."

I had a choice to make.

I could walk away from the story about the Kennedy killings right now and go back to the Victor Reyes story, a story that sadly no one really cared about but would bring me the pure satisfaction of doing the right thing.

Or I could pursue the Kennedy trail to wherever it might lead and maybe—just maybe—get a piece of a great story that could get me back onto the front page again.

Which meant, of course, that there was really no choice for me at all.

I closed the file on Victor Reyes and put it away in a drawer in my desk.

Even though I knew that by doing that I might be closing off something else—a chance, possibly my last chance—to become the person I once wanted to be.

PART TWO

GHOSTS
OF
DALLAS

CHAPTER 12

T HE *Daily News* broke the story on the front page the next day.
My stuff from the letter claiming responsibility for the two
murders and threatening more violence, including bombing Kennedy Airport. Plus all of Carrie Bratten's information about the
two seemingly unrelated murders being linked by the discovery of
the Kennedy half-dollars at each scene.

I sat in the same coffee shop reading the story, just like I had
the other morning. Except this time the story had my byline on it
as well as Bratten's.

'KENNEDY KILLER' LOOSE IN CITY
BY GIL MALLOY and CARRIE BRATTEN

THE DAILY NEWS has received a shocking letter
from someone who claims to have already killed two
people—and threatened more violence—in remem-
brance of the assassination of President John F. Kennedy.

The letter, left in an unmarked envelope at the newspaper's office, talks about plans to bomb Kennedy Airport as
some sort of bizarre and unexplained effort to seek justice

for what happened in Dallas on Nov. 22, 1963, when President Kennedy was cut down by bullets as he rode in a motorcade through the city.

The writer of the letter also claims responsibility for two recent murders in New York City: 28-year-old fashion photographer Shawn Kennedy, who was shot to death in Union Square; and a homeless man named Harold Daniels, found stabbed to death on the Bowery.

Police told the News that the letter appeared to be authentic because of previously undisclosed information that it contained about the two seemingly unconnected crime victims, Kennedy and Daniels. In both cases, a Kennedy half-dollar was found on or near the bodies—a fact that was not known by the public at the time of the crimes. The letter received by the News included a Kennedy half-dollar along with newspaper clippings about the two murders.

"The fact that the writer knows about the Kennedy half-dollars is confirmation that he or she must have been involved in the murders," Police Commissioner Ray Piersall said in a statement after authorities were notified of the letter received by the Daily News. "There is no other way this person could have been aware of this information. It appears we are dealing with a serial killer—perhaps set off by the coverage of the 50th anniversary of JFK's death. We don't know the motive, but for some unfathomable reason, the JFK assassination seems to be the catalyst."

I read the piece all the way through to the end. Then I went back to the beginning and read it again. It felt good to be back on the front page with a big story. It had been a long time since that had happened for me. But now . . . well, hell, it was as if I had never left. I still had the magic touch. No problem at all. Just like riding a bicycle, some things you just never forget.

Working with Carrie Bratten turned out to be my biggest problem.

First, she didn't want to share a byline with me. She wanted to write her own story about the Kennedy half-dollars being found on the two bodies. And then let me write my own story about the letter I received. Marilyn Staley, quite correctly, pointed out that they were both part of one big story. Ergo, we needed to write it as a single story, combining both of our stuff into one lead article for the paper.

Then there was the actual writing of the story itself. Just like she didn't want a double byline on the story, Carrie didn't want me to write it with her either. That was pretty hard to avoid, though. Normally, when a story has a double byline, one person does a lot of the reporting and the other actually writes the story. The question with Carrie and me was which one of us would write it. As it turned out, we managed to work out a compromise on this. Sort of. I wrote the part about receiving the letter. She did the stuff about the two murders she'd connected together with the Kennedy half-dollar. Then Staley edited the whole thing, putting together a coherent article.

I read through it all one more time in the coffee shop. Maybe a million people would read the *Daily News* today with my name on the page-one story. Maybe some of them would be other newspaper editors who might decide to give me another chance and offer me a real reporting job. Maybe my ex-wife would read it too, then realize what a mistake she made in giving up on me and would come crawling back pleading for my forgiveness. Maybe some of my ex-friends would start returning my phone messages or reach out to see how I was doing.

A waitress came over and asked if I wanted more coffee. She was young. Reddish hair, nice figure, cute face. I figured her for an aspiring actress. I flashed her a smile. The smile that used to open doors for me and convince people to tell me their innermost secrets and give up everything they had when I was a big star reporter. I hadn't used it very much in recent times. Not really much for me to smile about these days.

"That's me," I said, pointing to my byline in the paper. "I wrote the page-one story today."

"Really?" she said, clearly impressed by the customer she was serving.

I smiled again.

"Well, you deserve a free cup of coffee today," she said, filling my cup.

She smiled back at me. Then she walked off to wait on another customer. I picked up my coffee, sipped it slowly, and then headed for work.

What the hell, it was a start . . .

———

When I got to the office, Staley called Carrie and me to her office. She told us our story had become the big media news of the day; every other newspaper and TV station in town was chasing after our exclusive; the circulation department said copies of the *News* were flying off the newsstands this morning. Then she talked about some ideas we could work on for a follow-up story the next day. Finally, she asked Carrie and me if we had any questions.

"Why is his name first in the byline?" Carrie asked.

"That's your question?" Staley said.

"This really was my story. It was through my police contact that we first found out about the connections between the murders. All he did was get a letter."

"Which is why both of your names are in the byline."

"But his is first."

"There's really no significance to whoever's name is first."

"I think they just put them alphabetically," I said.

"My name is Bratten," she pointed out. "*B* comes before *M* in the alphabet, last time I looked."

"Oh, maybe they went by who's smarter, then."

"Malloy . . ." Staley said, glaring at me.

"Cuter?"

"Look," Staley said, "whether you two like it or not, you're going to be teamed up on this story. You're just going to have to learn to work together. Just like other teams have done in the past."

"Like Woodward and Bernstein," I suggested.

"Exactly."

"Huntley and Brinkley."

"Right."

"Leopold and Loeb."

Staley threw up her hands and stood up from her desk. "Okay, this meeting is over. You two figure it out. Handle the byline— handle all of it—any way you want. I don't care. Just don't screw it up."

Spoken like a true city editor.

———

"Leopold and Loeb?" Carrie said to me when we were back out in the city room.

"They were a pair of thrill killers back in the 1920s who murdered people and—"

"I know who Leopold and Loeb were," she said.

"Bad analogy, you think?

"Marilyn didn't seem to care for it too much."

"She wasn't that keen on your byline question either, was she, Carrie?"

She almost smiled at that, I thought.

"Look," I said, "Marilyn is right about this. We're going to have to work together, whether we like it or not. You know that, and I know that. We don't have to like each other. We don't even have to respect each other. But we do need to figure out some way to function together as an effective team."

She nodded.

"Like Woodward and Bernstein," I said.

"Or Leopold and Loeb," she said.

This time she did smile. No question about it. Ah, Malloy, they just melt when you turn on the charm. Even the ice-cold bitches like Carrie Bratten.

"Going forward," I told her, "maybe we should split up the two parts of this story. You keep working on the murders, looking for any connections on how the Kennedy half-dollars fit in. Me, I'll try to find out more about the letter. Not just the letter itself. The whole Kennedy assassination angle and how it could have set something like this off. There are still a lot of unanswered questions—always have been—about what happened that day in Dallas. Maybe one of them is the thing that set our killer off now. I want to go back and find the answers to those questions. That could be the answer to the questions we have today about these killings."

"What unanswered questions are you talking about?" she asked.

"Did Oswald kill Kennedy? Or was there a conspiracy and the real killers have gone free over all these years?"

She looked at me in amazement. "You're actually going to try to solve the Kennedy assassination?"

"I want to give it a shot."

"God, you really are crazy."

"It's the greatest murder mystery in history," I said. "I'm a reporter. I cover murders and look for answers. You do too, Carrie. So why not try to get to the bottom of the biggest murder ever?"

"And you think that somehow whatever you find out about the JFK assassination can help us figure out what's happening here now—who sent you this letter and who's killing people on the streets of New York City today?"

"Yes."

She shook her head.

"So what the hell are you going to do, Malloy?" Carrie asked. "Go back and read the whole goddamned Warren Commission Report looking for clues?"

"I don't have to read the Warren Commission Report."

"Why not?"

"I've already read it."

CHAPTER 13

MY FATHER USED to tell me that the Kennedy assassination was the most traumatic—and history-changing—event in his lifetime.

Like the Japanese sneak attack on Pearl Harbor was for his father's generation.

Or 9/11 would turn out to be for my generation.

A moment in time that changes you and the world you live in forever.

My father was in college when JFK was killed. This was before Vietnam, protests in the streets, the drug culture, and everything else we remember about the '60s. Students still believed in the government. John F. Kennedy had inspired them about politics and public service with his Peace Corps, his New Frontier, and his Camelot White House with youth and vigor and stirring speeches about changing the world.

But that unimaginable weekend in November 1963 changed everything for his generation, my father would say. The stunning and horrifying news of the assassination. The tears and grief of the young president's funeral in Washington. And, of course, the shooting that forever silenced the accused assassin, Lee Harvey

Oswald, in the basement of a Dallas police station by nightclub owner Jack Ruby.

Like many young men of his generation, my father became intrigued—maybe even obsessed—by the ongoing conspiracy theories about the JFK assassination as the years went on. He read books, watched documentaries, and talked about how there were so many unanswered questions about what happened that day in Dallas.

I don't think my father ever had a clear-cut opinion on who might have been involved in a conspiracy. He would rattle through the usual suspects: the mob, the CIA, the anti-Castro Cubans, right-wing fanatics, the FBI—or a combination of all of them. The only thing he was certain about was that the man the Warren Commission named as the lone assassin, Lee Harvey Oswald, could not have—and did not—carry out the assassination of John F. Kennedy on his own.

"Nothing about Oswald as the assassin makes sense," he would tell me. "It was the right wing that hated Kennedy, not the left. But Oswald proclaimed to be a Marxist and, in fact, had even lived in the Soviet Union. He wasn't a particularly good marksman in the Marines, but we're supposed to believe he hit Kennedy with shots from a window high above a moving motorcade—all in a span of a few seconds. With a cheap mail-order rifle known for misfiring and poor accuracy. And Oswald just happens to work in a building along the route the presidential motorcade decides to take that day. No, Oswald may have been involved in the conspiracy in some way, or maybe he was just a patsy the way he claimed to cops once he was in custody. But someone else was behind the plot that killed my president. And someday the truth will finally come out."

———

For me, none of this really mattered very much until after my father's death.

We had been very close, my father and me. You see, my mother died when I was only ten and my father raised me on his own. He was the circulation manager of a newspaper in Ohio where I grew up. He had once wanted to be a reporter, just like me, but he wound up on the business end of things instead. Maybe that's why he was always so proud of me and encouraged me to pursue journalism.

He died of a heart attack one night. No warning. He just went to bed and never woke up. This happened before I made it to New York. It was a difficult thing for me to deal with, and probably because of that I became curious and eventually obsessed for a while myself with some of the Kennedy assassination conspiracy theories. He had accumulated lots of books and records and documents on the subject, including the complete Warren Commission Report from 1964 that assured the American public a crazy lone assassin named Lee Harvey Oswald had killed Kennedy. After my father died, I read everything he had left and did some of the same kind of research into the assassination he had done. Somehow it felt like it brought him back to life for me while I was lost in the details. Of course, I—just like my father and all the others who have done the same thing—never came up with any persuasive answers. And, as time went on, it began to occupy a smaller and smaller part of my consciousness. By the time of 9/11, I had relegated the Kennedy assassination and all the unanswered questions about it to old history, just like most people had done.

But now here it was again.

The crime—maybe the greatest unsolved crime in history—that wouldn't go away even a half century later.

And now it might have something to do with new crimes and new murders that were happening today.

This wasn't just an exercise in history anymore.

More lives were at stake here.

All I had to do was find out why . . .

———

The Lee Harvey Oswald book coincidence still intrigued me. I wasn't sure why. Or what it might have to do with anything. But it was there. I needed to find out why both the book and the new violence were happening now. The best place to start was with Lee Harvey Oswald Jr. and his mysterious book.

I started by Googling Lee Harvey Oswald Jr. for some information or leads on the man. That turned out to be hopeless, of course. I was inundated with thousands of pieces about Lee Harvey Oswald. But none of them were about *my* Lee Harvey Oswald. No mention of a Lee Harvey Oswald Jr. Nothing on Facebook either. Or Myspace. Or Twitter or any other place I looked.

I called Nikki Reynolds's office. She wasn't there so I asked them to put me through to her voice mail. I left a message asking her to help me get in touch with her author. I didn't say why, of course, just that I was interested in doing a story about the book. I knew she'd figure it out—once she read my Kennedy story in the *Daily News*. But I was banking on the theory that Reynolds believed any kind of publicity for a client was good, even if it was controversial or potentially suspicious or criminal. I also thanked her on the message for our lunch and suggested we might have dinner some night soon. I told her how good it was to see her and, yes, how good she looked. I didn't actually offer to sleep with her, but I probably would have if I thought it would help me get to Lee Harvey Oswald Jr.

I dialed Oswald's number again. Still got the answering machine. I left another message, asking him to call me as soon as he could and saying again how anxious I was to do a story that could help publicize his book.

At that point, I was out of ideas. When that happens, my fallback plan is generally to get something to eat and then wait to see what develops. When the going gets tough, the tough get hungry.

On my way out of the newsroom, I passed by Carrie's desk.

"I just spoke to the medical examiner's office," she said. "They're doing an autopsy now on Daniels, the homeless guy, to see if there's any DNA or any other evidence that might connect his death directly to the Kennedy woman. I'm headed over there to get the results as soon as they come back. One way or another, this could be an angle for our story tomorrow."

"Absolutely."

"How about you?"

"Still scrambling."

"No leads at all?"

"Not yet."

That wasn't entirely true, of course, because I still hadn't told her about the Oswald book—but it wasn't a big lie either.

Just a little white lie.

———

When I got back to my desk later, my telephone was ringing. I picked it up.

"I'm looking for Gil Malloy, the newspaper reporter," a voice said.

"You got him."

"This is Lee Harvey Oswald Jr.," the voice on the other end said.

Damn! How about that?

"Thank you for calling back, Mr. Oswald," I said.

"Call me Lee."

"Sure, Lee."

"You asked me if you could do an interview about my book. Well, I would like that very much. I have a lot of things to say. Things that have gone unsaid for too long. I want the world to hear these things now. I want them to know the true story about Dallas and John F. Kennedy and my father."

CHAPTER 14

SAW YOUR NAME on the front page of the newspaper," Dr. Landis said. "The paper said it was an exclusive."

"Malloy's the name, exclusives are my game," I smiled.

Landis didn't smile back. The damn woman never smiled. She was wearing a blue pin-striped suit today that made her look even more prim and old-fashioned than she did the other times I was there. She sat erect in her chair, holding the ever-present notebook and pen in her lap. She had a concerned look on her face.

"Hey, how many psychiatrists does it take to change a lightbulb?" I asked her.

She didn't answer.

"Just one," I said. "But it takes a dozen office visits and the lightbulb really has to want to change."

No laugh, not even a smile.

"Wow, this is a tough room to work," I told her. "What's a guy gotta do to get a laugh around here."

Still nothing.

"Mr. Malloy," she said finally, "you and I have spoken before about your apparent tendency to make jokes to cover up your true feelings and emotions when you're talking in here."

She sighed and put the notebook down on a table next to her.

I took that as a sign that she was through listening to me for the moment and wanted me to listen to her. I was right.

"Let's talk about you and your defense mechanisms," Landis said. "You have other defense mechanisms that I think you rely on in the same way as this. One of them is the way you embrace and constantly refer to your job as a newspaper reporter. By doing that, it protects you from having to deal with the questions, the issues, the uncertainties of the world around you. It allows you to blank everything out except the story you're working on at that moment. You wrap yourself in journalism like it was a religion."

"It's my job."

"It's more than a job to you."

"Okay, I take my job very seriously."

"Which makes it even more terrifying for you when something happens that threatens to take that job away from you. Like the Houston story did."

I didn't say anything. I didn't want to talk to this woman anymore. I sure as hell didn't want to talk about Houston with her.

"Let's talk about 9/11," Landis said. "You've made numerous references to that since you've been coming to see me. Why is that?"

"Because I was there."

"So you witnessed a good deal of death and destruction?"

"Well, almost three thousand people died. And hundreds of tons of steel and concrete—where people worked, shopped, and visited—were vaporized into dust. So yes, I would say there was a great deal of death and destruction there. You've heard of 9/11, right? It was in all the papers."

She ignored the sarcasm.

"Did you know any of the victims?" she asked.

"I knew some of them. A few cops and firemen I'd worked

with over the years. A woman who worked for the Port Authority who was attending a breakfast at Windows on the World that morning. The husband of a neighbor of mine who'd just stopped in there on his way to work uptown to drop something off in one of the offices."

"And the other victims—the ones you didn't know—I assume you got to know a lot about them as you reported on the story during the weeks afterward?"

"I interviewed hundreds of families and friends and coworkers of the dead," I said. "I wrote their stories, I cried with them, I comforted them, and I raged with them against the cold-blooded terrorists who had carried out this horrendous act that took away so many good people and changed the lives of so many still living so irrevocably."

"How did all this tragedy affect you?"

"I'm not sure how to answer that."

"Were you ever overwhelmed with grief? Broke down in tears or had an emotional collapse? Felt like you couldn't go on anymore? Decided that you couldn't handle any more of the death and destruction and heartbreak that you were covering every day? That it was tearing you up too much inside to keep doing this? Did anything like that ever happen to you, Mr. Malloy?"

I snorted contemptuously.

"Boy, you just don't get it, do you? Being a reporter is my job. If a reporter lets his emotions take over, then he's no longer effective. You don't know anything about me or my job. And yet you sit there, all prim and proper with your degree on the wall, and take notes about me and tell me what you think I should be doing. Well, let me tell you something, lady . . . you don't have a clue to what being a reporter is all about. I shut all of that emotion out when I'm doing my job. It's the only way I can do my job. Sure, I could have broken down in tears that first day when the Twin Towers collapsed and I first saw and grasped the unimaginable horror that was happening in front of me. But I didn't. I did my job. I did it for a long time after that and I did it well. That's called being a reporter. And that's what I am. But I guess someone like you could never understand that."

I was angry, but it felt good. Felt good to let the anger out.

"I do understand," Landis said calmly. "I understand perfectly. And I think you've just done a very good job of making the point that I was trying to make to you. You use your job, you use being a reporter, as a defense mechanism. No matter how noble you try to make it—and it is a noble profession—being a reporter allows you to shut out emotion and avoid dealing with what's really inside you. So when this shield, this defense mechanism, is taken away from you, you are forced to confront things you never did before. I believe that's what happened to you after the Houston story fell apart. I believe the panic attacks came about because you couldn't handle the idea that you weren't a reporter anymore. And so you were forced to confront and to deal with all these emotions in your life for the first time without the shield of being a reporter you embraced for so long to protect you. When you couldn't do that, your body reacted by shutting down. Hence, the panic attacks. I believe it was the loss of your identity as a reporter—the thing you identified yourself by—that brought on the onset of the panic attacks." She shrugged. "Anyway, that's my working theory at the moment."

I stared at her. Desperately trying to hold myself together, even though this woman had just taken me and my life apart like I was a specimen in a medical lab.

"Is that the kind of stuff they teach you in psychiatry school?" I said.

"It doesn't make sense to you?"

I sighed. "Yes, it makes sense. Sort of . . . I guess."

"We need to get past you as a reporter," she said. "We need to find out about you as a person. This might be difficult for you. It might be upsetting at times. All I'm asking is that you try, Mr. Malloy. Will you do that for me?"

"I guess," I shrugged.

What the hell choice did I have?

"If you do, I think you'll help yourself get answers for some of the other things in your life you've talked about in here. The failure of your marriage. Loss of your friends. Difficulty getting along with people at work . . ."

"Hey, maybe it'll even bring my wife back, huh? You could add marriage consultant—hell, marriage fixer—to your headshrinker degree."

"Let's talk about your marriage. You said before that your wife left you in the aftermath of the Houston scandal. That the whole Houston thing not only cost you your job, but your wife and marriage too."

"Yes, she just couldn't handle the toll it took on me."

"That's kind of a convenient answer."

"What do you mean?"

"What was your life like before Houston? Was your marriage perfect? Did you and your wife ever fight? Were you madly in love all that time? And then, the minute you began having troubles as a reporter over the Houston scandal, it simply disassembled your marriage overnight? Is that what happened?"

Damn. This woman was good. She asked questions as relentlessly as I did as a reporter.

"No marriage is perfect," I told her. "There always are problems."

"How about your friends?" she asked. "Were they real friends? Or just people who liked being around you because you were a star reporter?"

I thought about Nikki Reynolds. The way she'd been my pal, my agent, and even my lover when I was riding high. How quickly she dropped me when it all went bad. Then came out of nowhere to be my friend again when she needed me to do something for her.

"I guess I had a lot of fake friends," I said.

"So it wasn't the Houston scandal that cost you your friends. They were never truly your friends. If it hadn't been the Houston scandal, it would have been something else for them probably. What do you think about that, Mr. Malloy?"

"I guess I need some better friends, huh?"

"You've got to stop blaming Houston for everything that's gone wrong in your life," Landis said.

CHAPTER 15

I F I THOUGHT there was going to be a quick and simple ending to this story—that an exclusive would drop right in my lap—that hope ended as soon as I saw Lee Harvey Oswald Jr.

Oswald was barely fifty, based on the information I knew about him, but he looked at least a decade older. He sat in a wheelchair, a thin, frail-looking man with an oxygen tube in his nose and a table stacked with bottles of pills and other medical paraphernalia next to him.

On the subway ride up there, it had all seemed so easy.

I'd imagined a scenario like this:

The previously unknown son of Lee Harvey Oswald spent his entire life frustrated by some sort of injustice that history had dealt to his father. Maybe he thought his father really was a patsy of some more sinister force, who had been set up as the fall guy for a conspiracy carried out by many. Maybe he thought his father was innocent altogether, just the wrong man in the wrong place at the wrong time. Whatever the reason, he set out to seek revenge for his father with a bizarre vendetta of murder and violence sparked by the fiftieth anniversary of Kennedy's death—and his father's too. Except one intrepid reporter (that would be me) figured it all out, broke the story, and became a media star all over again. It was a nice dream. But that's all it was.

Looking at Oswald now, it was hard to imagine that he had somehow made his way down to the Bowery and stabbed Harold Daniels to death.

It was even harder to believe he could have followed Shawn Kennedy into Union Square Park from the bar nearby and shot her to death.

"I have diabetes and emphysema," Oswald explained to me. "Some other things are wrong with me too, but those are the two biggest problems I'm dealing with now. I've already lost one leg to the diabetes, and the situation on the other one isn't looking good. That's where I was when you left your messages. At the hospital. The emphysema is the worst thing. That's what keeps me hooked up to this damn oxygen machine. Without it, I have real trouble breathing. The doctors give me six months, maybe a year tops to live."

"I'm sorry," I said.

It didn't seem enough. I felt like there was something more I should say, but I couldn't think of any words to fit the enormity of this man's situation.

"I'm really sorry," I repeated.

Oswald shrugged.

"They say stuff like this is all in your genes. A lot of it is predetermined before you even get into the world. I guess my parents didn't give me very good genes. Of course, my biological mother died when I was a baby. And my biological father. . . . well, you know what happened to him. Lee Harvey Oswald. He was twenty-four years old when he died. Can you believe that? Anyway, I can't find out much about my biological family's medical history because . . . well, because neither parent lived long enough to have much of a history."

I had decided not to ask him about the Kennedy murders for now, because I didn't want to spook him. I figured I'd just let him tell me about himself and his book and see where it all led.

He seemed happy to do that.

Without much prodding, he talked easily and openly about his life and the book and how he had discovered the facts about his past.

"I didn't know Oswald was my biological father for a long time. I knew I was adopted. My parents had told me that when I was growing up. But my mother didn't tell me who my biological father was until she got sick, right before she died. My father—the man who raised me—had died several years earlier. I was their only child, all that was left of the family. So I guess she wanted to make things right. To have some sort of closure or something. She told me the details of the adoption for the first time, that I was Lee Harvey Oswald's son. I know she was doing it because she thought it was the right thing to do, but in retrospect it was probably the worst thing that ever happened in my life.

"I had lived a relatively normal life until that point, I suppose. I was married with two children, a son and a daughter. I had a pretty good job as a salesman for an advertising agency in New Orleans, where I had grown up and spent most of my life. I never had any clue that I was different from any other American guy with a job and a family. But everything changed for me then. The realization that I was the offspring of Lee Harvey Oswald—this horrible man who had killed our president and changed history, or so I had been told—was difficult to accept. I would lie awake at night thinking about it. Wondering if whatever madness had driven him to do what he did was inside me somewhere too.

"I never told anyone, not even my wife and my children, not then, anyway. I kept the horrible truth inside me. I began to drink heavily, I couldn't concentrate on my job, I couldn't be there for my family. Finally, at some point, it all fell apart. My wife left me, my kids didn't want to talk to me, and I lost my job. For a while, I drifted like that. Going from sales job to sales job, drinking a lot and mostly feeling sorry for myself and who I was. It was a terrible burden to have to live with. I was Lee Harvey Oswald's son. My God, how could someone live with something like that?"

He told me that his name had been Lee Mathis. His adoptive parents had kept the first name his biological mother had given him—naming him after her secret love—but his last name had been the same as theirs for most of his life.

But then, when his health began to fade and he realized his own mortality, he decided to confront the demons he'd been avoiding. Rather than run away from the father he had never known, he decided to embrace his family heritage. Changed his name from Lee Mathis to Lee Harvey Oswald Jr. Proclaimed it to the world. Finally, about a year ago, he told his family the truth too. He wanted them to understand what he had been going through when he had drifted apart from them.

"How'd that go?" I asked.

"Not well."

"They didn't believe you?"

"Not at first. They told me that the alcohol had gone to my brain and ruined it. That I was crazy. That I needed some kind of psychiatric help. But then I showed them this."

He reached over to the table next to him, took a sheet of paper out of a file folder, and handed it to me.

"My birth certificate," he said. "I went back to New Orleans and dug through all the records for April 21, 1964, the day I was born."

I read the birth certificate. The name on it was indeed Lee Harvey Oswald Jr. The mother was Emily Springer. The father was listed as Lee Harvey Oswald (deceased).

"It could be someone else named Lee Harvey Oswald," I said.

"How many people named Lee Harvey Oswald do you think there are?"

"I don't know."

"I spoke to a relative of my birth mother—her sister, Laura—who said my mother was dating the same Lee Harvey Oswald who worked at the Texas School Book Depository in Dallas. The sister met him too."

I handed the document back to him.

"What about DNA proof?" I asked.

"A little hard, since my father's been in the ground for nearly half a century."

"Wasn't there some talk of digging him up for some kind of DNA testing a few years back?"

He nodded. "There were claims that it wasn't really his body in the ground. So they compared the DNA to make sure. It was him."

"So theoretically you could compare your DNA to that sample?"

"Theoretically."

"And practically?"

"I've never been allowed access to the DNA samples. All of that stuff is locked up tight. The FBI and CIA won't release it to allow for that kind of testing."

"But you would take a DNA test if you could?"

"Absolutely."

He told me next that he had decided to write the book to find out the truth about his father as part of his own desire to learn the secrets of who he really was.

"I didn't start out doing it to prove my father was innocent," he said to me now. "I just wanted to discover who he was and why he had done what he did. But the more I learned, the more I realized that a terrible injustice had been done to my father. I was never a conspiracy theorist. All my life I had just accepted the official 'lone gunman' version of the story. But there was a conspiracy. And my father was one of the victims. He was a victim, just like John F. Kennedy was a victim that day. That's what my book is all about."

He said he had moved to New York several months ago to work on the book. He felt it was important to be near the New York literary market to sell the manuscript. He knew he didn't have much time left to work on it—or sell it. He'd sent the rough draft of the manuscript out to a number of publishers and agents. One of them was Nikki Reynolds. He also sent copies of the nearly finished manuscript to his family a few weeks ago—his wife, son, and daughter. He said he wanted them to read it in case he died before getting it published.

Before I left, he handed me a copy of the manuscript. It was very thick, more than five hundred pages. He said I was welcome to take it and read it later, if it would help me write my article about the book for the *Daily News*. He also said I could quote any passages from it for the article.

It was time to get to the real reason for my visit.

"Mr. Oswald . . ."

"Lee."

"Lee, there've been two murders recently with some sort of link to John F. Kennedy and the assassination. A woman in Union

Square Park and a man on the Bowery. Both victims had Kennedy half-dollars near their bodies. In addition, I received a letter at the paper from someone claiming to have committed the murders and threatening to blow up Kennedy Airport and do more violence as some sort of way to remember the JFK assassination."

He looked confused. "What does this have to do with my book?"

"I was hoping you could tell me that. It just seems like an awfully big coincidence that these Kennedy-related killings happened at the same time as your book," I said.

"My God, you can't believe I could have had anything to do with these murders."

I looked at him sitting there in his wheelchair, hooked up to the oxygen tube. Looking like he was barely able to move around his own apartment.

"No, I guess not."

"You have to believe me!"

The truth was I did believe him.

I was hoping Lee Harvey Oswald Jr. might have some answers to help me make sense out of it all.

He didn't.

Maybe his book would.

CHAPTER 16

T HE TITLE OF the book was *The Kennedy Connection: Lee Harvey Oswald's Secret Son Searches for the Truth About Dallas.*

I took it home with me that night. Home was a one-bedroom apartment on the eleventh floor of a prewar building at 96th Street just off of Third Avenue. I'd moved there after Susan and I broke up. It was supposed to be a temporary place, until I figured out what I wanted to do. But like a lot of things in my life now, I'd never gotten around to making a decision about finding a new apartment. It wasn't a bad building or location, but the landlord wasn't exactly motivated to make repairs. I had peeling paint on the walls, bad plumbing, and—worst of all—air-conditioning that would inexplicably run at full blast in the middle of winter, then shut down completely in the summer. On hot summer nights like this one, the only way to get any kind of air into the place was to open a big picture window in the living room. But that meant bugs and dirt and noise from the outside came through too. It was always a tricky decision for me whether to leave that window open or closed. This time, I opted for the open window. Then I sat down in my living room to read Lee Harvey Oswald's book.

The beginning of the manuscript was devoted to Oswald's discovery of who his biological father was and his efforts to deal with the trauma that caused him.

He went on at some length about the effect all of this had had on him and his family and his life. He told of his descent from a normal existence into a cauldron of despair and depression after he found out about his biological father. About how that led to his estrangement from his wife and his two children. There were times, he said, when he contemplated suicide. Especially when he looked at pictures of Lee Harvey Oswald in history books and saw glimpses of himself in that face.

The turning point came for him one day when he tried to call his son, Eric, on the son's birthday. Eric Mathis had taken the Oswald news harder than anyone else, he recalled, directing all of his anger at his father even if that wasn't a logical target. That anger had culminated when Lee tried to make the birthday call. "I'd like to speak to Eric," he said. "This is his father." The person who answered the phone came back and said, "Eric said he doesn't have a father."

His daughter, Samantha, would speak to him, but only barely. And his wife, Carol, had remarried and moved to a new city. Everyone in his family, he said, wanted desperately to have nothing to do with him or with the evil it was now clear he had been spawned from.

For Lee himself, his rebirth had come, he wrote, when he decided to find out the truth about his infamous father, what he had actually done and why.

He soon found himself consumed by all the conspiracy theories about what happened that day in Dallas—all of them centered on the idea that Oswald was not a lone, deranged assassin and had, at worst, been caught up in something bigger than him that terrible day. "I'm just a patsy," Oswald had said in one of his few public comments after the arrest. His son decided to prove that was true. Maybe because he really believed it. Or maybe because he thought it was the only way he could save a bit of his own life too.

———

The Kennedy conspiracy stuff itself in the book—Oswald Jr.'s "investigation" and theories into what happened in Dallas—was disappointing to me. Maybe because I'd already heard all this so many times that this part of the manuscript had a stale, retold feel about it. No matter how hard Oswald Jr. tried to make the case that he was somehow looking at his father's life and death from a new, personal perspective.

A lot of it focused on the same questions and evidence about the investigation that had been analyzed, dissected, and argued about by historians, journalists, and conspiracy buffs many times before.

He started by giving the official version of the Kennedy assassination as we have always heard it. Lee Harvey Oswald firing three shots at the motorcade from the sixth floor of the Texas School Book Depository. Oswald fleeing the building afterward as the president was rushed to Parkland Memorial Hospital, where he was pronounced dead a short time later. Dallas Police Officer J. D. Tippit's fatal encounter with Oswald, who shot and killed Tippit when the policeman got out of his squad car to question him. Oswald's arrest in the Texas Theatre, a movie house nearby where he had fled after the Tippit shooting. His forty-eight hours of questioning by police as the nation grieved for the young president. And finally, of course, the death of Oswald himself when he was shot by Jack Ruby, who said he wanted to spare First Lady Jackie Kennedy the agony of an Oswald trial.

Then he laid out in the manuscript the key points that he believed proved his father was innocent or, at worst, only an unwilling participant in the tragic events. These were:

- If Oswald really acted alone, he would have had to fire all three shots from the window of the Book Depository building in approximately six seconds. This would have been almost impossible to do.
- There was never any visual sighting of Oswald on the sixth floor of the Book Depository building that day. No one actually saw Oswald crouching behind a box at the window getting ready to fire his shots at the presidential motorcade.
- There had to be other gunmen firing at Kennedy from some other point besides the Book Depository, most likely from the grassy knoll across the street from it. Ah, the grassy knoll. The holy grail of all JFK conspiracy theories. The facts on the grassy knoll that Oswald talked about in the book were the same ones I'd heard so many times before. The famous Zapruder film of the assassination shows Kennedy's head snapping back—not forward—from the impact of the final shot. That seemed to indicate the shot came from someplace in front of the motorcade—the grassy knoll—and not from behind in the direction of the Book Depository.

Anyway, Oswald Jr. had simply regurgitated all the familiar theories of a conspiracy without hard new evidence to back up any of it. There was no smoking gun here. Not on the grassy knoll. Or anywhere else either.

—

The thing that interested me more was the personal stuff.

Like the death of his mother when he was a baby—and his efforts to go back and determine the exact circumstances of what had happened to her.

The official version was pretty straightforward. Emily Springer, his mother, had worked as a dancer at a strip club in New Orleans. That was where she had met Oswald, who lived in the city during the spring and summer of 1963. One night in early 1964, not long after Lee Jr. was born, she got in her car, drove to a bridge over the nearby Mississippi River, and leaped to her death.

But digging deeper into the death of his mother, he had discovered some disturbing facts. His mother had been telling people in the days before her death that she had questions—and indicated she knew something—about the Kennedy assassination. Presumably based on her romantic relationship with Oswald in the months before the assassination. The Warren Commission was still meeting to prepare its report, and her coworkers said Emily Springer had said she wanted to talk to the commission about what she knew.

He speculated that this may have gotten back to other people, people who didn't want her talking to the Warren Commission or to anyone else.

He also said that Emily's sister, Laura, claimed that Emily had never talked about suicide or exhibited any suicidal tendencies. On the contrary, she had embraced the idea of being a single mother and raising the boy that was the result of her romance with Lee Harvey Oswald. Even more disturbing, he wrote, was that the sister had recalled his mother appeared nervous in the days before her death, complaining that she felt as if someone was following and watching her.

Oswald then compared his mother's death to the deaths of

other people linked to the JFK assassination in some way. From the moment Jack Ruby had silenced Oswald forever with a gunshot to the stomach two days after the assassination, people with ties to the events in Dallas had been dying mysteriously and in mind-boggling numbers.

The thing that made me think the most, though—the thing that made me sit bolt upright in my chair when I read it—was a clue to what his mother might have known about the assassination.

And might have been prepared to tell the Warren Commission, if she'd ever gotten the chance.

An alibi for Lee Harvey Oswald.

———

On that fateful morning, Laura Springer had received a phone call from Emily.

She remembered it vividly because the call had woken her up at six in the morning.

Emily said she was at the New Orleans bus station and that Lee Harvey Oswald was with her. She had just bought him a bus ticket for an eight-hour ride back to Dallas, and he was about to board the bus. He had taken the bus in from Dallas to New Orleans the previous day to see her. When he had gotten there, Oswald told Emily there were big changes coming in his life—exciting changes, the big break he had been hoping for—and that he wanted to share it all with her. They had stayed up all night talking about how he would leave his wife, Marina, and their family in Dallas, then come to live with Emily and the baby they would have together.

At one point, Emily put Oswald on the phone with her sister. Laura remembered asking him about his job at the Book Depository and how he got the time off to go to New Orleans. She said he just laughed and said, "Don't worry, that's all been taken care of. I'm taking a bus back to Dallas now. All I have to do is be there in time to meet someone this afternoon. Someone very important. Someone who is finally going to change my life. Everything's going to be different from now on."

It was, of course, the last time Emily Springer would ever see him.

Later, when Emily saw Oswald all over the news and eventually watched him gunned down on TV, she took out the receipt for the ticket she'd bought him that day. She told her sister she would keep it forever. As a memory of that wonderful last time they spent together.

Lee Mathis, who now called himself Lee Harvey Oswald Jr., said in the manuscript after writing this account:

What was the big opportunity—the big change in his life— my father thought he was going to get? Who was he sup- posed to meet that afternoon instead of going to work at the Book Depository? What did he mean when he said he didn't have to go to work that day because "it had all been taken care of"?

There had always been stories of Oswald "doubles." Sightings of my father in the weeks before the assassina- tion that seemed staged, as if it wasn't really him, but some- one who wanted to make it seem like it was. These Oswald "sightings" included a trip to Mexico to meet with Com- munist officials at the Soviet embassy; an incident at a rifle range where he seemed to go out of his way to make a pub- lic display of anger against the U.S.; even a famous picture of him holding the assassination rifle in his backyard before

November 22 had been accused by some of being a phony
photo with a double. So what if the people who saw my
father the day of the assassination—who said he was in the
Book Depository—actually saw another "Oswald double"?
Someone who was instructed to make himself noticeable as
Oswald that fateful day?

And where was the meeting he had that afternoon in
Dallas? Could that have been why he went into the Texas
Theatre where he was captured? To meet what he thought
was going to be a contact who could change his life? Instead, he walked into a trap that set him up to be the greatest villain in history.

I don't know the answers to all of these questions.

But let me ask this simple—but crucial—question:

If my mother had bought Oswald a bus ticket for an
eight-hour ride back to Dallas at six a.m., how could he have
gotten there in time to assassinate the president at 12:30?

CHAPTER 17

WANT TO GO to Dallas," I said.

"What's in Dallas?" Marilyn Staley asked.

"The scene of the JFK assassination."

"What's the point of going there now?"

"Whoever wrote that note to me and killed those two people is motivated for some reason by the JFK assassination. It doesn't make any sense, of course. What happened in Dallas all those years ago that could possibly motivate someone today to commit murders in New York City? Nothing any logical mind could fathom. But then murderers—especially serial killers—generally don't have logical minds.

"So I go to Dallas and try to figure out what that motivation might be. I go to Dealey Plaza. The Texas School Book Depository where Oswald supposedly fired the shots from the sixth-floor window. The Dallas police station where he was shot by Jack Ruby two days later. The rooming house where he lived. The movie theater he fled into just before he was arrested. All of the spots that are a part of the JFK assassination history.

"Maybe I stumble on some answers that help us figure out what's going on here now. Maybe I don't. But I think there's an answer there. Somewhere. There has to be. Something we're not seeing, some connection that I might be able to figure out by re-tracing the steps of the assassination.

"And even if I don't, we still get a good story out of it. An in-depth feature piece. Talking about the two Kennedy murders here and how we went to Dallas looking for answers from the past, etc. C'mon, Marilyn, even if I just wind up asking a lot of questions without answers, it could still be a nice read."

We were sitting in Staley's office. Me, her, and Carrie Bratten. Carrie didn't look happy. She kept glaring at me with a tight look on her mouth as I talked about the trip to Dallas and my idea for a feature story. I'd expected that reaction from her. To be honest, I actually had looked forward to it.

The arrogant little bitch. I hadn't told her about any of this before we went into Staley's office. I hadn't told her about what was coming up next either.

"That could be a good Sunday feature," Staley said. "You go to Dallas, soak up the local color for a few days, and then write it up for the weekend edition. I like that, Gil."

The smile on Carrie's face got tighter.

"Meanwhile, Carrie can add some of the live stuff here from the police investigation into the murders for tomorrow to keep the story going until your weekend piece. What do you think, Carrie?"

"Uh . . . well, I'll have to make some calls to see what I can come up with," she said, obviously rattled and a bit off her game. "I'm sure I'll be able to find something new and . . ."

"Actually, I have something for tomorrow too," I said.

I took out Lee Harvey Oswald Jr.'s manuscript and plopped it down on Staley's desk.

"Are you saying that you think the person who wrote this book could have done the Kennedy killings now out of some sort of weird revenge motive or quest for justice over what happened to Lee Harvey Oswald in 1963?" Staley asked with amazement after I'd told her what I found in the manuscript.

"Doubtful."

I explained his serious health issues and the wheelchair and the oxygen tube tied to him.

"He could be faking the illness," she pointed out.

"I don't think so. I spent time with him. He looks very frail; he's in pretty bad shape. I'm sure he's really incapacitated."

"Maybe he hired someone to carry out the murders for him," she suggested.

"Possible, but unlikely. He doesn't seem like a violent or angry man. More tragic than anything. His whole life was destroyed by being Lee Harvey Oswald's son. And now he is dying. Which is why he wrote the book."

"And you think he's telling the truth about this?"

"As far as I can tell. At least, he believes it. The birth certificate seems genuine. Of course, DNA testing could tell for sure. But yes, I think it's very possible he is the secret son of Lee Harvey Oswald."

Staley skimmed through the pages of the manuscript, stopping once in a while to read a paragraph or two.

"Let me see if I understand this," she said finally. "You don't think that the person who wrote this manuscript—even though he could well be Lee Harvey Oswald's secret son—murdered those two people, left Kennedy half-dollars with their bodies as a sick clue, or wrote you a letter warning of new violence at Kennedy Airport? Or that he is responsible for anything else going on in the city now?"

"Right."

"Then what's the story?"

"That is the story," I said. "It's a helluva connection. Someone is killing people and claiming to have done it to mark the JFK assassination. At the same time, the unknown son of Lee Harvey Oswald emerges with this claim that his father was secretly set up for the killing. We lay it all out for the readers just like that. We talk about Lee Harvey Oswald Jr. and the book and his claim of his father's innocence. And we simply point out that this is all happening at the same time as the other killings and threats taking place. That's all."

"And this Oswald character—or whatever his real name is— he's okay with you quoting stuff from the manuscript?"

"He wants this information out there," I said. "I want this information out there too. It works for both of us. We get a good story out of this, and he gets publicity for the book. Hell, we'll probably make it a best seller before this is all over. It's a win-win situation for everyone, Marilyn."

———

After we left Staley's office, Carrie didn't speak to me until we got back to her desk in the newsroom.

"Why didn't you tell me about any of this stuff you were working on?" she asked. "I thought we were working as a team."

"C'mon, Carrie," I said. "Let's be honest here. Just you and me talking. If you had something hot like this manuscript—an exclusive dropped right into your lap—would you have told me about it? Honestly?"

"Yes," she said. "I would have."

I looked at her face again. The tightness around her mouth was still there. The anger too. But there was something else I saw this time. Shock. She looked as if I had just slapped her across the face.

This wasn't working out the way I had hoped. I had thought about—eagerly anticipated, truth be told—Carrie's reaction to my big scoop. I'd reveled in the fact that she would find out about it at the same time I told Staley and how much that would piss her off. I thought it would be an incredibly satisfying moment for me. But now it didn't seem so satisfying at all.

"Look, Carrie, I'm sorry," I said. "You're right, I should have told you first. I owed you that much. If it helps you feel any better, we can put your name on the byline too. The same as we did before. And I promise to—"

"You're an asshole, Malloy!" she said in a loud voice.

Loud enough that other people in the newsroom looked around at us.

Then she stormed away from her desk and out of the newsroom. I waited a few minutes to see if she would come back. She didn't. Eventually, I walked to my own desk. I picked up Oswald's manuscript and started reading through portions of it again for my story. But I couldn't stop thinking about what had just happened with Carrie Bratten.

Because I didn't like being called an asshole.

Because I didn't like that she'd done it in a public setting where other people in the newsroom heard it.

And also because—well, the thing that really bothered me the most about it all, I guess—she was right.

Dammit.

I had acted like an asshole.

CHAPTER 18

ON THE NIGHT I wrote the Lee Harvey Oswald Jr. story, I waited around for the first editions of the *Daily News* to roll off the presses and arrive in the newsroom. I picked up a copy and looked at the front page. The headline said REVEALED: JFK ASSASSIN HAD SECRET SON. Underneath that, a subhead read LEE HARVEY OSWALD JR. EMERGES IN NYC AS MYSTERY DEEPENS OVER NEW KENNEDY KILLINGS. The picture was a split of Oswald Jr. taken in his Washington Heights apartment and a mug shot of Lee Harvey Oswald himself from the Dallas police files in 1963. In big bold letters on the front page, the byline said EXCUSIVE BY GIL MALLOY and CARRIE BRATTEN.

I read the story from beginning to end. Then I grabbed a few extra papers from the stack, stuck them under my arm, and headed for home. On the way out, one of the guys at the copy desk looked up, smiled, and gave me a big thumbs-up. "Nice story, Gil," he said. It had been a long time since anyone at the *News* had said that to me. I'd almost forgotten how good it felt.

———

The next morning my desk was piled high with messages from people trying to reach me. Some of them were from TV shows and magazines and even a few other newspapers that were trying to follow up on Oswald Jr. and wanted to interview me about him and the book. Other messages were from people I'd known in the past who had disappeared from my life in recent times after my career went into a tailspin after the Houston mess. People who had not only not called me since then but also had never returned my phone messages or ignored me when I ran into them on the street or at events.

A few of the other papers in town did point out my troubled past. Without actually coming out and saying so, they tried to imply that there could be some question about the validity of my reporting because of the Houston business. But this was different from Houston. This time I had a real flesh-and-blood person I was writing about in Lee Harvey Oswald Jr. and his book about his infamous father.

The one person I had not heard from whom I expected to was Nikki Reynolds. I figured she must be ecstatic over the story on her author. So I finally called her.

"Who loves ya, baby?" I said when she came on the line. "Did I come through for you? Huh?"

"Thank you, Gil," she said, but not with a lot of emotion.

"That's it?"

"What do you want me to say?"

"I'm not feeling the love here, Nikki."

"Sorry, I guess I'm still a bit stunned that this all wound up on page one like this."

"That was what you wanted, wasn't it?" I said. "Lots of publicity? This is great for you, Nikki. And for your client. Hey, I'll tell you what. Let's go out for dinner tonight. To celebrate."

"I'm pretty busy right now. Some other time."

Except she didn't sound busy. Just tense. Maybe even a little scared.

"When, then?"

"I gotta go . . ."

"What's wrong with you, Nikki?"

There was a long pause on the other end.

"Look, I probably shouldn't say anything. But be careful, Gil. Just watch out for yourself."

"Careful of what? Nikki, what the hell's going on?"

She hung up before I could say anything else.

———

I didn't go straight home that night. Instead, I stopped at an apartment house near Gramercy Park. It was a brownstone on 19th Street between Third Avenue and Irving Place. I looked through the names on the buzzer in the lobby until I found one for Susan Endicott. Who used to be Susan Malloy. My ex-wife. I pressed the buzzer.

A few seconds later, I heard her voice over the intercom in the lobby.

"Yes? Who is it?"

"Gil."

There was silence.

"Gil Malloy."

More silence.

"Your husband."

Still nothing.

"Ex-husband."

"What do you want, Gil?"

"I wanted to apologize to you."

"What exactly are you apologizing for?"

"The last time we talked."

"So you're apologizing for calling me a bitch?"

"Yes."

"Apologizing for saying I ruined your life?"

"That too."

"Apologizing for—"

"I'm apologizing for everything. Can I come up?"

———

It was the first time I'd been in her new apartment. We'd both found new places after we split up. Me on the Upper East Side, her in Gramercy Park, the same neighborhood where we'd lived together when we were man and wife in another lifetime. I'd driven by her place a few times but never gotten up the courage to try to go in until now.

Some of the furniture in the living room I recognized as stuff she'd taken from our old place. Other things were new. There was a picture on the coffee table of her and a dark-haired, good-looking guy that had been taken at some kind of formal event. She was dressed in an evening gown and he was in a tux. I figured that was her fiancé. I think his name was Dave. My replacement in her life.

Next to it was a copy of the *Daily News*, open to my story from today.

I wondered if she'd been reading it when I showed up.

Susan sat down in a chair across from me. She was wearing jeans and a sweatshirt, and didn't have any makeup on. She obviously wasn't expecting visitors tonight. But she still looked good. I'd almost forgotten how good she looked. It had been awhile.

"Is that the new boyfriend?" I said, looking over toward the picture on the coffee table in front of us.

"That's my fiancé."

"Dave, right?

"Dale."

"Whatever."

I picked up the picture and looked at him again.

"What does he do again?"

"He's a commodities trader."

"I don't even know what that really is. I mean, is it legal?"

She glared at me.

"So you guys don't live together?" I said, putting the picture back down on the table.

"Not that it's any of your business, but no. We have separate apartments right now. We're thinking about buying a place together on Second Avenue, near Stuyvesant Town, after the marriage. We're getting married in December. The wedding will be at Trinity Church in lower Manhattan. The reception afterward is at the National Arts Club. We've decided on chicken as the main menu course at the reception dinner, but we're still vacillating between strip steak, lamb chops, or some kind of seafood as the alternate. Is there anything else you'd like to know?"

"Will I be invited?"

She actually laughed at that one. I remembered that laugh. It was a nice laugh.

She'd laughed like that the first time I met her. She was a young law school student interning in the Manhattan DA's office, and I was a young reporter doing a feature on summer internships in city government. I cracked some kind of a joke during the interview, and she laughed. God, I don't even remember what the joke was anymore, but I remember the laugh. I think I probably fell in love with her at that moment. I guess I'm just a sucker for a good audience.

I asked her out to lunch after the interview and told her more jokes, which she seemed to appreciate. I was so impressed that I asked her out for dinner that night too. Afterward, we went back to my apartment and she spent the night. She never really left. That weekend we moved all of her stuff in. Three months later, we got married. Maybe it was too much, too soon, but—back then, anyway—it all seemed great.

Both of our careers skyrocketed. While I was making a name for myself with page-one exclusives at the *Daily News*, Susan was climbing the ladder as an ambitious young lawyer at the DA's office. From intern to ADA to senior investigator. We were the perfect Manhattan power couple back then, Susan and me. The hotshot reporter and the superstar prosecutor. Until I went and screwed everything up.

It didn't stop Susan, though. She kept moving up the hierarchy at the DA's office, and she was now the right-hand person for the district attorney himself. There was even talk of her possibly running for district attorney at some point in the future when her boss decided to step down.

All of this caused changes in our relationship. I was angry at myself, jealous of Susan for all her success, and mostly acted like a jerk until she couldn't take it anymore. And so now here I was sitting in her apartment, looking at a picture of the man she was going to marry after me, and talking about her new life.

"Look," I said, "I'm not here to argue with you or give you a hard time about anything. I just felt bad about the way things went down the last time we talked. The things I said. I guess I just want some kind of closure. You mean too much to me—and I hope I mean too much to you—to leave it like that. I know we're not together anymore, but we had something pretty good for a while.

Something pretty special. I just wanted you to know that, and to know that I'm okay with everything. That's all."

She nodded. "Interesting that you just happened to pick this day to show up on my doorstep to tell me all this."

"What do you mean?"

She picked up the *Daily News* from the table and pointed to my byline on page one. "The same day you get a front-page exclusive."

"What does one thing have to do with the other?"

"That fight we had happened weeks ago. You didn't apologize then. Or in any of the days or weeks after that. No, you wait until you're back on top at the *Daily News* to try for this 'closure' you say you want for us. You've got your self-confidence back. But do you really think it makes some kind of difference to me that you're a big man at the paper again? That's never been what it was about for me. Sure, I like the fact that you somehow seem to have resurrected your career. But I loved you before you were ever a big-shot reporter. Remember, Gil? But that was a long time ago. And you changed. You changed long before the bottom dropped out of your life with the Houston scandal. Well, I've moved on with my life since then. But you're still stuck in the same old bullshit, just like you've always been. I know you too well, and I know that's the truth. You know that too. You just don't want to admit it."

I didn't stay very long after that.

I didn't want to argue with her anymore.

And there wasn't much more to say.

And so I mumbled a few perfunctory words about it being good to see her again, gave her my best wishes for the wedding, and got the hell out of there as soon as I could.

As she walked me to the door, Susan glanced back at the *Daily News* on the table where we'd been sitting.

"Hey," she said, "it really was a good article."

"Thanks," I said.

"You're still a helluva reporter."

I tried to think of a snappy comeback for my farewell line.

But it didn't matter.

She'd already shut the door behind me.

CHAPTER 19

WHAT DID YOU think was going to happen with your ex-wife?" Dr. Landis asked.

"I hoped she'd realize what a terrible mistake she had made, she'd call off her engagement to the friggin' stock trader—Dan or Dale or Dave or whatever his name is—we'd run off and get re-married that night, and then the two of us would live happily ever after."

"Seriously?"

"No."

"What was your motivation, then?"

"Sex. I wanted to have sex with her one last time. Bang her all night, give her the best sex she'd ever had so she'd remember it the rest of her life. Every time she'd have sex with her husband, she'd remember what she missed out on with me."

"Sex? That was the real reason you went there?"

"I told you I haven't been with a woman in a long time. I'm ready. I'm horny as hell, or at least I was that night. I'm also pretty good in bed, if I do say so myself. I remember one time when I . . ."

"Mr. Malloy."

"Yes?"

"You didn't have sex with her."

"Uh, no."

"And you didn't go there to have sex with her either, did you?"

"Well, it would have been nice . . ."

"So—one more time—why did you go there?"

I sighed.

"Look, I was just feeling very good about myself because I had a front-page story in the paper. I wanted to share that with someone. And I thought about Susan. I'd always felt bad about the way it ended for us. Especially that last conversation when she told me she was getting engaged. I was at my low point then, I wasn't in very good shape and I reacted badly. I wanted to talk to her again when I felt better about myself. I wanted her to see the real me. Not that other guy I've been for a while now. That's why I went to see her that night. That's all. And that's the truth."

Landis wrote that in her notebook.

"Once again, everything revolves around your work as a reporter. That's how you measure everything in your life. As I've said, I believe that's why you began having the panic attacks. Once you could no longer be the reporter you wanted to be, you had nothing else in your life to fall back on. Being a reporter is a very good—at times a very noble—way to spend your life. But it can't be your entire life. Except for you it is. And somehow you need to change that. You have to build a life that's about something more than just being an ace reporter."

I sighed.

"Being a reporter was always more than just a job for me. It gave me a purpose, a meaning to my life. I felt invulnerable, I felt indestructible, I felt there was nothing I couldn't accomplish as a reporter. It was a feeling of invincibility that stayed with me for a long, long time. Right up until Houston. And so—get ready, here comes the answer to your question—I guess that's what I was trying to do when I went to Susan's apartment. For just a minute there, with my article on page one and everyone telling me again how good I was, I felt the way I used to feel. I wanted Susan to see me like that again."

CHAPTER 20

A T SIX THE next morning, I was on a flight to Dallas. I tried to get a little sleep before we landed, but I couldn't. Just as I finally started to drift off, the pilot announced that we were making our final landing approach to Dallas's Love Field airport.

A half hour later, I was in a rented car driving into downtown Dallas. The air-conditioning was going full blast, but I was still covered in sweat just from the walk to the rental agency parking lot. I remembered from my reading that November 22, 1963, had been a really warm day in Dallas too. So I guess it shouldn't have been a surprise to me that Dallas was sweltering hot in the summer. But this summer heat was definitely more brutal than the weather I'd left behind in New York City.

As I approached Dealey Plaza, I saw all of the landmarks I'd read and heard about all my life. The grassy knoll, the foundation of so many conspiracy theories that had gunmen firing at the Kennedy motorcade from behind the fence at the top of the incline. The highway overpass ahead that would have given Kennedy protection from the gunshots if the motorcade had been going just a little faster. And, of course, my first destination: the Texas School Book Depository, where the Warren Commission concluded that

Lee Harvey Oswald fired all the shots that killed Kennedy from a sixth-floor window.

The Texas School Book Depository Company that had been housed there was long gone by now. A few years after the assassination, the book company had moved out. The building sat empty for a long time. There was talk of converting it to other office or warehouse space, but that never happened. It was a reminder of the worst moment in Dallas history, and many people wanted them to just tear down the damn building. But eventually the decision was made to turn it into a John F. Kennedy Museum, devoted to the "life, death and legacy" of the president. Which is what it was now, with the name of the Sixth Floor Museum at Dealey Plaza.

The museum itself was on the sixth floor, with stores and shops on the seventh floor. Walking around in the museum was like going in a time machine back to the early '60s. I wasn't even around then, but I'd read so much about it and heard so many things from my father that it was fascinating to see some of this stuff come alive again at the exact spot where the JFK dream died.

As I wandered around, I found one area that had been devoted to the location where Oswald supposedly crouched with his rifle in wait for Kennedy and the motorcade to pass by. The museum had labeled that area of the sixth floor "The Sniper's Perch." Standing there and looking out at Elm Street and Dealey Plaza sent a shiver through me. If Oswald had been here that day, as the Warren Commission and so many others claimed, then I was standing in the same spot where he fired at Kennedy. Now, of course, there was just ordinary morning traffic on Elm Street. But in my mind, the Kennedy motorcade—with JFK waving to the crowd and Jackie in her pink suit and pillbox hat and carrying the flowers they'd been given as a welcoming gift when they arrived—came alive for me from all the old news clips I'd seen over the years.

In another part of the sixth floor, there was an exhibit of pictures and home movies collected from many of those who had been in Dealey Plaza on that day. People who wanted to record Kennedy's visit—and instead wound up recording history.

The most famous of these was the home video known as the Zapruder tape. Abraham Zapruder had brought his video camera to Dealey Plaza that day to record the president's motorcade through the streets of Dallas. He captured in horrifying frame-by-frame detail those last forty-five seconds of the young president's life.

I'd seen the Zapruder film before, of course. Most people have. Or snippets of it, anyway. But of all the cameras that day in Dealey Plaza, his was the only one that captured the presidential motorcade from the moment it made the turn onto Elm Street, made its way past the Texas School Book Depository, and then recorded the shots that killed Kennedy. And watching it in its entirety now, in the building where the history of the world had changed that day, made it seem even more moving and powerful and sad than ever.

First, you saw the joy and the anticipation of the president's visit. Much of Dallas had turned out to greet JFK. They lined the streets of the city, holding signs welcoming him and Jackie, cheering them and waving. "Well, Mr. President, you can't say Dallas doesn't love you," Nellie Connally, who was sitting in the front seat of the presidential limousine with her husband, Texas governor John Connally, had said shortly before the shots rang out.

The motorcade—without the bubble top on the limousine so Kennedy could greet the crowd—moved slowly, fatally slowly,

past the Book Depository and the grassy knoll area. Then, the gun-
fire. When the first bullet hits the president, you see him grab at
his throat. Jackie turns to look at him. It's clear on the film that
something is wrong, but no one is sure what happened at that
point. At almost the same time as President Kennedy clutched his
throat, John Connally was hit in the front seat. This was the
so-called magic bullet. According to the Warren Commission Report, it exited Kennedy's throat and then hit Connally in at least
three places, seeming to change direction at several points. Connally turns and then yells in pain, his face in anguish on the Zapruder film. "My God, they're going to kill us all," he screamed
out, his wife would recall afterward.

For a second or two, there is nothing. Just the president clutch-
ing his throat, Jackie looking over at him, Connally wounded in
the front seat—until the last shot rang out. That's the one that
blew Kennedy's head off. Even now, all these years later, watching
it on this grainy old color film, it's hard to take. Secret Service
agent Clint Hill jumps on the back of the presidential limousine
and we see the famous picture of Jackie Kennedy crawling onto
the back of the car to help him get aboard. But it was too late.
Even the first lady knew this. "They've killed Jack," she is supposed to have said, cradling her husband in her arms. "I have his
brains in my hands."

When the Zapruder film was over, I played it again. And again.
There were options to watch it in slow motion and in freeze frames.
I did all that too. I took detailed notes as I watched. But no matter
how many times I watched it, I still had questions about what I
was seeing on the screen.

I walked over to the reception desk for the museum and asked
a young woman there if she could help me. She did have answers
for a few of my questions, but she admitted that she had just

started working at the museum and wasn't as much of an expert on Kennedy assassination details as were others who worked there.

"Eric knows more about the Zapruder film than anyone," she said. "He could tell you everything you want to know."

"Can I talk to him?"

"Oh, Eric's not here now."

"When will he be back?"

"Soon, I hope," she grinned.

I looked through some of the other exhibits. There was lots of film from the assassination and the days afterward. The scene at Parkland Memorial Hospital where the president was declared dead. The police discovery of a rifle on the sixth floor of the Book Depository. Oswald being led through the Dallas police station and telling reporters, "I didn't kill anyone . . . I'm just a patsy." And finally the scene in the basement of the police station on the Sunday morning after the assassination when Jack Ruby fatally shot Oswald, silencing him forever and setting in motion all the conspiracy scenarios that exist to this day. I watched that scene over and over again too. Oswald being led out of the elevator, then through the basement of the station toward a waiting armored car. Oswald looking over toward Ruby just before the shooting. (Did he recognize Ruby? Did he suddenly realize what was about to happen?) Then you saw Jack Ruby, wearing a black hat and holding a gun in his hand, shooting Oswald before being swarmed over and arrested by Dallas police.

As I wandered back through the museum, I passed by a couple in their sixties watching the Zapruder tape. They watched in stunned silence, then horror, and finally in tears as the young president was cut down in front of their eyes.

I decided to interview them. They said they had been in college then, just like my father. They told me how Kennedy had inspired them with his talk of a new generation and the Peace Corps and the idea that being a politician was a noble thing and how they really believed back then that they could help change the world. And how that had all changed forever in those six seconds in Dallas.

They began to cry again.

I felt like crying too.

Not because of Kennedy's assassination. That had happened a long time ago, before I was even born, and nothing could change that. No, I was crying for myself. I'd come here looking for a story. I had a story. Sort of. But not the one I wanted.

This was simply a museum, a historic landmark. That was all it was. I'd come looking for answers to what was happening in New York City, but there were none. At least none that I could see. I'm not sure what I was looking for, but I sure hadn't found it.

And I feared I was wasting my time here in Dallas chasing ghosts while Carrie Bratten was back in New York working on the real story.

CHAPTER 21

MY MOOD DIDN'T improve at all when I checked in with the office.

"Hey, stuff's happening here," Carrie told me excitedly on the phone.

She said the cops had found a receipt in Shawn Kennedy's apartment that had put her on the Bowery a few days before her death. That gave her a possible connection with Harold Daniels, the dead guy on the Bowery. It was a few blocks away from where his body was found, but he was a transient who moved around the entire neighborhood. So it was possible that their paths had somehow crossed that day. That still didn't explain why they both turned up dead. But it was something, and the police were pursuing the angle to see if they could find any witnesses who could put the two of them together at any point.

"The Kennedy woman was a photographer," Carrie pointed out. "What if she was taking pictures down on the Bowery that day she was there? What if one of them was a picture of Daniels? What if that picture showed something someone didn't want anyone else to see?"

"You're kind of reaching there," I said, even though the same thought had crossed my mind.

"It's just a theory."

She'd gotten autopsy results on Kennedy and Daniels. They pretty much confirmed what we already knew, but they added a few new details.

Kennedy had been shot twice at relatively close range—no more than a few feet away—by someone with a .40 caliber Glock pistol. The first shot hit her in the back, which indicated she was fleeing from her assailant. The second shot appeared to have been fired into her chest when she was down on the ground. She may have already been dead at that point. The bottom line was it appeared she knew she was in danger, tried to run, and was shot from behind.

Daniels died of stab wounds. The weapon was identified as a knife with a six-inch blade, which the cops said was the kind of knife many people on the Bowery carried—either for protection or to use on someone else. Daniels's blood alcohol level at time of his death was somewhere around 0.25, which indicated he was pretty much dead drunk and probably unconscious. Based on that and the pattern of blood from the wounds and lack of any defensive-looking wounds on him, the autopsy report concluded he had been asleep or unconscious at the time of his death. Probably never even aware of what was happening to him.

It all made for an interesting story, but Carrie saved her biggest update for last.

"I got an interview with Daniels's ex-wife," she said. "I tracked her down to Lodi, New Jersey, where she still lives with their four kids. She told me all about the guy's descent from a hardworking family guy to a homeless street person. How the unemployment and the alcohol and the drug addictions changed him from the man she married into a total stranger. She said she hadn't heard from him in two years, and she'd assumed that he might already be dead. Because she knew it was inevitable. But she still cried. Can you believe that? And I got a picture from her of Daniels in happier times—all dressed up in a suit with a couple of the kids for some school event. It's real exclusive stuff, Gil. Marilyn says they're going to put it on the front page."

Carrie had done everything right, of course. Everything I would have done on the story if I had been there. Instead, I was sitting here twelve hundred miles away from the crime scene in Dallas spinning my wheels.

"How are you doing there?" she asked me now.

"I'm working on some leads."

"Tell me about them."

"Hey, I gotta go," I said. "Lots of stuff is happening here too. I'll fill you in later."

———

My original plan had been to start at the Book Depository and then work my way through all of the historical spots that played such a key role in the events that day in Dallas. As I'd told Staley, I figured it would make a good color piece to detail this stuff all over again in the context of the new Kennedy murders and the revelation of the book written by Oswald's never-before-known son. But the truth is I'd hoped for more. Hoped for some lead, some clue that could help me make sense out of everything that was happening now. And maybe, just maybe, I would figure out how it all tied in with the assassination that happened so long ago.

But now, after my visit to the museum, I realized that I was just looking for a needle in a haystack, a needle that had been there for a very long time and that I wasn't even sure existed.

I started by visiting the grassy knoll. The place where—according to pretty much every conspiracy theory out there—another gunman, or more than one gunman, lay in ambush in the trees or behind the picket fence to fire on the approaching motorcade. Many people at the scene said they thought they heard shots coming from there, which soon led to the grassy knoll assassination scenarios. I'd heard about the grassy knoll all my life. It was a piece of history. But in real life it didn't seem that historical at all. It just seemed . . . well, ordinary.

I stood there looking onto Elm Street, where the motorcade had passed by. It had been filled with people that day, people who came to see the president, people who witnessed history. This was the spot where, according to virtually every conspiracy theory you listened to, someone else—marksmen with high-powered weapons, probably—had been firing at Kennedy and the motorcade. The grassy knoll was supposed to be the secret assassins' nest where the conspirators actually shot Kennedy. The key to solving the assassination. But it didn't look like an assassins' nest now. It just looked like a grassy area with a clump of trees. On the street in front of me, traffic moved steadily, the occupants of the vehicles seemingly unaware of or indifferent to the historical impact of their route.

My next stop was the rooming house at 1026 North Beckley Avenue where Oswald had lived at the time. He had gone home that day after the Kennedy shooting, changed his clothes, got a handgun, and left the house hurriedly. No one ever saw where he was going. But his landlady claimed that a Dallas police car pulled up in front of the house and honked several times—like some sort of a signal—and then drove away. The conspiracy buffs had a field day with that one. Of course, no one ever determined if there really was a police car in front of Oswald's house that day or why they might have honked. But that landlady was long gone. The house was just another tourist stop for JFK assassination buffs now. I visited the intersection of East 10th Street and North Patton Avenue, in the Oak Cliff section of the city about five minutes away. That's where Police Officer J. D. Tippit was shot to death less than an hour after JFK. There were various theories and scenarios of what happened. But according to the Warren Commission and other official law enforcement findings, Oswald shot Tippit after the police officer got out of his squad car and approached him on the street. Like everything else, the corner of 10th and Patton didn't look like a place where history had taken place. There were a few cars, a few pedestrians passing by, and that was it. It was just a quiet intersection in Dallas now, nothing else.

After the Tippit shooting, Oswald fled into the Texas Theatre. The movie playing that afternoon was *War Heroes*. Oswald ran in without paying, which aroused enough suspicion for people at the theater to call police. When the police got there and turned up the theater lights, Oswald was sitting in a back row. Approached by officers, he pulled out the gun, pointed it at them, and yelled, "It's all over now!" But the gun didn't go off and he was subdued after a brief struggle and taken to the police station. The theater building itself was still there, but it had closed down in the mid-'90s. There was a movement afoot to turn it into some kind of historical spot like the Book Depository. But for now it just sat there empty.

Finally, I went to the Dallas police station where Oswald had been held for close to forty-eight hours and charged with the murders of Kennedy and Tippit.

By the time I got back to Dealey Plaza, I had a notebook filled with details on the stuff I'd seen. I had enough to write the color scene piece I'd promised Staley, but I wanted more. I looked back up at the Texas Depository. I still hadn't gotten all my questions answered at the museum. I had plenty of time to file my story. It was a Sunday piece so the *News* wasn't going to deal with it until the end of the week. So I went back to the Kennedy museum.

————

There was a different receptionist on duty at the desk now.

An older woman, in her mid fifties, with gray hair. She had a tag on the front of her blouse that identified her as a museum manager. I asked if she was in charge.

"Oh, I'm in charge," she said. "I'm also answering the phone. The receptionist who was supposed to work this shift is sick. We're awfully thin in personnel right now. People calling in sick, people quitting. I'm in charge, all right. I'm in charge of myself."

I smiled. I didn't give a damn about her being overworked. But I'd learned how to pretend to care about people like her. It helped open doors and get them to talk about the things I wanted them to talk about. So we chatted for a while about all the stress she was under and how hard it was to find good help.

"I do have some questions about the Zapruder tape," I said finally. "I watched it here earlier today and then asked the young woman who was here a few questions about it. She didn't know the answers. But she said someone named Eric probably would. That he was an expert on the Zapruder tape and a lot of other things about the Kennedy assassination."

"Eric's not here," she said.

"When do you think he'll be back?"

"Eric's not coming back."

"He doesn't work here anymore?"

"He quit."

"Gee, the woman I talked to before didn't tell me that. Just that he wasn't around at the moment."

"I haven't told anyone yet. I guess at first I hoped he might show up. But now I realize that's not going to happen. The damn kid just left me a few weeks ago without any reason or any notice. No apology. No nothing. And, even worse, he took a bunch of stuff from the museum with him."

"What kind of stuff?"

"Stuff about Lee Harvey Oswald, including a video of him at the Dallas police station just before he was shot. Dammit, we need that material. It's not easy finding good people you can trust to work for you these days. Eric Mathis just up and left me in the lurch."

The name sounded familiar. At first, I couldn't figure out why. And then it hit me.

"Eric's last name is Mathis?" I asked.

"That's right."

Mathis was the real name of Lee Harvey Oswald Jr.

Lee Mathis.

And Lee Mathis had a son named Eric.

"Do you know Eric?" she asked.

"I think I do."

CHAPTER 22

RIC MATHIS HAD begun working at the Sixth Floor Museum a year earlier.

Lee Mathis said his son had gotten very upset and refused to speak to him at about that time when he told him he had changed his name to Lee Harvey Oswald Jr. and was writing a book about his infamous father—the same time that Eric Mathis apparently moved to Dallas and took the job at the Kennedy museum.

Then, a few weeks ago, Mathis sent his son a copy of the manuscript he was working on about the Oswald family connection.

Shortly after that, Eric disappeared from his job at the museum—taking a lot of Lee Harvey Oswald historical material with him.

So what did it all mean? Well, I wouldn't know for sure until I tracked down Eric. But there was a pretty clear pattern here that was hard to ignore. The circumstantial evidence was definitely starting to build up. Lee Mathis aka Lee Harvey Oswald Jr. wrote a book about the injustice he believed was done to his father. Two people in New York were shot dead by some Kennedy assassination–obsessed killer. And Oswald Jr.'s apparently Kennedy assassination–obsessed son had disappeared suddenly from his job at the time of the murders.

Was Eric Mathis in New York City right now killing people?

Leaving a Kennedy half-dollar behind with his victims as some kind of a bizarre calling card?

Threatening to blow up Kennedy Airport simply because of the name?

And, if all this were true, there was another question still unanswered.

Why?

———

The woman at the Kennedy museum, whose name was Janet Gooding, turned out to be very helpful after I told her who I was and about the story I was working on.

I didn't tell her anything about the murders. Or even about the Oswald connection. Just that I was doing a story on a book written by Eric's father about the Kennedy assassination and would like to talk to him to get his input too.

She went through Eric's desk with me. There was a typewritten list that contained a series of Lee Harvey Oswald items and artifacts at the museum. These included various tapes and accounts of the shooting of Oswald; Oswald's police mug shot; a copy of his arrest warrant; a receipt for the mail-order rifle he'd bought, which authorities declared to be the murder weapon; a picture of him holding the rifle in his backyard from several months earlier, which Oswald always claimed was a phony; and the transcript of what Oswald said to police during the forty-eight hours he was held in custody before being gunned down.

Gooding said all of these items were now missing from the museum. Damn! I was on the trail of a hot story here. Eric Mathis was the key. He was the one who could give me the answers I was looking for. All I had to do now was find him.

Before I left the museum, Janet Gooding—after some prod-ding—gave me Eric's home address.

"I don't think he's there, though," she said. "I tried to call him a number of times when he didn't show up for work, but there was no answer."

"Maybe he's sick or something," I said, even though I didn't really believe that. "I'll go over there and check it out."

"If you do find him," she said, "please ask him to return the documents and materials he took. Those things are invaluable to us at the museum, and they are irreplaceable as historical artifacts. Otherwise, I'll have to report him to officials of the museum and to authorities. He could get in a lot of trouble. Tell him that, will you, Mr. Malloy?"

I thanked her for her help, took his address, and left. I didn't tell her that Eric Mathis was probably already in trouble.

Big trouble.

Bigger trouble than Janet Gooding could ever imagine.

———

Mathis had lived on the ground floor of a two-family house on a quiet street about a fifteen-minute drive from the museum.

I rang the front doorbell even though I didn't expect anyone to answer. Like Janet Gooding, I was pretty sure he wasn't there. But you never know. I rang it a second time and then a third. Still no-body. I turned the doorknob. Unlocked.

I looked around at the street behind me. It was all quiet. No cars. No neighbors outside. No one looking at me out windows that I could see.

There are all sorts of rules and guidelines about what a journal-ist is supposed to do or not do. Some are clear-cut and inflexible no matter how much you try or want to bend them. Others . . .

well, sometimes it's not so clear-cut. There are lines that all journalists cross sometimes in the pursuit of a story. Some journalists cross those lines more than others. Me, I was always willing to push the envelope if doing so could get me an exclusive. I took one more look behind me to make sure no one was watching. Then I pushed open the door and went inside.

The place consisted of a living room, kitchen, and two bedrooms. One of the bedrooms had been converted into some kind of a study. Wherever the Mathis kid had gone, it looked like he had left in a hurry. Newspapers and magazines were scattered around the living room, unwashed dishes filled the sink, an unfinished TV dinner sat on the kitchen counter, and clothes were strewn around the bedroom, where the bed was unmade.

The study was more interesting. If there was any question about Eric Mathis's obsession with his Oswald family background, it was answered by the wealth of Oswald stuff there. Pictures on the wall of the JFK assassination. Newspaper clippings about Oswald on a bulletin board next to the desk. A huge poster for the movie *JFK*, which is, of course, all about Oswald not being the lone assassin. Stacks of videos and books about conspiracy theories and a second (and third) gunman and every other imaginable scenario of what happened that day in Dallas.

I also found, on top of the desk and scattered in other places around the study and the rest of the apartment, some of the Lee Harvey Oswald items that Eric Mathis had taken from the museum. Wherever he had gone, he left in so much of a hurry that he didn't even bother to take them all with him.

I looked through a lot of other material in the room too. Things in the drawers of the desk and in a filing cabinet next to it. Everything was about Lee Harvey Oswald and the assassination. Particularly a detailed account of what Oswald was doing in New

Orleans that summer before the assassination. And about his potential connections with Cuban radicals and mobsters and even
renegade elements of the U.S. intelligence community who might
have drawn Oswald into something so far over his head that he
didn't realize how much trouble he was in until it was too late.

It was pretty clear what Eric Mathis was trying to do. He desperately wanted to find out if Lee Harvey Oswald—the man he
now knew to be his biological grandfather—really was the lone
assassin of President John F. Kennedy or whether history had
done Oswald a horrible wrong.

No question about it, he was obsessed.

Whatever his father had set in motion by telling his son about
his own father being Lee Harvey Oswald had culminated in this
obsession. An obsession that I now believed led the son for some
reason into a murderous rage on the streets of New York City,
where his father now lived. It was the only logical explanation.

I found notes Eric had written to himself. Extensive details
about the assassination and Oswald and everything that happened
that day in Dallas. There were also notes he had clearly made to
himself after reading his father's manuscript. Things about Emily
Springer and the birth certificate for his father at the New Orleans
hospital and even the strip club where Emily Springer had met
Oswald.

The most recent entry seemed to be on a yellow legal pad left
on top of his desk with a pen next to it—as if it might have been
the last thing he was doing before he left.

There was a name and an address written at the bottom of the
top sheet.

The name was Howard Crenshaw.

Underneath that was "New Orleans."

Howard Crenshaw could have been anyone, of course. A friend

or a family member or someone else Eric Mathis knew from growing up in New Orleans. But New Orleans was clearly the key to all
this. New Orleans was the city where Lee Harvey Oswald had
been born and lived much of his short life until coming to Dallas.
Where he spent the summer of 1963 before the assassination.
Where Oswald had impregnated Emily Springer with the baby
that would become Lee Harvey Oswald Jr. According to Lee
Mathis's book, Oswald had actually been in New Orleans on the
day of the assassination, eagerly making plans for a new life with
Emily Springer.

There are various degrees of crossing the line for a reporter.

Sometimes what you do is pretty much in a gray area in terms
of following the letter of the law and rules; other times it goes beyond that. I'd crossed the line when I entered—and then
searched—Eric Mathis's home. That was clear without a doubt.
So was what I did next. Now that I was already across that line of
right and wrong, I decided to hurtle over it with both feet. I
scooped up as much of the material about Oswald and Kennedy
and Dallas as I could find, stuffed it all into the luggage I'd been
carrying around with me all day, and made my way out of there.

I still hadn't checked into my hotel.

But it was too late for that now.

I called the hotel, canceled my reservation, and boarded the
first flight I could get to New Orleans.

CHAPTER 23

HOWARD CRENSHAW TURNED out to be an attorney. I found that out when I Googled his name and address and other information before the flight to New Orleans. There was a website with a bio and specific directions on how to get to his office.

The bio said the law firm had been started by his father, Benjamin Crenshaw, in 1958. His father had taken him on as a partner when he graduated from law school in 1986. Howard Crenshaw had taken over the business when his father retired in 1999. There was a long list of legal honors and civic awards he had won. A picture of him and his family too. But what I found the most interesting was the type of law he practiced. His specialty was adoption law. He worked with families looking for children and facilitated adoptions with individuals and agencies trying to find children homes.

It was evening by the time my plane touched down in New Orleans. I called the number listed on Crenshaw's website and got a voice mail telling me his office hours were from nine to five. I left a message asking for an appointment in the morning.

I checked into my hotel before doing anything else this time. I'd never been to New Orleans before. To be honest, my image of it mostly came from the devastation I'd seen on TV after Hurricane Katrina, and also the scenes I'd watched on the HBO series *Treme*. But people who had been there always told me what a great city it was. The Cajun food. The jazz clubs and the music.

But it had been a long day, starting with my waking up at four in the morning to catch the early flight out of New York to Dallas, and I just wanted to get some sleep. I sat down on the bed for a second to review my notes from the day. That was the last thing I remembered until I woke up to the sound of my cell phone ringing.

I sleepily looked over at the clock. It said 11 p.m. I picked up the cell phone to see who was calling. The number was blocked. That meant it wasn't the office or Carrie or anyone else I could think of. I thought for a second about letting it go to voice mail but decided to answer it.

"Who is this?" I asked.

There was a long silence on the other end.

"Hello, who's there?" I said.

Finally a voice came on. A low, husky, almost gravelly voice. It sounded like a voice someone was using to disguise who he was.

"Get off this story, Malloy," the voice said.

"I don't know what you're talking about."

"John F. Kennedy is dead. He's been dead for fifty years. Just let him rest in peace. Let us all rest in peace. Leave it alone."

"And why should I do that?"

"Because it would be healthy for you, Malloy."

"Are you threatening me?"

"A lot of people who asked too many questions—or knew too much—about the Kennedy assassination have died. But then you already know that, don't you, Malloy. So just make sure you're not one of them."

Then the phone went dead.

I was getting deeper and deeper into something I didn't completely understand. Someone out there knew it, and he wanted to stop me. Maybe it was Eric Mathis. Maybe it was his father, even though that didn't make a lot of sense to me. Or maybe it was someone else I didn't know about yet but who knew about me.

I realized I was probably just being paranoid, but I suddenly had this fear that someone was watching me right now. I walked over to the window and pulled the blinds shut. Then I made sure the door was locked and the chain bolt on. Whoever was out there wanted to scare me. Scare me enough so that I got on a plane and went back to New York. I was scared, I'll admit that. But not quite that scared. After a while, the paranoia passed and I realized that no one was going to come after me in my locked hotel room that night. I watched TV, and then fell back asleep.

———

At eleven the next morning, I was sitting across from Howard Crenshaw at the desk in his office.

"I understand you're interested in having me help you with an adoption," Crenshaw said.

"Actually, I'm not here to talk to you about adopting a child."

"But my secretary said you told her—"

"I lied to your secretary,"

"Why would you do that?"

"Because I needed to get in here. I needed to see you. And I figured lying was the best way to do that since I probably couldn't have gotten the appointment if I told the truth."

"So why are you here?"

"To ask you about a previous adoption. One from a long time ago. I think someone at this firm—probably your father—handled it. And I'm pretty sure you had another visitor recently asking you about it too. Eric Mathis."

"I'm sorry," he said softly, "but I can't discuss the details of any adoption case. Those facts are confidential and privileged."

Crenshaw was about as nondescript-looking a lawyer as one could imagine. I was used to New York lawyers. Charismatic, colorful, oversized egos, always looking to outsmart you somehow. Crenshaw was a plain-looking middle-aged guy of about fifty, with thinning hair, a slight but noticeable paunch, and wearing a conservative, and not very expensive-looking, blue serge suit. I'm pretty good at reading people. I read him to be a guy who didn't have a lot of ambition, wasn't looking to get rich—he just wanted to run a nice quiet business like his father had done before him. I was more comfortable with the loud, flashy New York lawyers. Them, I understood. I had a plan to get this guy to tell me what I wanted to know; I just hoped it would work on him.

I showed him my press credentials. Then I told him about the story I was doing and why I was interested in finding out if Eric Mathis had indeed been in contact with him and what he wanted to know.

"As I said, Mr. Malloy," he told me when I was finished, "I cannot discuss the details of any adoption business with anyone else, including you. Now, if you'll excuse me, I have a long day ahead of me so—"

"I'm afraid that's not good enough," I said.

"What do you mean?"

"I'm a newspaper reporter, Mr. Crenshaw. A good newspaper reporter doesn't take no for an answer on a story. Not in New York. And not in New Orleans either."

Crenshaw shrugged. "I don't care about that. The fact that you're a newspaper reporter means nothing to me. You still have no legal right to such confidential information."

"I'm not talking about legal here," I said.

He shook his head. Confused.

"What are you talking about?"

"A quid pro quo."

"Quid pro quo?"

"It means you give something to me, and in return I give something to you."

"I know what a quid pro quo is, Mr. Malloy. And I certainly know what it is you want from me. But what is it you have to give me in return? Because if you're talking about offering me money, I must remind you that I'm a member of the bar and I adhere to all ethical guidelines."

"I'm not talking about money."

"What else do you have that could persuade me to talk to you about this matter?"

"The power of the press. I work for the *New York Daily News*. One of the biggest newspapers in the country. This is a big story. A story with national implications. It's already gotten coverage from media outlets across the country. This story's only going to get bigger. And I'm the reporter for the *Daily News* working on the story. Ergo, the power of the press."

Crenshaw stared at me over the desk. The moment of truth. I still wasn't sure whether this was going to work or not.

"What you're saying is if I cooperate with you, you can make me into some kind of a star lawyer. Write about me, play me up in your article and make me a national figure. Fame, not fortune, that's what you're offering me, huh?"

"It's one option you have," I said.

"Well, I'm sorry to disappoint you. But that sort of thing has never been very important to me. In fact, I go out of my way to avoid publicity. I've had opportunities in the past to be a much higher-profile lawyer than I am, but I stay out of the spotlight.

Maybe this kind of I'll-make-you-a-star approach works on lawyers back in New York City. But I'm very happy with my law practice and my life here the way it is. So you can take your offer to write about me in your story . . . and get out of here."

"No," I said, "the offer is that I *not* write about you in the story."

That stopped him for a second.

"Look, Mr. Crenshaw," I said, "a long time ago your father handled an adoption for a woman here whose sister had died. He may not have even known who the biological father of the child was at the time, probably didn't. It was just another adoption case to him. But it wasn't. Because the biological father was Lee Harvey Oswald, still one of the most reviled and hated people in U.S. history. If I write that your father—and your firm—handled the adoption fifty years ago, your entire little world—your quiet life here—is going to come crashing down. TV crews will be parked outside your door. Reporters like me will be clamoring for interviews with you. Crazy people, conspiracy theorists, quick-buck artists—they'll all want to talk to you too. Some people will blame you for what happened, that's how nuts this kind of thing can get. Do you really want the world to know you are linked to Lee Harvey Oswald's son like that? Do you want your father's life—his entire legacy—to be remembered by this? I don't know if your father is still alive, Mr. Crenshaw, but even if it's just for his memory—"

"My father is alive," Crenshaw said slowly. "He lives in Boca Raton, Florida, now. I lost my mother about a year ago. He's very frail; the doctors say he's got a bad heart. It's important not to agitate him. I guess that's why I didn't tell him about Eric Mathis's visit to me."

"I don't want to upset your father," I said. "You don't have to upset your father. You don't have to change your life or his in any way. Everything can go on for you the same way it always has, the way you want it. I can keep both of you out of this story. That's the quid pro quo I'm offering you."

"In other words, you're threatening me with publicity to get me to talk to you."

I'd actually walked into his office with a different plan. That one had been the opposite, to make him a media star. But, like I said, I'm good at reading people. And I read Howard Crenshaw as a man who wasn't looking for fame or even fortune. He just wanted to live a normal, quiet life. And taking that away from him was the biggest threat I had. I wasn't proud of what I was doing. But then I'm never proud of a lot of things I do as a reporter. The most important thing for me has always been getting the story, no matter what it takes. And the truth is, I wasn't really going to expose his sick father to public scrutiny or turn Crenshaw's life upside down. I just needed him to think that.

"Eric Mathis was here," he said finally.

"What did he want?"

"Details about his adoption."

"And you gave them to him?"

"Yes. After I verified who he was. He has a right to that information as a relative of the person who was adopted."

Crenshaw took out the case file from a drawer and told me the same things he'd told Mathis. About who the birth mother was. And the father. That the baby—Eric Mathis's father—had been conceived while Oswald was in New Orleans in the summer of 1963 prior to the assassination. That shortly after the baby was born, Emily Springer jumped off the Huey P. Long Bridge into the Mississippi River and killed herself. Her family—a mother and a younger sister—thought about trying to raise the baby, but it was too much for them. That's when they made arrangements for the adoption, which was handled by Crenshaw's father, to the Mathis family.

"What else did Eric ask you, Mr. Crenshaw?"

"He wanted to know how to get in touch with the family of his birth mother."

"Did you tell him?"

Crenshaw shrugged. "I told him what I had. But it's been so long . . . the parents of his biological mother—the ones who came to my father to give up the baby for adoption—must be long dead. The only member of the family who might still be alive is a sister. I believe she was a few years younger than Emily had been. At least from what I saw in my father's adoption records. I gave Eric the last contact information I had on the sister. Although even that was very old. If she is still alive, I'm sure she must have moved on since then."

"Tell me the name of the sister."

"Laura Springer," he said.

The same woman the author who called himself Lee Harvey Oswald Jr. had written about in his book.

CHAPTER 24

AMAZINGLY, LAURA SPRINGER still lived at the home of her parents, which had been listed during the adoption proceedings. When I called her, she said I could come over that afternoon if I wanted to talk to her. I didn't tell her why a reporter from New York City wanted to interview her, and she didn't ask. I was pretty sure she already knew.

I spent the rest of the morning visiting the section of the city where Lee Harvey Oswald had been during the summer of 1963.

I was especially interested in 544 Camp Street. It was the building Oswald had worked out of that summer, handing out pamphlets for a pro-Castro group called Fair Play for Cuba. He had also been arrested on Camp Street after a battle on the street with anti-Castro demonstrators. From what we knew about Oswald, the Camp Street area had been where he'd spent most of his time that summer, talking about being a Marxist and openly advertising the time he'd spent living in the Soviet Union before returning to the United States in the early '60s.

The building wasn't there anymore. But I stood at the site where it used to be fifty years ago. The problem—as many investigators and Kennedy conspiracy theorists had pointed out over the years—was that Oswald's presence in the building, in this neighborhood back then, made no sense at all.

Because the building in the early '60s housed tenants who had been anti-Castro activists, not pro-Castro as Oswald claimed to be, as well as many right-wing organizations known for their connections to the American intelligence community. Also, nearby were headquarters of Navy Intelligence, the Secret Service, and various CIA-connected fronts and groups. The entire U.S. intelligence community in New Orleans in those days was on Camp Street, and there too—right in the middle of it—was Lee Harvey Oswald. Which raised real questions about what Oswald was really doing in New Orleans during the months before the assassination of President Kennedy.

I thought about a quote I'd read in Mathis's book. From someone on the House Assassinations Committee who investigated the JFK killing again in 1979: "In the months leading up to the assassination, I think Oswald got in over his head. He was no longer sure who he was working for or why. Somebody was using him."

Standing there on this hot summer day, I thought about how Lee Harvey Oswald walked this same street a half century earlier, and wondered what he might have been thinking about back then.

I wondered too if Eric Mathis, Oswald's grandson, had walked this street too not long before me, trying to find the same kind of answers as I was now.

And, most of all, I wondered where Eric Mathis was and what he was doing.

———

Laura Springer was still a handsome woman, even though she must have been close to seventy. She had silver hair and piercing blue eyes, and was wearing jeans and a T-shirt pullover that revealed a still more than decent body when she opened the door for me.

She told me she'd done some modeling over the years when she was younger, then got married and settled down to being a full-time wife and mother. There were pictures of her family all over her living room where we sat talking. Even though the house was very old, the furniture was more contemporary. She wasn't some old lady living in the past. She pointed out her husband in one of the pictures. Her three children. Two grandkids. And one very old picture, worn and faded now, which she said was her as a young girl with her sister Emily. Emily was holding a baby in her arms in the picture.

"Is that the baby from the affair she had with Lee Harvey Oswald?" I asked.

"You get right to the point, don't you, Mr. Malloy?"

"I'm a newspaperman. I like to put the lead in the first graph."

I smiled. She smiled back. Ah, you still got it, Malloy. Women melt when you turn on the charm. At least senior citizens do. The thing was I liked Laura Springer. She had a real elegance, a presence about her. I asked her to tell me whatever she remembered about her sister Emily and the events of that summer when she met Oswald and eventually had his baby.

"My gosh, that was so long ago," she said, looking at the picture of her sister as she talked. "I was just seventeen years old then. Emmy was twenty-one. She was my big sister, and I idolized her. I wanted to be just like Emmy. I tried to dress like her, wear my hair like her, I wanted to be my big sister back then. We were very close, despite the age difference. I told her all my secrets, and she shared hers with me. Even the things that . . . well, the things that sometimes I wish now that I'd never known."

"You mean like having the affair with Lee Harvey Oswald and getting pregnant with his baby?"

"Yes."

"How did she meet him?"

"At the strip club."

"The strip club where she worked. How did your sister—this sister whom you idolized—wind up working at a strip club?"

"It's a long story."

"I've got plenty of time, and that's what I'm here for." I smiled.

She told me that her sister had fought with their parents about everything, the way teenagers do—clothes, makeup, friends, and, most of all, boys. At some point, things had escalated from normal teenage trauma with her parents to all-out war. Emily ran away from home a few times but came back. Then she left for good. She found a place to live and struggled to make it on her own. She worked for a while as a clerk in a grocery store, then as a waitress at a coffee shop, and finally—because she was such a beautiful girl—she got the job at the strip club.

" 'It's just for a little while, Laura.' That's what she told me," her sister said. " 'Until I figure out what I want to do with my life. The pay is better than bagging groceries or waiting on tables, and it's really not that bad. Most of the men are actually very nice.' "

"And that's where she met Oswald?" I asked.

Laura Springer nodded.

"She told you about the affair with Oswald? Is it possible she just made it up for some reason after the assassination?"

"Oh, I met him. Before that day in Dallas. She couldn't come back to our house because of the fight with our parents. So I would meet her places. A couple of times Oswald was with her. She introduced me to him. And then, of course, I recognized him after I saw his picture on television after President Kennedy was shot."

"What was Oswald like?"

"I didn't like him. I know it's easy to say that now, but I really felt that way at the time. He was very volatile, very moody, very preoccupied—he seemed angry a lot. He talked politics all the time. Going on about communism and living in Russia and Castro in Cuba and a lot of other things I didn't really understand then. He thought a lot of himself. He acted like he was destined for some kind of greatness, even though he was just struggling along in a low-level job. Plus, of course, there was the fact that he was married with a family. He even had another baby on the way with his wife, Marina. I thought he was all wrong for my sister. I told her that. But she didn't listen to me."

"So he was with Marina at the same time he was dating your sister?"

"That's right. He grew up in New Orleans, you know. Then, that spring before the JFK assassination, he and Marina and their baby daughter moved back here. Marina was pregnant with their second child. That's when he started going to the strip club and met my sister. They saw each other throughout that summer until Oswald's wife was about to give birth to the second child, and then they moved back to Dallas."

"Did Oswald know Emily was pregnant with his baby?"

"She told him. I think that might be why he moved back to Dallas. I always wondered if Marina might have found out and made him go back to Dallas to keep him away from Emily."

I shook my head sadly. If it were all true, and I had no reason to disbelieve anything this woman was telling me, history could have been changed by this encounter between her sister and Oswald in the strip club. If they hadn't met, if she hadn't gotten pregnant with his child, if Oswald hadn't gone back to Dallas before the president arrived . . . so many ifs.

She said that she and her sister had watched the events in Dallas unfold together with shock and disbelief. When Oswald's face came on the screen as the assassin—when he was fatally shot by Jack Ruby—Emily cried. She was several months pregnant at that time. She could have aborted the child, but abortion was much more difficult for a woman in the South in those days. For whatever reason, she decided to go ahead and have the baby. No one else but her sister knew who the baby's father was at that point. But Emily did put it on the birth certificate, for some reason.

"I think she wanted someone to know that the baby had a father," Laura Springer said. "No matter who that father was. Every baby has a right to have a father."

I had been taking notes prolifically during the interview with her. I stopped for a second now and looked over at the picture of Emily Springer, holding the son of Lee Harvey Oswald in her arms.

"So what happened to the baby?" I asked. "How did he wind up being adopted?"

"Emmy died about six months later after Lee was killed. My parents didn't want to raise him, and I was too young. So they arranged for the adoption with Mr. Crenshaw."

"Tell me about your sister's death."

"She jumped off the Huey P. Long Bridge and drowned. Not far from here. Committed suicide. At least, that's what the official report said."

"It sounds like you don't necessarily believe that."

"After the assassination and Oswald's death, Emmy told me she thought people were following her. Spying on her. Watching her. I told her she was just being paranoid, but she began to believe it more and more. She told me she thought she was in danger, but she wasn't sure from whom. And then suddenly she was dead. Suicide, the authorities said. Pretty convenient if someone really wanted her dead, I say."

"You don't think your sister killed herself?"

"Emmy never seemed suicidal to me. Just scared."

"Did you tell the authorities your sister thought she was in danger from someone?"

"Yes, but they didn't take it seriously. They said it was just an example of the delusional state she was in, which led her to take her own life. I wasn't sure myself at the time. But later, when I heard about all the mysterious deaths of people connected to the assassination in some way . . ."

"And you never told anyone else about any of this until now?"

"No."

"Why not?"

"At some point, I guess I decided there was nothing to be gained by talking about it. No one seemed to care about Emmy. Why would they care what I had to say? Maybe I was a bit afraid too. Afraid that I might wind up dead like her. So I just pretty much pretended it never happened. I went on with my life, got married, raised my family—all in the same house where Emmy and I were raised. My parents are long dead, of course. My husband too; he had a heart attack about ten years ago. My three children are grown up and on their own. I'm all alone in this house now. But it's been a good life. I just wish Emmy could have enjoyed a life like I have, instead of it ending so quickly."

She looked over at the picture of her long-dead sister again.

"I just tried to pretend it all never happened," she muttered, more to the picture than to me.

"Until Lee Harvey Oswald Jr.—your sister's child—contacted you?" I asked.

She nodded.

"And you told him everything?"

"Everything I know."

"Why?"

"I thought he had a right to know. And I guess I thought someone else should know. Finally talking about it with him has had an interesting effect on me. I'm not afraid anymore. I thought it was time to tell the story. To him. And now, I guess, to you too."

"And Eric Mathis?"

"Yes, he was here too."

"When?"

"A few weeks ago."

"What did he say?"

"He said he was Emily's grandson. He said he wanted to know the truth about her and about Lee and about how his father came into this world. And so I told him. He got very upset. Very angry. He stormed out of here, and I haven't heard from him since."

CHAPTER 25

W E NEED TO talk about Eric," I said to Lee Mathis, who now called himself Lee Harvey Oswald Jr.

"What does my son have to do with this?"

We were sitting in the living room of his Washington Heights apartment again. I'd called him on my way back from Dallas and set up the new interview. I took a cab directly to his place after my plane landed. Didn't go back to my apartment or to the office. I wanted to get to him as soon as possible.

"You told Eric you had changed your name to Lee Harvey Oswald Jr. and that you were writing a book about being his secret son and all the rest of it approximately a year ago, right?"

"Yes."

"The same time as Eric moved to Dallas and went to work at the JFK museum in Dealey Plaza?"

"I guess."

"Then a few weeks ago you sent him a copy of the manuscript?"

He nodded.

"What was his reaction?"

"He was very . . . well, very upset."

"And you haven't heard from him since."

"No. He won't answer any of my phone calls or email messages. What's wrong, Mr. Malloy? Why are you asking me all of these questions about Eric? Has something happened to him?"

I'd gone over and over it all again in my head on the trip back from Dallas. There was only one logical scenario. Eric had become obsessed with the JFK assassination after he learned his father had changed his name to embrace his own biological father, who he now believed was innocent and not the horrendous villain he'd been made out to be. Then, when Eric had read his father's book, he disappeared from his job and began some kind of journey to find out the truth for himself. Did that journey take him to New York City? And was he now out there in this city somewhere killing people as part of his own vendetta to avenge the injustices he believed had been done to the man he now knew was his own grandfather?

I told it all to Oswald now. Everything I'd found out in Dallas. And the trip to the adoption lawyer in New Orleans and then to his biological mother's sister. The same sister he had talked to who provided Lee Harvey Oswald with an alibi for that day in Dallas. By the time I had finished, I could see the anguish in his face. Maybe he had suspected his son was involved somehow. Feared it as the evidence piled up. But he'd probably told himself it couldn't be true, had tried to blot the possibility from his mind that his son could be responsible for what was happening. But it was out there now, and he couldn't ignore it anymore.

"Do you think your son could have done these killings?" I asked him.

He didn't answer me.

"Do you think he sent me this note threatening to blow up Kennedy Airport?"

Still nothing.

"I believe he did," I said. "I think you believe that too. Because it's the only possible answer that can explain why this is happening now at the same time as your book. You know that's right, don't you, Mr. Oswald?"

He nodded sadly, almost imperceptibly.

"This book," he said, "this damn book. I wish I'd never written it. I wish I'd never changed my name. I wish I'd never found out who my real father was. I meddled with the past. With the ghosts from the past. I woke up those sleeping ghosts from the past . . . and now I don't know how to undo it."

———

I raced back to the *Daily News*, excited about my big scoop that I thought would be all over the front page of the paper the next day.

Except it didn't work out exactly that way.

That's the thing about a big story. A big story is like a living, breathing organism. A big story keeps moving. No matter how good a job you think you did on it, no matter how much time you spent on it, it sometimes doesn't matter in the end. If something new or shocking or unexpected happens . . . well, breaking news always trumps everything in this business.

Which is what happened here.

"I've got the page-one story!" Carrie Bratten suddenly screamed across the newsroom, standing up from her desk and starting to run toward Marilyn Staley's office.

I started to say that I had the page-one story.

That it was all mine too, and she couldn't be a part of it.

But even before Carrie said her next words, I knew exactly what they were going to be.

"There's been another Kennedy murder," she shouted to me over her shoulder as she headed for Staley's office.

PART THREE

CAMELOT AND OTHER MYTHS

CHAPTER 26

THE NAME OF the new victim was Marjorie Balzano.

She was a seventy-nine-year-old widow and grandmother who had lived in the city for her entire life. Her apartment was on West 83rd Street, just off Riverside Drive. At some point, shortly after ten the night before, she had gone out to a bodega on Columbus Avenue to buy milk, bread, and assorted other groceries. She was killed on the way home, apparently by a blow to the head.

A neighbor found her body sprawled on West 83rd Street just a few doors away from her apartment house at approximately ten forty-five. There was a large gash on her head and blood flowing from it. The groceries she'd just bought were scattered on the sidewalk near her. Her purse was there too. The money and credit cards inside it had been taken.

On the face of it, this looked to be a pretty clear-cut mugging that somehow turned fatal. Someone assaulted the elderly woman walking home along on the dark street, she resisted, there was an altercation—and she died.

Except for one thing.

They found something in her purse.

A Kennedy half-dollar.

Inside an envelope.

The outside of the envelope said simply: "No. 3."

The cops didn't make that angle public right away. We did. Well, Carrie actually. She got a tip about it from her source in the police department, and the *Daily News* broke the story.

The page-one headline said simply KENNEDY KILLER STRIKES AGAIN!

There was a press conference in the afternoon at police headquarters. The police commissioner was there, flanked by some of his top lieutenants. Commissioner Ray Piersall went through the details of what they knew about Balzano's death and the Kennedy killings in general, then asked if there were any questions.

There were a lot of questions.

"Why do you think the killer robbed this victim?" someone asked.

"Maybe the killer needed money."

"But the killer didn't take any money or jewelry from Shawn Kennedy," another reporter said. "And he certainly didn't take anything from Harold Daniels on the Bowery because Daniels didn't have anything."

"Those are the facts as we know them," the commissioner said.

"Why rob now and not rob the Kennedy woman who had more valuable items to be taken?"

"We don't have the answer to that at this point."

Someone else brought up the one thing that was consistent in all the killings. "Do you think there is any significance to the fact that all the killings have happened in Manhattan? Not in the same area, but still all in the same borough. Do you think that means the killer lives in Manhattan?"

"That is a likely scenario," Piersall said. "Either that the killer lives in Manhattan or he is more familiar with Manhattan. Manhattan is fairly easy to navigate, even for someone who doesn't know the city very well. Brooklyn, Queens, and the other boroughs are not. So yes, there is a good chance the killer either lives in Manhattan or is at least comfortable there—compared to other parts of the city. That's the profile of the killer we project at this point."

Or someone from out of town who didn't know the city very well, I thought to myself.

Someone like Eric Mathis.

If Mathis had come to New York to start killing people, he very likely would do that in Manhattan instead of a borough where he might get lost or confused by directions.

Carrie asked a question then. I knew she would. I figured she'd want the opportunity to get some face time in front of the cameras and all the press there.

"I notice you said 'he' when you were referring to the killer," she said to the commissioner. "That suggests you have information that the killer is a man. Do you know that for a fact and, if so, how did you obtain that information?"

"Uh, no . . . we have no such information."

"So it would be correct to say that you have no idea if the killer is a woman or a man at this point?"

"We don't have the answer to that question right now."

Carrie smiled. She had made her point. Now she went for the kill.

"So, to recap here, Commissioner, you don't know if the killer is a man or a woman. You don't know what the connection might be between any of the victims. You don't why the killer—he or she—used a different method to kill each time. You don't know why he or she has struck in completely different parts of Manhattan, against completely different kinds of victims and for what seems to be different motives. And you don't know why he or she has only killed in Manhattan. Ergo, you seem to be saying that you have no idea who the killer is or how to catch him. Or her."

There was laughter all around the room. Piersall looked flustered. He looked at his aides, like he was hoping to get some kind of help from them. But no one said anything. This was not going well for Commissioner Piersall or the New York City Police Department.

"We are pursuing the investigation vigorously at all levels," Commissioner Piersall said defensively. "All the resources of the NYPD are being thrown into this investigation. I personally can assure the people of New York City that we are doing everything we can to capture the person committing these crimes."

"But you have absolutely no idea who that is right now or why he or she is doing it," Carrie repeated.

"Not at this point," the commissioner said.

Maybe he didn't.

But I did.

CHAPTER 27

WE BROKE THE Eric Mathis story the next day. The headline practically jumped out at you off the newsstands that morning.

OSWALD GRANDSON HUNTED IN KENNEDY KILLINGS, the front-page banner head screamed.

Below that, a smaller headline: KIN OF JFK ASSASSIN IS NOW SOUGHT FOR QUESTIONING ABOUT 3 NEW NYC MURDERS.

And then the byline:

EXCLUSIVE BY GIL MALLOY and CARRIE BRATTEN.

The story itself ran on all of pages two and three of the paper. With a picture of Eric Mathis I'd been able to grab from the file at the Book Depository in Dallas, which was positioned for maximum effect next to the mug shot taken of Lee Harvey Oswald following his arrest after the JFK murder. There were also pictures of Lee Mathis from my interview with him; pictures of the three murder victims; old file shots of the JFK assassination, including the famous one of Jackie in the backseat of the car holding her dying husband in her arms.

Everything in the forty inches of my story was pretty much the way I had written it. Marilyn Staley and the copy desk had barely changed a word. And why should they? This was a friggin' perfect story.

A MAN BELIEVED to be the grandson of JFK assassin Lee Harvey Oswald is being sought for questioning
by police in connection with three recent New York
City murders linked to President Kennedy's death in
Dallas a half century ago, the Daily News has learned.

The suspect was identified as Eric Mathis, 27, who
recently disappeared from his job at the Texas School
Book Depository museum in Dallas—taking with him
materials about Oswald and the JFK assassination.

"He's definitely a person of interest," Police Commissioner Ray Piersall told the News exclusively last
night. "Based on new evidence and information provided by the Daily News, we are searching for Eric
Mathis here and across the country."

The TV cameras descended on us later that day. The local New
York stations, the cable outfits, the national news, and network
magazine shows—all of them were there. They wanted to interview me. They wanted to interview Carrie. Some of them interviewed Marilyn or anyone else they could find. Or they just stood
in front of the News building and quoted from my story. That's the
thing about TV news. Everyone always says newspapers are dying,
and all that matters are TV and the Internet. But when a big story
breaks, it's still usually a newspaper reporter who breaks it, and
TV and all the rest of the so-called new media just follow along.

I wondered if somebody would ask me about my past. My
checkered newspaper history with the Houston incident and my
disappearance from the front page for so long. I wasn't sure how
I'd answer that question. I'd played around with several re-
sponses—making a joke of it, expressing remorse, refusing to answer anything that wasn't about the current story. But no one

asked. It was as if Houston had never happened. Everything was the way it used to be for me again. The media attention. The journalistic acclaim. The thrill—that incomparable high I hadn't felt in so long—of being the star reporter on the biggest story around. Just as quickly as all that had disappeared from my life, it was all back.

For Carrie, this was a whole new experience. She'd had a few big stories, but she'd never been in the media spotlight like this before. I could tell she liked it, of course, but she was also a bit taken aback—maybe even intimidated—by the glare of the cameras and all the attention she was getting.

That surprised me a little.

I figured she was so full of herself and so arrogant that she didn't have any of those kinds of insecurities.

But what the hell, she was only twenty-five years old, and it was all happening very quickly for her.

The other thing that surprised me was the way she talked about me in the interviews. I heard her saying "we" or "Gil and I" about the story. When I talked about the story on air, I just said "I." Hardly ever mentioned Carrie. I felt a little guilty about that after I heard her. So I started making a few references to her too. Why not? There was enough fame to go around with this story.

In the middle of all this, we still had to write a story for the next day's paper. Carrie and I worked the phones, then put our heads together for a follow-up angle on the police search for Eric Mathis and wrote it all up in time for the early copy deadline at seven thirty. Marilyn read it, made only a few edits, and sent it to the copy desk.

"You know what I think we should do next?" she said.

"Think about a story for the next day," Carrie said. "I have an idea—"

"No, not now." Staley smiled. "There's something much more important we have to do now. Go to Headlines to celebrate."

———

Headlines was a newspaper bar where a lot of *Daily News* reporters hung out. It was a tradition that had been honored for as long as I'd been at the paper. Whenever you broke a big story—whenever the paper pulled off some sort of journalistic coup—the reporter who broke the story got feted with drinks at Headlines.

We drank there for a few hours. Me, Carrie, Marilyn. And a lot of other editors and reporters at the paper.

"Let me make a toast," Marilyn said at one point, standing at the bar and holding up a glass a bit unsteadily after a few drinks. "To the most unlikely journalistic duo of all time. Gil Malloy and Carrie Bratten."

"Beauty and the beast," someone said.

"Malloy, isn't he dead?" another person yelled out.

"Joke if you will, but they make one helluva reporting team," Marilyn shouted to the crowd.

Behind her, the TV over the bar was playing an interview with us. I couldn't hear my words over the din in the bar, but I could see my face on the screen and the words written underneath: "Daily News Reporter Gil Malloy, who broke the exclusive story about the Kennedy killings."

It was a great night.

At some point, I wandered outside to get a breath of fresh air. Carrie was there, standing on the sidewalk and smoking a cigarette. Looking a little dazed by it all, I thought at first. But as I got closer to her, I realized it was more than that. She was pretty drunk.

"Gil Malloy," she said to me with glassy eyes. "Gil Malloy and Carrie Bratten. Like Marilyn said in there, we make a helluva team, don't we?"

She took a step toward me, then slipped and almost fell onto the sidewalk. I caught her before she went down. She leaned against me closely for support.

"Let's go back in for another drink," she said.

I shook my head.

"I've gotta go. I don't want to get home too late; it's going to be another big day tomorrow."

"You don't have to, you know."

"I don't have to what?"

"Go home for the night."

She looked up at me. Her face was only a few inches away from mine now. She was clearly drunk. But it was also pretty clear what she was proposing to me.

"My place is not far from here," she said. "We could just head over there for a nightcap . . ."

"I'm going home," I said.

"Oh, don't be like that."

"I think you should go home too."

"It's a real nice apartment. Great views. Especially from the bedroom . . ."

"I'm going home," I said again.

I got her a cab, then somehow managed to put her in the back-seat and gave the driver her address.

Then I went back into the bar and had another drink.

By myself.

And thought about how I'd dodged a very big bullet.

CHAPTER 28

"A GUY WALKS INTO a psychiatrist's office with a chicken on his head," I said to Dr. Landis. "The psychiatrist says, 'I can see you've got a real problem.' The guy doesn't say anything. But the chicken tells the psychiatrist, 'You're telling me. How do I get this jerk from under my ass?'"

She didn't even smile. Just sat there with a pen in her hand and notebook on her lap. My God, did this woman ever loosen up at all?

"You didn't laugh."

"I've heard the joke before."

"Still could have laughed."

"I've heard it many times."

Landis looked down at the notebook. She paged through it for a second or two.

"What did you think of my big page-one story? I've been on TV too. Everyone is talking about me and this story. I'm a star again."

"To be honest, I have conflicting emotions about it."

"Hey, what I've done over the past few days is damn impressive. Why can't you just be happy for me? Why do you have to analyze and dissect everything about me? I was about as down as

I could be when I first started coming to see you. Now I'm up again, everything is going right in my life. So what the hell is your problem?"

"My problem, as you put it, Mr. Malloy, is that you came to me with some serious psychological issues that I believe led to the panic attacks you were having and had greatly impacted you and your life. I thought you—I thought we—were making significant headway on these issues. I told you in some of our previous sessions that I thought one of your biggest problems was that you tend to evaluate your life based on your worth as a reporter. So when you were a big star, you felt good about yourself. When you weren't, you fell apart and found yourself experiencing the panic attacks. Now you're on top as a reporter again, which is good. But you can't allow that to camouflage the serious underlying issues about you as a person that caused you to have the panic attacks in the first place."

"I haven't had any more of the panic attacks," I said.

"For now. But what happens when the story goes away? And you're not the star reporter anymore? That's why you need to deal with the realities of yourself as a person. Not as a reporter. I need you to evaluate your life as a complete entity, not just based on how many front-page bylines you get."

My comment about having no more panic attacks hadn't been completely true. I'd felt the beginnings of one when I was in Dallas and thought the story was getting away from me. But I sure as hell wasn't going to tell her about that.

"You make it sound like doing well at my job is a bad thing," I said.

"No, it's a good thing. But it's not the only thing. You don't feel like a complete person, as someone worthy of being loved, without that star reporter label on you. That's why I'm concerned about the impact all of this recent success will have on you. Yes, I'm happy for you as a reporter. But I'm worried about you as a person."

———

At some point, she started asking me questions about my personal life.

"Have you tried to make contact with your ex-wife again?"

"No, not since the time I went to her apartment that I told you about already."

That wasn't completely true either. On the night my story had broken all over page one, I'd gone back to her place. After I left the bar, I just stood outside Susan's apartment for a while. I'm not sure why. I thought about going in and showing her the paper and trying to get her to change her mind about everything again. But I didn't. I just stayed there on the street and watched the lights in her apartment until they went out. Then I went home.

"What about Carrie Bratten?" she asked.

A warning bell went off in my head. Did I say something about what happened at the bar the other night? I didn't think so. But then how else would she know? Why was she suddenly asking personal questions about me and Carrie?

"The only reason I asked," she said, "is that you've talked about her a few times in the past. Not in a flattering way. But I just wondered if that had changed at all. What's the Bratten woman like?"

"Young. Arrogant. Very, very ambitious. She'd do anything to get ahead as a reporter."

"Does that remind you of anyone?"

I didn't say anything.

"Is she attractive?"

"She's okay."

"Describe her."

I did.

"That sounds attractive," Landis said when I was finished. "But you're not interested in her? Sexually, that is?"

"Like I told you, I haven't had sex in a long time. I'm pretty horny. A lot of women attract me sexually these days. But Carrie would not be at the top of my list. Too much trouble. Definitely high-maintenance. And working together like we do . . . well, it just wouldn't be worth the trouble."

"Does she feel the same way about you?"

The image of her that night outside the bar—holding on to me, her lips close to mine, her eyes filled with passion—crossed my mind.

"I can't imagine that she'd have any interest in me," I said.

"I'm glad to hear that," Landis said. "Because I did wonder if all this success the two of you are having as a team on this story might somehow draw you closer together, closer in many ways, one of them possibly even sexually. I must tell you, I think that would be a very bad thing to happen. You do need to find someone to share your life with again. But I think it should be someone without any connection to your job. For the reasons we discussed earlier. Your life needs to be about more than your job. And so I would advise strongly against you beginning any kind of a personal relationship with anyone at the *News*, especially the Bratten woman."

"I'm with you there, Doc," I said. "Don't worry, the one thing I'm not going to do is sleep with Carrie Bratten."

———

Toward the end of the session she brought up something I wasn't expecting.

"What happened with the Victor Reyes story?" she asked.

"I stopped doing it."

"Why?"

"Because the other story—this big opportunity—came along."

"You were very enthusiastic about the Reyes story when you first came here. You talked about how if you could do this one story right again, you'd feel better about yourself. Not just as a reporter, but as a person. I was very impressed by that."

"I didn't know what else to do then," I said. "I was desperate. But then I got lucky. I got the JFK story dropped into my lap. That's the thing about being a reporter. Being good has a lot to do with the job. But sometimes you just have to be lucky. So much of it is luck. Being in the right place at the right time. That's what happened to me."

———

As she was walking me to the door at the end of the session, Landis started talking about our next appointment.

"How about next Tuesday?" she asked. "Same time? Four p.m.?"

"I don't think so."

"Tuesday at four doesn't work for you?"

"I don't think I'm coming back. I'm done with this little charade we've been doing here. I came here before because the *Daily News* made me after the panic attacks. I told you, I'm not having the panic attacks anymore. And the *Daily News* . . . well, they can't make me see you. All they care about is that I keep busting exclusives on this story. They don't care about this doctor bullshit anymore either. And, even if they did, I don't have to listen to them now. I'm a reporter again, not a patient. A real reporter. That's what it's all about for me, Doc. As long as I can do that, all the rest of it will take care of itself. That means I don't need you."

I thought she'd be surprised. But she didn't seem to be. Almost like she was expecting it.

"I don't suppose there's anything I can say that would change your mind."

"Not a thing."

She looked at me sadly.

"Look, I'm cured," I told her. "That's what I'm going to tell my editors at the *News*. And that's what you should tell them too. You did your job. The sessions were a big success. I'm cured."

I pushed open the door and started out of the office.

I looked around at her.

She was still standing there looking at me with that sad expression on her face.

"I'm sorry, Doc," I told her.

"So am I," she said.

CHAPTER 29

E RIC MATHIS WAS the key to this.

His life had been turned upside down when he found out about his family background and the connection with Lee Harvey Oswald. Then all the hullaballoo about the fiftieth anniversary of JFK's death must have upset him even more. He devoted his life to the assassination, finding some sort of comfort or whatever in being around the events of that day in Dallas. But then, when he read the book his father was writing, which would make this all public, he couldn't handle it anymore. Maybe there was something specific in the book that set him off. Maybe it was just the thought of his story becoming public and him being forever branded to the world as Lee Harvey Oswald's grandson that he couldn't handle. For whatever reason, he embarked on this violent rampage that he somehow linked to the JFK assassination.

Sitting at my desk in the newsroom, I took out the documents and other materials I'd grabbed from Eric Mathis's place in Dallas and read through as much of it as I could.

Most of the materials dealt with Lee Harvey Oswald's time in New Orleans the summer before the assassination, the same time period when Oswald had supposedly gotten Emily Springer pregnant with Eric's father.

There was much speculation in the material—some of it presumably substantiated, a lot of it not—about Oswald's relationship with both the mob and U.S. intelligence groups in New Orleans.

Much of it seemed to focus on a mob boss named Carlos Marcello, who had run the New Orleans crime family back then. Of all the conspiracy theories floating around about the killing of John F. Kennedy, the ones that always made the most sense to many people involved Marcello as the man who ordered the assassination. Marcello had been one of the primary targets of both President Kennedy and his brother Bobby as attorney general in their attempts to go after organized crime.

There was evidence too that Oswald had had a relationship with David Ferrie, a colorful New Orleans pilot and right-wing activist who had dealings with Marcello at times. Ferrie and Oswald had belonged to the same youth group when they were both growing up together in New Orleans. And Ferrie—who had been played as a wacky but lovable character by Joe Pesci in the movie *JFK*—had aroused suspicion because he suddenly drove from New Orleans to Dallas on the night before the assassination.

Mathis also seemed to dwell a lot on the presence of Oswald in the Camp Street area of New Orleans and the potential significance of him being in the heart of all the ultraconservative political groups based there. Mathis specifically had collected a lot of articles about a right-wing ex–FBI agent named Guy Banister, who operated a private detective agency out of 544 Camp Street. Many people who thought Oswald was secretly working for the CIA, posing as a left-wing activist, also speculated that Banister—with his deep U.S. intelligence connections—might have been Oswald's "handler" during the early '60s.

Then there was the shooting of Oswald himself. Mathis had

accumulated all sorts of materials—again much of it based on speculation or rumor or innuendo—that Jack Ruby had had connections with both the mob and Oswald. The angle Mathis was pursuing on Ruby seemed clear: Someone didn't want Oswald to tell what he knew about the assassination and a conspiracy behind it; they wanted Oswald to take the sole blame for it instead. So they got Jack Ruby to kill him.

There was only one problem with all of this.

Jack Ruby was dead. So were Carlos Marcello, David Ferrie, and Guy Banister.

There was no one alive to go after to confirm any of it, no clear-cut trail to follow for anyone to pursue the scenario that Oswald was not the lone assassin, that he was the "patsy" who got caught up in it and wound up taking the fall instead of the men really responsible for killing the president.

I could see that now.

And, more important, Lee Mathis must have seen the futility of it too.

So what did Eric Mathis do next?

———

"Have you heard from your son?" I asked Lee Mathis.

"No."

"Are you sure about that?"

"Of course, I'm sure."

"Would you tell me if he did call you?"

"Yes."

I stared at him without saying anything.

"Okay, I wouldn't tell you," he said.

I kept staring.

"Maybe I would, maybe I wouldn't. I'm not sure."

"Well, that pretty much covers all the possibilities," I said.

"But he hasn't tried to contact me. That's the truth. I wish he would, I'm so concerned about him. The last contact I had with him was several weeks ago, when I tried to reach him on the phone and he refused to talk to me."

Mathis himself didn't look good. He seemed much weaker and more frail than the previous time I was there. It wasn't just his physical appearance. His voice sounded weak, and there was none of the emotion and excitement about the book he'd had when he talked to me about it before.

"One thing's for sure," I told him. "The publicity for all this is going to make everyone want to read your book. I know you wish it didn't have to happen this way, but at least people will read your book and listen to what you have to say. That should give you some solace."

"No, it doesn't give me any satisfaction at all," he said. "I wanted to do the book, but now I've lost my son because of it. That's not a very good trade, is it? I should have left well enough alone. I shouldn't have messed with the past. I started these things, set all of this in motion. I wish I hadn't done that. But it's too late now to undo the damage I've done."

"Well, it should make your agent happy anyway," I told him, mostly because I couldn't think of anything else to say. "Nikki Reynolds is probably ecstatic about all this publicity. She always says there's no bad publicity for a book, that any publicity is good."

"Nikki Reynolds isn't my agent anymore," he said.

"When did this happen?"

"A few days ago."

"Just about the same time the news broke about Eric and the connection to the murders here?"

"Yes."

"So you fired her?"

"Actually, she fired me."

"I don't understand."

"She said she didn't want to represent me or this book."

"Why not?"

"She wouldn't say. She just said she didn't want to be my agent and then hung up. I called back, but she wouldn't take the call. Or any other calls I've made to her. I don't understand why."

Neither did I. That didn't make any sense at all. Nikki had been willing to try to sell the book when no one else knew him or had any reason to believe any of it at all. Now everyone knew about him and the book and was following the news about Lee Harvey Oswald's secret son and grandson. So Nikki should have wanted to represent the book more than ever. Instead, she walked away from a likely best seller. Hell, it sounded like she ran away from it. Why? I made a note to call her to ask what was behind her sudden change of heart.

I tried to ask him some more questions about his son and about his revelations about Lee Harvey Oswald and about how he thought the JFK assassination could possibly be connected to what was going on here now. But he was fading fast. He told me he was tired and didn't feel up to talking anymore.

"Read the book," he said to me just before I finally gave up and left his apartment. "Everything I know is there. It's all in that damn book."

CHAPTER 30

IT WAS CLOSE to the end of the day by the time I got back to the *Daily News*. The Oswald manuscript was in a drawer of my desk. My plan was to take it home with me that night and read it all again from cover to cover, to look for any angles or leads I might have missed.

The phone on my desk was ringing when I got there. I picked it up.

"Mr. Malloy, this is Camille Reyes," the voice on the other end said.

For just a second, I had trouble placing the name. It had been a long time and a lot of things had changed for me since that day I'd sat in her living room in the Bronx and talked to her about her son.

"How are you?" I said finally.

"Did I call at a bad time?"

"No, this is fine."

"I just wondered . . . well, I never heard back from you . . . so I wanted to ask if you'd found out anything more about who shot my son?"

There it was again. The moment of truth. It happens to every reporter. No matter how many stories you break, no matter how many exclusives you're responsible for, there's always the guilt about the stories you never did. I'd felt the first pangs of that guilt in Dr. Landis's office when she brought up Victor Reyes. Now here it was all over again, but this time like a slap in the face from Reyes's mother asking me what I'd done about the promises I'd made back then. Well, I hadn't done much.

"I really haven't been able to find out anything about your son's shooting," I told her.

"I was afraid of that."

"I did make some checks, did some interviews . . ."

"But no one knew anything?"

"It's been a long time, Mrs. Reyes."

"I understand."

There was a silence on the other end of the phone that probably lasted only a few seconds, but it seemed to me to go on forever.

"I'll make some more calls when I can," I said. "I'll try to do some more digging. I promise to get back to you if I find out anything at all about your son."

"Thank you very much, Mr. Malloy. I appreciate your effort," she said, even though—and maybe this was just my imagination—she probably had a feeling she would never hear from me again.

———

I tried to put Camille Reyes out of my mind. But the guilt was still eating away at me. At some point, I reached into a drawer and took out the file I'd put together on the Reyes case that I'd walked away from once I started doing the Kennedy story.

I paged through it again, refreshing myself on what I had done and what I hadn't done about Victor Reyes. The one obvious missing piece was still Bobby Ortiz, whom the police had identified as the prime suspect in the shooting fifteen years ago. I remembered that Brad Lawton, then one of the investigating detectives and now a deputy police commissioner, had told me he'd try to check on whatever happened to Ortiz. I still had his card with a direct office line on it. I dialed that now, figuring it was unlikely he'd pick up the phone this late. But he did.

"I wish I could help you," Lawton said after I told him what I wanted. "But I did do a check on Ortiz. He disappeared afterward, got arrested on a DUI charge in Poughkeepsie a few months later—but the cops there let him go on bail before they knew he was wanted for questioning as a suspect in a shooting. No sign of him since then. Best theory is he's dead. Killed in some kind of gang violence. Not a long life span for guys like Bobby Ortiz in the Bronx."

I'd figured as much, but I was still disappointed. If Ortiz had been the one who shot Reyes, and he was dead now, that was probably my last chance to find out what happened that night. Christ, fifteen years was a long time to go back on a case like this. I should have realized that at the beginning before I made promises to Camille Reyes and to Santiago's widow too. Promises that were impossible to keep.

"From what I see, it looks like you've got plenty on your plate already," Lawton said. "I've been following your coverage of the Kennedy killings. You've really been leading the way on that."

"Are you involved in that investigation at all?" I asked Lawton.

"Nah, that's being handled directly out of Commissioner Piersall's office. He's personally spearheading the search for the Mathis kid."

"If you do hear anything about the whereabouts of Mathis—or even more information on the search for him—I'd appreciate it if you could give me a heads-up call."

"No problem," Lawton said, then added with a laugh before

hanging up, "But it sounds like you know more about this case than I do. It's a helluva story. To be honest, I don't understand why you'd even care about Ortiz or Reyes at this point. Kinda pales next to the hunt for Eric Mathis, huh?"

He was right, of course. But just for the hell of it I paged through the Reyes file again after I got off the phone with Lawton. There were some other leads there I could follow. More calls I could even make that night. But that would take time. And the only thing I wanted to do was reread the Oswald manuscript. That's the story I cared about. Not Victor Reyes. Like Lawton had said, Reyes sure paled in comparison to what Eric Mathis had done—and might still be doing out there.

I closed the Victor Reyes file and stuck it back in my desk drawer.

I grabbed the Oswald manuscript and headed for home.

I had a long night of reading ahead of me.

CHAPTER 31

IT WAS A SWELTERING August night in New York City. The temperature hit 100° at one point in the afternoon. It had dropped a bit in the early evening, but was still in the 90s. By the time I got to my apartment, the place was like a sauna.

Just for the hell of it, I made one more try to see if the air conditioner might miraculously come back to life. It didn't. I wasn't sure that it would help much, but I opened the big window in my living room as far as I could. Then I opened all the other windows in the place, in the hope of getting some kind of cross ventilation going.

But all that accomplished was convincing me again how much I needed to move. When my job at the *Daily News* had been on the line, I'd been reluctant to spend money on a better place. But I didn't have to worry about losing my job anymore. I resolved to go apartment hunting as soon as this story was over and I had some free time.

The first time I'd read Lee Mathis's Oswald book I'd been in a hurry to get to the stuff I thought was the most important. About his father and the new evidence on the JFK assassination. So I skipped over lots of sections in the manuscript. This time I decided to read it all. Maybe I'd find some answers there.

Before I started on it, I checked my email for messages. There were a lot, including one from Carrie asking if I'd gotten anything good from Lee Mathis. I didn't answer any of them. Instead, I went into the kitchen, opened a bottle of Amstel Lite, and took it back to the living room.

Then I picked up the TV remote and surfed around the cable channels until I came to a reality show of some sort. It involved a bunch of people living in a house who were trying to lose weight and also trying to find someone to date or something like that. Perfect. I wanted something so forgettable in the background that I wouldn't pay attention to it—but at the same time I wanted to feel as though I wasn't sitting alone in an empty house.

As I picked up the manuscript and took a sip of the Amstel, I was struck by the incongruity of it all. A half century ago, when JFK died, there was no email. There were no reality TV shows. There was barely even color TV. But here I was, reading a book about a crime that happened in 1963 and trying to find some clue as to how it could possibly relate to what was going on in my current world.

A lot of the stuff I'd skipped through the first time was the material Lee Mathis—or Lee Harvey Oswald Jr., as he now called himself—had written about the Kennedy presidency, the so-called Camelot era in American politics when people were inspired by politicians like John Kennedy and thought they could change the world. I read it all now, as he argued against the Camelot myth, using all the things we've found out about JFK since then and saying that nothing in the Kennedy presidency was what it seemed to be.

There were the sexual escapades, of course, which had all gone unreported at the time as the American people bought the fairy tale of Jack and Jackie's idyllic marriage. He talked about Judith Exner, Marilyn Monroe, and all the rest of Kennedy's affairs.

There were the mob connections to some of these women, as well as the Kennedy family's connections in the past with unsavory characters from the underworld. His family's money and financial tactics, not always completely ethical and aboveboard. The debate over whether he was simply a rich kid whose father had bought him the presidency. His nepotism—appointing Bobby attorney general over more-qualified candidates and helping Teddy get elected to the Senate as well as all the other Kennedy family members and cronies who advanced in the so-called New Frontier.

And, most of all, the book talked about the failures of Kennedy's policies and actions, focusing a lot on the disastrous Bay of Pigs invasion of Cuba. But that was just the most notable failure, he argued. He said that despite his lofty speeches and promises to the American people, Kennedy had accomplished very little during his years in office—while at the same time engaging in numerous dubious activities, some of which might have been illegal.

He even speculated that if Kennedy had lived and been reelected in 1964, he might have become immersed in scandal during his second term the way Richard Nixon was. Nixon left the presidency in disgrace, Kennedy left as a legend—all because he got himself shot before any of the sordid details came out, Oswald wrote in the manuscript.

The Vietnam stuff too was damning to the feel-good image of the Camelot presidency, although less so. The line we always hear about the JFK presidency is, "If Kennedy had lived, he never would have gotten us bogged down in Vietnam the way Lyndon Johnson did. It would have changed everything about the history of the '60s."

Oswald Jr. attempted to dismantle that theory by detailing the Kennedy policies that resulted in a continued buildup of U.S.

forces in Vietnam through "military advisers"—a buildup of military presence there even greater than his predecessor, Dwight Eisenhower, had dared attempt.

Particularly troublesome was Kennedy's role in the coup against and subsequent assassination of South Vietnamese president Ngo Dinh Diem in the fall of 1963, just weeks before JFK's own assassination. There was no credible evidence that he sanctioned the killing of Diem as part of the coup. But it was evident that Kennedy's actions played a role in the events that led to Diem's assassination just before the events in Dallas.

I went to the kitchen for another Amstel. I took a sip and thought about what Oswald was saying. A lot of it was the truth, of course. Camelot was a choreographed, artificial myth that was sold to the American people, and they bought into the myth wholeheartedly. There were no twenty-four-hour news cycles back then, no countless cable channels, no Internet, no Twitter, no real hard coverage of what was truly going on behind the façade of the Camelot myth. I get that. We all get that now.

But I still believed there was something special about JFK's presidency, something unique in modern American politics. Maybe he would have had problems in his second term and maybe he would have led us into Vietnam like LBJ did. But a lot of people, and I was one of them, still believed that American history would have been very different if JFK had lived.

———

Next I read through all the chapters on his father, Lee Harvey Oswald, and why Jr. believed he was innocent. The first time I'd read it was before I'd met Laura Springer. Now I put together what she told me with the book, and the results were pretty clear-cut.

Lee Harvey Oswald had gone to New Orleans on November 21 to see his girlfriend, Emily, who was carrying his unborn son. He spent the night in New Orleans with her. At six the next morning, he went with her to the New Orleans bus station, where he caught the 6:32 bus back to Dallas. It was an eight-hour ride, and he said he had to meet someone in Dallas that afternoon.

The president was shot at 12:30. People claimed they saw Oswald at work that day and also saw him in the lunchroom there soon after the shooting. Except it couldn't have been Lee Harvey Oswald because he was on a bus. So who did these people see?

There was only one answer: If it wasn't Oswald at the Book Depository the day Kennedy was shot, it had to be someone posing as Oswald.

Why would anyone go to all that trouble?

To set him up as the fall guy for the murder. A murder that happened while he was still on a bus heading back to Dallas. Ergo, Oswald was innocent. Someone else had killed John F. Kennedy. And gone through elaborate efforts to pin the crime on Oswald.

The end of the book was an opinionated look at the investigations that had been done into the assassination. The Warren Commission. The congressional subcommittee that conducted its own investigation from 1976 to 1978. The Dallas police. The FBI. He talked about a massive cover-up that allowed the government to keep the secrets of the biggest crime in American history from the people all these years.

He wrote: "Now it is finally time to tell the truth about what happened that day. Time for the government to tell us the truth and tell us how an innocent man, my father, could have been blamed while the real culprits, the people who murdered the president, walked free and were never held accountable for their despicable act."

I looked at my watch. It was nearly eleven. I'd been reading for hours, but I had no more of a clue to where Eric was or what he was doing than when I started.

I put the manuscript down and went into the kitchen. I was hungry. I took out a wedge of Italian bread, cut it in two, then filled it with salami, Swiss cheese, pickles, mustard, and anything else I could find in the kitchen. I opened the refrigerator and grabbed another bottle of Amstel.

I took the sandwich and the beer back out into the living room. The reality show was over. I switched around to a bunch of other channels, looking for something to watch. I thought again about how much the world had changed since November 22, 1963. If John F. Kennedy somehow were to come back to life, he wouldn't recognize America as the same place he knew in the 1960s.

And yet, despite all the changes that had taken place since then, one thing remained the same: We didn't know any more now than we did then about who murdered JFK—and why.

I walked over to the open window and looked down at the lights of the traffic and the buildings below. Shimmering in the hot summer night air. It had been a hot day in Dallas too. And America may very well have blamed the wrong man for the crime.

"It is finally time for us to find out what happened that day," Mathis/Oswald Jr. had written at the end of the book. "Time for the government to tell us the truth."

That's when it hit me.

I knew what my follow-up story was going to be.

CHAPTER 32

I WANT TO CALL on the government to reopen the Kennedy assassination investigation," I said to Marilyn Staley.

"C'mon, Gil." Staley snorted.

"I'm serious."

"No, you're not."

"It's really not that crazy."

"Yes, it is."

"Just listen to me for a second."

She put her fingers in her ears.

"That's pretty immature," I said.

"But effective."

"Okay, if you don't want to hear my idea, just say so."

"I don't want to hear your idea," she said.

I told her anyway. Carrie was in Marilyn's office too. She had never mentioned anything to me after her drunken bedroom invitation about the incident. Maybe she didn't remember doing it. Anyway, I'd alerted Carrie to what I was going to say to Staley. I figured I owed her that much at this point in our professional relationship.

"We've come up with new evidence that shows Lee Harvey Oswald couldn't have done the shooting, that he was on a bus from New Orleans at the time of the assassination," I said. "So that leaves the obvious question of who really killed JFK. We demand that authorities reopen the investigation all over again. That happens all the time in cold cases, especially murders. Except it won't happen here because the law enforcement people won't ever do it. Not on their own. So we do it. Or at least we force them to do it by calling on public opinion. I write—or rather we write," I said, looking over at the silent Carrie, "a front-page editorial calling for a reopening of the Kennedy investigation. This isn't just some conspiracy nut calling for it. It's the *New York Daily News.* And we're doing it for a viable reason. We have new evidence that shows the man believed to have been responsible for killing the president couldn't have done it. So we call on Congress, the president, the FBI, and whoever else to start all over again. To go back to Dallas now and look at the case from a fresh angle."

Staley looked over at Carrie, who still hadn't said anything.

"What do you think about all this?" Staley asked her.

"I think it's a good idea," Carrie said.

That surprised me a little.

I think it surprised Staley too.

"You do?"

"It makes perfect sense when you think about it."

"You're as crazy as he is," Staley said.

She looked back at me now.

"Let me get this straight," she said. "You want the *Daily News* to run a front-page story asking the U.S. government to reopen the entire Kennedy investigation?"

"Yes."

"To prove Oswald didn't do it."

"That's right."

"And to find out who really did."

"Maybe."

"Maybe?"

"I don't know if it's possible at this point to pin down the real murderer. Or murderers."

"Why not?"

"It's been half a century. The trail is cold. It's not like I think we're going to be able to parade the perp in front of a TV camera or anything like that. It's been too long."

"Then why do this?"

"It's a helluva story," I said.

———

Later, as Carrie and I were walking out, Staley called out to me. She asked if she could have a second with me alone. Carrie gave me a what's-this-all-about? look, shrugged, and left. I shut the door behind her and sat down again in front of Staley's desk.

"I understand you've stopped going to the appointments with the psychiatrist," she said.

"That's right. I don't need them anymore."

I wasn't sure what she was going to do or say next. Was she going to order me to go back to see that damn Landis woman? Now, with all the big stuff happening for us with this story? I needed to devote myself to the story, not waste time sitting in some shrink's office.

"I'm not going to make you go back," Staley said.

"Good."

"You probably wouldn't listen to me even if I did."

"Probably."

"I guess I just want to talk to you about everything that's been happening recently. I know I was pretty hard on you before about your future as a reporter here. But now . . . well, now things are different. I never thought you could come back like this, but you've really surprised me. So I just want to clear the air between us. I gotta be honest with you. When this all started, and you first came to me with the Kennedy letter you got claiming responsibility for the murders and warning of more violence to come . . . well, I wasn't sure."

"You thought I might have made it up? Wrote the letter myself to get in on a big story? Done anything to get back on top?"

"I wasn't sure," she repeated. "Not then."

"And now?"

"I'm sure about you."

"Thanks, I think."

"Look, I just want you to know that I've got your back. You've been through an awful lot, you've gone through the worst hell that a reporter could go through, and somehow you survived that. And now you're back on top. I've never seen that happen quite like it did for you. But I'm happy for you. You got a second chance. Lots of people don't get a first chance. You're a very lucky man. I hope you're back on the front page for good now."

"Me too," I said.

CHAPTER **33**

T HE CALL FOR a new investigation into the JFK assassination, based on the new evidence we'd uncovered, succeeded beyond our wildest expectations.

Everyone jumped on it. The TV networks and cable outlets camped outside the *News* building, trying to get Carrie and me on camera for interviews. All the other papers in town—and across the country—started to pick up on the story too. Politicians jumped on the bandwagon, demanding a new assassination probe by the Senate, the House of Representatives, and even the White House.

And, of course, the Internet was ablaze with comments, controversy, and speculation. For the conspiracy theorists, it was like a gift from heaven. For everyone else, it was just downright compelling. The bottom line was people were talking about it now.

There was also lots of speculation about suspects, who might have been behind the assassination if you eliminated Oswald from the equation. All the familiar names were hauled out. Jimmy Hoffa, the mob, Fidel Castro, Cuban exiles, J. Edgar Hoover, LBJ, Richard Nixon. One new website sprang up called Who Killed JFK?

Meanwhile, videos related to the assassination—including edited versions of the Zapruder tape and Jack Ruby's shooting of Oswald—went viral online, getting hundreds of thousands of hits from people who hadn't seen them the first time.

Half a century after his death, everyone was still obsessed with John F. Kennedy and the story of what happened to Camelot.

And, of course, the bizarre connection to a series of murders in New York City happening now.

On the day after the article appeared, I got another envelope in the mail. It looked the same as the first one I got with the two newspaper clippings about the victims, the threatening letter, and the Kennedy half-dollar. Addressed again to me at the *Daily News*.

Inside was another Kennedy half-dollar and a list that someone had printed off the Internet of all the mysterious deaths that had occurred over the years to people connected with the JFK investigation. There were more than fifty names on the list. At the bottom, in bright red marker, another name had been written. My name. That was all. But the message was clear.

Of course, anyone could have sent this one. It didn't have to be from the same person doing the killing. But along with the threatening phone call I'd received in New Orleans, it sure looked like someone was damn intent on getting me off this story. Which just made me more certain than ever that I was on the right path.

———

At the height of all the media frenzy over our JFK story, Carrie and I found ourselves being interviewed for the *NBC Nightly News*. We rode up the elevator at 30 Rock, which I'd seen on television so many times. The TV show with Tina Fey. *Saturday Night Live.* Conan and then later Fallon. I'm pretty sure I saw one of the *Sat-*

urday Night Live people as I got on the elevator. No question about it, I got a kick out of being there. And I could see Carrie was completely captivated by the glamour and history of the place. I had a feeling that she could imagine herself as a TV star here one day.

"Who do you think killed JFK?" the on-air person asked us at one point during the interview.

"We don't know," Carrie said. "Which is why the *Daily News* is calling for the new investigation. It's finally time to find some answers. We demand the answers. Not just for us, but for all Americans. We deserve those answers."

"But you don't think Lee Harvey Oswald pulled the trigger in Dallas?"

"The new evidence indicates that he wasn't even in Dallas until after the assassination happened," I said. "Which means he couldn't have shot Kennedy. But the evidence also shows that someone wanted to make Oswald look like the shooter. The lone shooter."

"And you believe that this is all connected somehow to the murders of three people in New York City in recent weeks?"

"Yes. We don't know how. And we don't know why. But maybe when we get the answers from one of these crimes—either from the JFK assassination or the so-called Kennedy killings that are happening now—well, it will help us find the answers to all the rest of it too."

They interspersed the interview with clips of the assassination, JFK's funeral, and shots of Carrie and me at work in the *Daily News* city room—typing on computers, talking on the phone, and conversing with other reporters and editors.

There's an outdoor bar in the center of Rockefeller Plaza that's open in the summer, in the same place as the ice rink during the Christmas season and winter months. Carrie suggested that we stop for a drink there after the interview. Sitting in the center of 30 Rock, with all the Manhattan traffic and the glamour and the New York feeling around me, I savored my moment in the sun. I was back on top of the media world. Me and Carrie.

"We're really a lot alike, Gil," Carrie said.

"How's that?"

"Well, we're both very smart people."

"Can't argue with you there."

"We're both very ambitious."

"Okay. Maybe you more than me. But I'm still with you."

"And we're both great reporters who will do anything it takes to get the story—to get it first, to get it best. The story is all that matters to people like you and me. It's our lives, it defines us, it's what we're all about. There're not a lot of people who have that kind of dedication to being a reporter the way we do. That's the special bond you and I have. You know that as well as I do."

I wasn't sure I agreed with all that. I didn't want to say I was just like her. There were a lot of things about Carrie I didn't like. She was a great reporter, but the jury was still out on her as a person as far as I was concerned. I had to admit one thing, though. She was damn hot. Sitting there with her on the hot summer night, I couldn't help but be very aware she was wearing a low-cut blouse, very tight blue jeans, and big open-toed sandals that she kept dangling from her perfectly shaped and manicured feet as we talked. I'd resisted the urge to take her home after she got drunk in the bar. But I sure as hell remembered the way she came on to me that night. Sexy. Flirtatious. Needy. Not at all like she acted in the office when she was all business and ice-cold professionalism. Now she was drinking again, and slipping a bit more into that mode. Maybe if I just hung out with Carrie when she was drinking, I'd like her better.

"So maybe we should just roll the dice," Carrie said.

"Excuse me?"

"You and me."

"What about us?"

"Together."

"We are together. Just like Woodward and Bernstein, remember."

"No, silly." She giggled, and I realized she was definitely getting drunk again. "I mean you and I together as . . . well, you know." She drained the rest of her drink, then signaled the bartender for another. "I mean that offer to come over to my apartment is still open."

"I don't think that's a good idea."

"How come?"

"We could ruin our professional working relationship."

"Or we could expand it into a different kind of a relationship." She giggled again. "A fun relationship."

"But what if it doesn't work out?"

"What if it does? What if you and I turned out to be great together? Even greater than we are as a reporting duo. It's possible, you know. We might light up the bedroom the same way we light up the front page. Wouldn't you like to find out if we can do that? I would."

"It's a nice offer, and I'm very flattered, Carrie. But I don't think so . . ."

"Take me to my place for one more drink. Just a nightcap in my apartment. That's all. Then you go home. And tomorrow morning we go back to work on the story."

"A nightcap? That's all you want from me? Honestly?"

"Cross my heart and hope to die," she said, putting her hand over her chest. Then she reached over, took my hand, and put it there too.

She had a spacious two-bedroom apartment overlooking the East River. You could see the UN, the East Side of Manhattan and across the river to Queens from different parts of the place. It was expensively furnished too, or at least it looked that way to me. There was a huge velvet couch, a fancy easy chair, lots of artwork on the walls, and a thick shag carpet on the floor. Nicer than my place. A lot nicer. So how did she afford all this on a starting reporter's salary? Probably her plastic surgeon father, making sure his little girl was well taken care of in the big city. Damn, he must have to do a lot of Botox and face-lifts to pay the rent on a place like this.

She went into the kitchen, made me a drink and one for herself, then brought them out and sat on the velvet couch beside me. Without any warning, she suddenly leaned over and kissed me. I kissed her back. Our hands quickly and passionately began exploring each other's bodies. I buried my face in her hair, smelling expensive shampoo. I could smell her perfume too as well as getting a whiff of the booze on her breath as she kissed me. It was all good. I realized I'd been fantasizing about doing this with her for a long time, even as we sat in news meetings in Staley's office. I wanted her. I needed her. And for whatever reason, she wanted and needed me too.

We tore each other's clothing off as we moved into the bedroom. I caressed her breasts and explored the rest of her body. She did the same to me. It had been a long time since I'd been with a woman, and I thought I'd feel uncomfortable and awkward in this situation after all this time. But the passion I felt at that moment superseded all that. Even as I did this with her, I couldn't believe it was happening. I was making love to Carrie Bratten. But it was also as if I was releasing all my demons and uncertainty and self-doubt at the same time. Like I was being reborn completely at that moment. All of that stuff was going through my mind while I was in bed with Carrie. Of course, the alcohol may have played a role in it all too.

When it was over, neither of us said much. She asked me if I wanted to spend the night there. I said yes. We discussed the logistics a bit: I'd have to get up early in the morning, go back to my place, and grab a change of clothes for the office. She even tried to get me to talk a bit about what we were going to do next on the Kennedy story, but I was in no mood for that. I just laughed, said we'd pick up the conversation at the office in the morning, and then rolled over and went to sleep.

A few hours later, I woke up and saw the bed next to me was empty. No sign of Carrie. I got up, walked out into the hallway, and heard her in the second bedroom, which she had turned into a study. She was sitting at a desk, typing into a computer. Some of the articles we'd done on the Kennedy killings were spread out in front of her. Jesus, she was working on the story. This kid was a helluva dedicated reporter. I watched her for a few minutes as she typed. She didn't see me. She was too focused on what she was doing. I went back into the bedroom.

I sat on the bed, wide-awake now, looking out at the expanse of New York City from the window.

And I had a flashback to another time I sat in a woman's fancy apartment like this, looking out at the city and realizing that it was all out there for me—New York City, the whole damn world.

That had been with Nikki Reynolds. Right before everything went bad with Houston. And now I was doing the same thing all over again.

Maybe it was just my own insecurity and paranoia.

Or maybe it was some kind of karma or omen or supernatural warning or something for me.

But later, when the Kevin Gallagher thing happened, I remembered it came right after that night I spent at Carrie's apartment.

That's when it all started to go wrong.

CHAPTER 34

KEVIN GALLAGHER HAD been a part of this story briefly at the beginning. He was the bartender at the Union Square bar where Shawn Kennedy had been drinking the night she was murdered, and—as far as anyone knew—Gallagher was the last person to talk to her that night before the murder.

At first, the cops considered him to be a potential suspect. But he had an alibi. He'd been working at the bar until two o'clock, a few hours after Shawn Kennedy was murdered, according to the time of death determined by the medical examiner.

So the police moved on to other theories of what happened to her. An ex-boyfriend. A mugging in the park that went bad. Even a drug deal gone awry.

That was at first, of course.

Then, once the Kennedy half-dollar she had was connected to other murders with the same coin left with the victims, the investigation moved in a new direction: serial killer. Shawn Kennedy was not killed for any reason other than to make a statement by an obsessed killer—presumably now Eric Mathis—about the Kennedy assassination anniversary. Maybe the fact that her name was Kennedy played a part in it. Or maybe that was just a coincidence.

But for Kevin Gallagher, his brief moment in the spotlight was over. He gave a few interviews about his encounter with the Kennedy woman that night, talked about how shocking it was that a beautiful girl like her got murdered after leaving the bar where he worked, and then pretty much faded from public view and wasn't heard from again.

Until he was arrested.

This happened in the East Village, outside a small apartment building near Avenue C. A young woman said she'd been followed home from a nearby bar by a man whose advances she'd rejected repeatedly earlier that night. The man had trailed her after she left, then accosted her outside her front door, saying he wanted to come up to her apartment. Then he tried to kiss her. When she resisted, he punched her and then smashed her facedown onto the sidewalk so hard it required thirty stitches to stop the bleeding afterward and she had fractured orbital bones around one eye. As she lay there bleeding and moaning in pain on the street, she said he told her, "Stop whining, bitch. It could be worse. You're lucky you're not winding up dead like that other bitch who didn't want to kiss me in Union Square Park." She later identified her assailant as Gallagher.

When the police picked him up, he denied everything. At first.

But then his story began to fall apart piece by piece.

The first story he told was that nothing had happened. He hadn't followed the woman home, he had never left the bar until much later, and she had mistaken him for someone else.

Under intense interrogation, he changed his story a bit. He said he had followed her from the bar, but only because he was concerned about her safety and wanted to make sure she got home all right. He had never approached her, certainly had not hit her, and he had no idea who did.

A bruise on his hand matched up with one of the wounds on the woman's face. The cops also found blood on his shirt. They suspected it was the woman's blood that splashed on him after he hit her and threw her down to the sidewalk. They pointed out to him that once they got the tests back from the lab showing it was her blood on his shirt, then they'd know for sure he was lying.

That's when he changed his story again. This time he admitted he did hit her but claimed it was self-defense because she attacked him when he tried to kiss her. He continued to deny that he bragged to her—or mentioned anything—about killing the Kennedy woman in Union Square Park. The questioning went on for several hours. Eventually, he admitted he might have mentioned something about his involvement in the Union Square case. But only because he was trying to impress the woman on the street with how important he was and how he had his name in the newspapers. Not because he really knew anything about it other than that.

It all fell apart, though, when police found the gun. While they were interviewing him, the cops got a search warrant for his apartment. That's when they found the gun. A Glock. The same kind of gun that had killed Shawn Kennedy. I'm still surprised by how stupid people are. I've never killed anyone. But if I ever did, I sure as hell wouldn't leave the evidence in my apartment for someone to find. I'd drop it off a bridge somewhere or bury it or whatever. But not Gallagher. He took the gun home with him, stuck it in a drawer, and seemingly forgot all about it.

The cops didn't even have to wait for the ballistics report to come back to clear the case.

Gallagher gave it all up as soon as he saw the gun.

Signed a full confession right then and there.

The details went like this: He had tried to hit on the Kennedy woman at the bar. Especially when she got a call from her date saying he couldn't make it. When she left the bar, he followed her into Union Square Park as she headed for the subway station. She confronted him, told him to get away, and then—when he didn't— began to scream. He took out the gun, which he claimed he just wanted to use to scare her enough to shut up, but she screamed even more.

He said the first shot hit her in the back as she turned away to run. He claimed it was an accident. The gun just went off in his hand. Then, when he realized what had happened, he was afraid if she lived and identified him he'd go to jail. So he stood over her and fired another shot into her as a coup de grâce to make sure she could never tell anyone about him. Then he went back to the bar and finished his shift.

The owner of the bar had backed up his alibi for a couple of reasons. One, Gallagher was selling him drugs and he didn't want to cut off that supply. Second, Gallagher knew about violations at the bar that could have gotten it shut down if he went to authorities. The owner insisted, however, that he never lied with any idea that Gallagher might have actually committed the crime. He said he just went along with Gallagher's story because he didn't want to see him get in any trouble, which was probably true. In the end, the owner was arrested too and charged with lying to law enforcement officers. The Union Square bar was padlocked and shut down.

So this was no longer an unsolved Kennedy Killer case.

Shawn Kennedy's murderer had been caught, and the case was closed.

That just left Harold Daniels and Marjorie Balzano.

———

"It doesn't make sense," Carrie said to me as she read the account.

"I know."

"If Gallagher killed the girl because she spurned him that night, why was the Kennedy half-dollar there with her? Could it really just have been a coincidence she had the coin? Like the cops thought at first. What about the half-dollars found with Harold Daniels and Marjorie Balzano? If the first one was an accident, how did they get there?"

"I don't understand any of it, Carrie."

We were both stunned by these developments. The arrest of Gallagher had been announced by the police so everyone in the media found out at the same time. That didn't make us happy either. It was the first time we hadn't broken the news with an exclusive on this story. I didn't like not being first. Neither did Carrie.

It didn't help any either that I was still trying to figure out what was going on between Carrie and me outside the office. That's what happens when you sleep with someone you work with. Things get confused.

Carrie and I hadn't spoken about the night at her apartment. Just like the incident with the cab the other time, she was all business the next day in the newsroom and acted as if nothing had happened between us.

Except it did happen. Again. Two nights later. As we were leaving the office, she invited me back to her apartment. I went, of course. We made love in the big bed with the view of the East River again. I stayed the night again. I figured this time maybe we could at least talk about it in the morning. But I was wrong. When I woke up, the other side of the bed was empty again. The apartment too. She'd left me a note saying she had to get to work early to make some calls and do some research. By the time I got to work, she was already writing a story for the next day. She showed it to me, I made some suggestions, she put the revisions into the story, and then went back to her desk. There was no mention of our roll in the sack the night before.

And so that's where we stood right now, me and Carrie.

I was confused about the status of our relationship.

I was confused about what was happening with the Kennedy story.

I was confused about pretty much everything.

"Okay, so Gallagher killed the Kennedy woman," Carrie was saying. "The Kennedy half-dollar just happens to be there. Or Gallagher puts it there for some reason. But then how do Kennedy half-dollars show up at the other two crime scenes? And where does Eric Mathis fit into all this? I gotta tell you, Gil, this Kennedy half-dollar thing doesn't make sense now."

"Nothing makes sense," I said.

CHAPTER 35

NOT LONG AFTER Gallagher confessed to the Shawn Kennedy murder, someone used Marjorie Balzano's ATM card. Her ATM card—along with her wallet, ID, credit cards, and money—had been missing when cops arrived at the scene after getting the 911 call from the neighbor.

The ATM hit happened at a bodega in the Bedford-Stuyvesant neighborhood in Brooklyn. Someone had withdrawn $800, the maximum allowed to be taken out at any one time. There was a security camera in the bodega, which showed the person who used the ATM. The owner of the bodega identified him from the video as Anthony Davis, a high school dropout who came into the bodega from time to time.

Police arrested Davis later that day at his mother's house a few blocks away. He said he didn't know anything about the Marjorie Balzano murder. He said he hadn't even been in Manhattan in months. When he was confronted with the threat of a murder charge, he copped to using Balzano's card at the ATM but said he bought it from a guy in the neighborhood named Tyrone Greene.

Greene made a bit more sense as Marjorie Balzano's killer than Anthony Davis did. He ran with a gang known for violent crimes and had a rap sheet of drug ripoffs, assaults, muggings, and possession of a weapon. The cops found him at his girlfriend's house. They were both in bed, high on drugs at two in the afternoon. A search of the place turned up the rest of the stolen contents of Marjorie Balzano's purse, including credit cards and cash. The cops took them both in for questioning about the murders.

At first, Greene insisted he'd found the contents of the purse. He was going through a garbage can and just stumbled across it, so he simply took advantage of the situation. He admitted selling the ATM card to Davis but said that was all he did.

The girlfriend, however, was more helpful. She was a junkie who had the habit bad—and was willing to do about anything to get her next fix. She said that Greene had not killed Marjorie Balzano. She said someone else had done the killing. His name was Franklin Jackson. Jackson had told them he mugged the old lady, took her ATM and credit cards and wanted to sell them. He and Greene argued about the price, and Greene wound up killing Jackson. The girlfriend even led them to a vacant lot where Franklin Jackson's body was found. Greene then confessed to everything, claiming Jackson had attacked him and he killed Jackson in self-defense. For the record, none of them—Greene, his girlfriend, or Davis—knew anything about a Kennedy half-dollar.

It was a tragic crime story, the kind I'd seen so many times in New York. They always bothered me. But this one bothered me even more than usual. Because—as with Shawn Kennedy's murder—I didn't understand what was happening or why it was happening.

Marjorie Balzano had been killed during a mugging. The mugger took the contents of her purse, then tried to sell them. He got killed. And the person who killed him got caught along with the person who tried to access the dead woman's bank account. But what did any of this have to do with the "Kennedy killings"?

Where did the Kennedy half-dollar come from that connected the dead Balzano woman to the other cases? And, most important, where was Eric Mathis and how did he figure into all of this?

By the time I got to the *Daily News*, the city room was in an uproar.

"Marilyn wants to know what's going on with our story," Carrie said to me. "I don't know what to tell her. I've been up all night thinking about this. I can't sleep. I can't eat. This is not good."

I could hear the tension in her voice, see it on her face. I realized this had probably never happened to her before. Every story she'd ever done, every assignment she'd worked on, was a big success. She never had to deal with a story blowing up in her face like this. I was like that for a long time too.

I remember when the first questions began to be asked, the first doubts about the Houston story. This was suddenly starting to feel the same way. A big story falling apart. It hadn't reached Houston proportions yet, but I kept thinking about Houston. How could a story that had been going so good go bad so quickly? I desperately wanted to do something to put it back on course—to fix whatever was wrong—but I didn't know how. I didn't even understand what was going wrong. So there was no way to fix it.

For just a brief period, I started to feel short of breath again. Oh, God, not another panic attack, I thought to myself. Not here in the newsroom in front of everyone. Not in front of Carrie. I excused myself and raced into the bathroom. I locked myself in a stall, took deep breaths, and tried to calm myself down. After a little while, I felt better. I came out of the stall, splashed water on my face, and tried to pull myself together before walking back out to my desk. Carrie looked quizzically at me when I came back, like she wondered what I'd been doing for the past twenty minutes. But she didn't say anything.

The meeting in Marilyn's office later didn't go well. It was only a few days earlier that she was telling me how great I was and how proud she was of my rehabilitation as an ace reporter. It was a beautiful moment. But that was in the past. Staley was all business this time. Asking questions, demanding answers we couldn't give her. Staley looked tense too.

We agreed to do a story for the next day's paper summing up all the new developments and doing our best to put them in some sort of perspective to the overall "Kennedy killings" story. She wanted us to quote the police extensively. The police were as confused as we were. So if we put the confusion on them, it took some of the heat directly off of us and our front-page exclusives about the case that now seemed a long time ago.

"Where is Eric Mathis in all this?" Staley asked.

"The police are still looking for him."

"No leads whatsoever?"

"Nope. He's just gone."

"Well, someone better find him soon."

"What happens then?" Carrie asked.

"We get some answers from him," I said.

"Hopefully, they're the answers we want to hear."

"So where the hell is Eric Mathis?" Staley asked.

CHAPTER 36

THEY FOUND Eric Mathis two days later.

New York City police had a massive manhunt on for him. The search concentrated on Manhattan but also fanned out into the adjoining boroughs and suburbs of the tristate area. They had a watch on airports, train stations, bus depots, hotels, subways, rental car places, and everywhere else for him. Posters of him were plastered throughout the city.

"New York is a big city, but he can't hide from us forever," Police Commissioner Piersall had proclaimed at one of his press conferences. "If he's still here, we'll find him. Wherever he is, we'll find him."

But when someone did finally find him, it wasn't in New York City at all.

Not even close.

It was one thousand miles away.

A fishing boat found a body floating in the Mississippi River outside New Orleans while trolling for its morning catch. The body got scooped up along with the fish in the net, and when they emptied the contents of the net on the deck of the boat they discovered the body of a young man. When the local authorities arrived, they reported that the body looked as if it had been in the water for a while. They said there was no sign of physical trauma or injury beyond what might have been expected from being in the water for some time.

The police did a search of the area, and at a spot overlooking the water, not terribly far from where the body had been found, discovered a man's wallet with a room key that had been left there. The wallet identified him as Eric Mathis. The key was for a motel room on the outskirts of New Orleans. When police questioned the motel owner, he said that a man who fit Mathis's description had stayed there several weeks earlier but then disappeared without paying his bill. He left his belongings behind. Because he wasn't sure if the man might come back to claim them—and hopefully pay his bill—the motel owner had packed up the belongings in a closet.

Police went through the stuff and found the rest of the materials Mathis had taken from the Kennedy museum. Pictures of Lee Harvey Oswald. Videos of the assassinations. Eyewitness accounts. Stuff that he had apparently taken with him to New Orleans, just like the stuff I'd found at his home in Dallas. The material looked as if it had been neatly organized at one point—in different-colored file folders with labels—but it was now a disorganized mess. Maybe that had happened when the motel owner packed them in the closet. Or maybe, at some point, Mathis simply stopped caring about keeping it all organized.

The police found something else too.

A suicide note.

Eric Mathis explained in the note why he had made the decision to kill himself.

You go through your entire life thinking you're one person. That you know yourself. You know your father and mother.

You know where you came from. And then one day, out of the blue, you find out that's all wrong. You know nothing about who you are and, more important, about the genes you carry inside you and what you might someday be capable of.

I know now that my father is the son of Lee Harvey Oswald, which makes me the grandson of Lee Harvey Oswald. And I can no longer live with that fact. Because whatever Oswald did or didn't do that day in Dallas, the people of America will never forgive him. I can never forgive him either.

And I can never forgive my father for opening up this Pandora's box of trouble for me. Why couldn't he have just left well enough alone? I tried to deal with it. Tried for a long time. I thought by learning as much as I could about my grandfather and what happened in Dallas, I could somehow better handle the reality of who I was and where I came from.

But then my father wrote the book. And once I read it, I knew there was no hope for me, no future and no reason to live. The entire world would know me only as Lee Harvey Oswald's grandson. I don't want to be that man. I can't bear the shame that it will bring. This is the only way out for me.

He talked about plans to jump off of a bridge near where his body was found, pointing out he would die the same way as his grandmother Emily Springer had. He seemed to take some solace in that, saying he hoped it would provide him with "final closure" from the nightmare he had found himself caught up in. The note was signed simply, "Goodbye, Eric Mathis."

The writing was authenticated to be Mathis's after compari-
sons with other documents he had signed at the Texas School
Book Depository. The body in the water was also officially identified as him. The ME's office determined that Mathis died of
drowning—his lungs were filled with water while he was still
alive—and that there was no other apparent cause of death. Which
meant he had, as he said in the suicide note, simply jumped off the
bridge in a deliberate effort to die.

Even more important, though, the ME delivered an approxi-
mate time of death: about three weeks before his body was found.

Which was right after he had disappeared from the motel.

And before any of the New York City murders.

———

The story had broken overnight and the night rewrite crew handled it.

They put the story of Mathis's death on the front page, but it
was a pretty straightforward, factual story. It had all the basic information in it. But it didn't deal with the implications, especially
the part about how long ago he had died.

I'd been up for hours, ever since one of the night editors called
me with the news. I tried to help out with the story as best I could,
feeding some background material to the rewrite man handling it
in the office. No way I could go back to sleep after that. I went
online to read some of the other reports, watched the cable news
on TV too. Eventually, I just got dressed and went into the office
at the crack of dawn, when hardly anyone else was there.

I sat there in the empty newsroom for a long time, reading the
article in the *News* and thinking about everything that had happened. After an hour or two, people began streaming into work.

No Carrie, though. That was unusual. She was usually one of the first reporters in the office. I tried her cell phone a bunch of times, but it kept going right to voice mail.

"Hey, kid, we've got a problem," I said as I left her a message. "Call me right away."

But she never did.

She could have still been asleep, of course. Or shut her phone off for some reason. Or been too busy trying to work on the new developments herself to get back to me right away. But I realized now that she had seemed to be distancing herself from me ever since the questions about the story had started with the bartender's confession of killing Shawn Kennedy. Sure, we'd slept together a few times after that first night at her place. We still never talked about it, just pretended the next day that none of it had happened as she went back to being Carrie Bratten, star girl reporter. But once cracks in the Kennedy story began to clearly emerge, there had been no more bedroom invitations. Even on the work front, she was going more her own way. I had a flashback to the way so many people distanced themselves from me after the Houston debacle. I kept trying to convince myself that it couldn't be happening all over again. But it was pretty hard to ignore the signs that my life was falling apart.

I'd had another panic attack in my apartment as I was getting ready to come to work. A bad one. So bad I thought I might have to dial 911 for help. But, like most of the previous attacks, it passed and I was able to make it into the *Daily News* office without any more incidents. I just hoped that nothing happened in the office again. I couldn't handle that. Whenever the panic attacks happened, in the middle of them, I always had the fear that I was going to die. If I did die from a panic attack, I wanted to be alone in my apartment or somewhere else far away from the *Daily News* so that no one could ever see me like that. I didn't want to die in the newsroom. That somehow seemed a very important thing for me at that point.

I went over it all again in my head, just as I'd been doing ever since I got that phone call in the middle of the night telling me the news of Eric Mathis's death. No matter how many times I did it, no matter how many different scenarios I tried to imagine, the answers were always the same.

Kevin Gallagher had confessed to Shawn Kennedy's murder when she rejected his advances. Why would he confess if he didn't do it? Besides, the gun that killed her was found hidden in his apartment. So this was clearly now a crime of passion and anger and panic that had nothing to do with the other two killings.

Similarly, Franklin Jackson had robbed Marjorie Balzano, then died when he attempted to sell her ATM and credit cards to Tyrone Greene—which meant that killing too could no longer be listed as part of the "Kennedy killings" equation.

The Harold Daniels killing was still unsolved. But now, with everything that had happened in the other two cases, that was looking more and more like what was initially believed. A senseless murder of a bum on the Bowery, probably committed by someone else living on the Bowery.

And in any case, Eric Mathis—whom I had pinpointed as the most likely suspect to have killed all three of them as part of some Kennedy assassination anniversary vendetta—couldn't have committed any of the murders.

Because he was already dead at the time they happened.

Which left the question of the Kennedy half-dollars. That completely baffled me. If the crimes weren't connected, if none of

them had anything to do with Eric Mathis's Kennedy obsession—
or anyone else's Kennedy obsession—then why were the coins at
all the crime scenes?

And how did they get there?

Who the hell could have put them there besides the killer?

I tried Carrie again on her cell phone. Still no answer. I didn't
leave a message this time. I wondered where she was and why she
wasn't checking her phone. She must have known by now about
Mathis's death. Marilyn Staley wasn't in yet either. I wasn't looking
forward to talking to Staley that morning, but I knew I needed to
have that conversation and wanted to get it over with as soon as
possible.

At about nine o'clock they both walked in.

Staley and Carrie.

Together.

That's when I realized what had happened. Carrie wasn't answering my calls because she wanted to talk to Staley herself. She
was cutting her losses. She wanted to distance herself from the
damage that was being done here. Maybe she met Staley for breakfast somewhere. Or maybe she just waited outside the building to
grab her before she came into the office. But they had already
discussed what had happened overnight; I knew that now. And I
was on the outside looking in.

Neither of them looked at me.

They just walked into Staley's office and shut the door behind
them.

After a while, Staley came out, looked over at me, and shouted
across the newsroom, "Malloy, in here now."

There was no warmth in her voice like there had been a few
days earlier.

This was not going to be a friendly chat like that.

Someone had to take the fall for what was going on.

And I knew at that moment who it was going to be.

Like Lee Harvey Oswald had said a half century ago, "I'm just the patsy."

CHAPTER **37**

T HE HOUSTON NIGHTMARE had begun slowly, with a few questions at the beginning about the story and then a few more until the entire thing imploded in my face. No one comes right out and asks you if you made a story up the first day. Or demands answers about your fact checking. Or questions you about your thoroughness or—most important—your integrity as a reporter. No, that all comes later when a story goes bad.

At first, it starts as a "we" thing. "We have to find out what's wrong," "We have to do more research," and, of course, "We have a problem." With Houston, it took a while before the "we" became "you." I could tell it wasn't going to take nearly as long for the finger-pointing to start this time.

"I'm sure you understand that this puts the paper in a very vulnerable position," Staley said when she finally met that morning with Carrie and me. "We've been out in front on this story. We've been the impetus behind the investigation into the Kennedy connection to the murders. And now it appears there may not be a connection. That raises some serious concerns for us and the newspaper. How do we deal with this? How do we take a hard look at our reporting and our overall performance on this story? And where do we go from here with this story?"

"The facts in the story, no matter what has transpired in the last few days, are all accurate," I said, trying not to sound defensive about it but hearing that tone in my voice as I spoke the words.

"I'm not questioning the facts or the reporting you've done," Staley said.

"Thank you."

"I'm just trying to determine the best way to handle this story going forward knowing what we now know about the facts and the lack of any apparent connection between these murders."

"Fair enough."

"So what do we do for a follow at this point?"

"Well, we know for a fact that three people—Shawn Kennedy, Harold Daniels, and Marjorie Balzano—were murdered. A Kennedy half-dollar was found with all three crime victims."

"But if the bartender killed the Kennedy woman and the drug dealer killed the old woman on the Upper West Side, then it would appear the murders are not connected. So how do you explain the presence of the Kennedy half-dollars at each of the three crime scenes?"

"I can't," I said.

"What else?" Staley asked.

"We know that I received a letter from someone—presumably the killer, because the letter talks about the Kennedy half-dollars. And whoever wrote the letter claimed responsibility for the murders and threatened more violence."

"Except it can't be the killer if we now know that at least two of the murders, probably all three, were never connected at all."

"There has to be something else going on here that we are missing. I still want to find out what that is."

"And then there's Eric Mathis," Staley said.

I shrugged.

"Look, the facts about Mathis are what they are. We know that he was upset with his father's going public with the Lee Harvey Oswald family connection. We know he became obsessed with Oswald and the Kennedy assassination, to the point of moving to Dallas taking a job at the Sixth Floor Museum. And we know that he disappeared right before the murders started and he discovered the book his father was writing that would make public their family connection to Oswald. We took those basic facts and put together a scenario of what appeared to be happening. A scenario that pointed toward Mathis as the lead suspect in the killings. It was, and it is, a legitimate scenario. Even though it may not be the accurate scenario given the new information we now have. I know that makes us look bad, Marilyn, but I still stand by all the reporting that Carrie and I have done on this story."

Staley looked over at Carrie, who hadn't said a word yet, then back at me.

"There's another factor we have to deal with here, Gil," Staley said. "That factor is you. You and your background. We can't ignore that. I'm sure you understand that it's going to be an issue here."

There it was, the elephant in the room. Out there in the open now. Gil Malloy, the guy who screwed up the Houston story. Now he was working on a new story that got all screwed up. Anybody see a pattern here?

Carrie spoke for the first time. "I think what we need to do is write an open, candid story for tomorrow raising all these new questions. Just spell out what we know and what we don't know. Be honest with our readers. Transparency is what we should be striving for here to make it clear we have nothing to hide."

"Transparency?" I said. "What the hell does that mean?"

"We make clear to our readers that we have nothing to hide and we're sharing with them everything we know at the moment about the story. Including what went wrong. We give it to them warts and all."

She said it in a patronizing kind of way, like it was barely worth her time to explain it to me. The way she used to talk to me before we started working together. And before we started sleeping together. I was pretty sure that we would not be sleeping together again.

Staley nodded in agreement to the "transparency" and "warts and all" comments suggested by Carrie, as if she'd never heard them before. But I figured they'd gone over all this together that morning before coming into the office and sitting down with me.

Staley then said Carrie should write the story as quickly as possible. She added that Carrie should do this story herself under her byline, not the joint byline we'd been using on all the previous Kennedy stuff. She didn't say why, but she didn't have to. She asked Carrie a series of questions about what she was going to write and how she was going to do it. They discussed all of this at some length between themselves as if I wasn't even in the room.

Staley didn't ask me any questions at all for the rest of the meeting.

Which was okay with me.

Because I was all out of answers.

———

The police didn't have many answers either. Commissioner Ray Piersall held a press conference to deal with the stunning new developments. The press conference would be described in the papers the next day as "painful," "extraordinarily embarrassing," and—on the editorial page of the *New York Times*—"potentially career ending for the commissioner."

"So are you saying there's no serial killer, that these were all individual killings with no connections to each other whatsoever?" a reporter yelled out.

"How could you spend weeks, devote all the resources of your department, searching for a 'serial killer' who didn't exist, and looking for a suspect who was already dead before any of these murders took place?" someone else asked.

"What about the letter that claimed to take responsibility for the killings? The Kennedy letter. Who wrote that?" another person shouted out to him.

Piersall attempted painfully to run through the details of the case, to explain the changes in the direction of the investigation, to defend the department and himself for their actions.

He even made a personal appeal to the room to remember that they had now solved two of the three cases, and how maybe that wouldn't have happened if they hadn't pursued the relationship with the Kennedy angle so intensely until they finally got to the truth about the real culprits.

But no one was buying it.

He couldn't answer the question of why the Kennedy half-dollars were found at all three crime scenes any more than I could. It didn't make any kind of sense. The coins seemed to indicate a serial killer who wanted to make some sort of political point about Kennedy. But now that the cases no longer seemed to be related, how did the coins fit in? Unless it really was just a coincidence that all the victims had a Kennedy half-dollar on them at the time of their death. There were still a million or so of the coins in circulation, so it was possible—if not probable—that these three people had one of them with them at the time of their deaths.

Piersall also couldn't answer the question of how so much of the police department's resources had been used to chase after a suspect who couldn't have had any connection with the murders. His only answer was that they had pursued the investigation in the direction it had seemed to be heading, until the facts of the case changed. Eric Mathis appeared to be a likely suspect at the time, even though now it was clear that he wasn't.

He also pointed out that the media had played up the Mathis angle too—often from investigative reporting beyond what the police were doing—so the media bore some of the responsibility for the mistakes that were made. He didn't specifically mention me or the *Daily News*. I think he wanted to. But to suggest that the police manhunt for the Mathis kid had been set in motion because of a reporter's lead—even if that was the truth—would be even more embarrassing than taking the responsibility himself for everything that had gone wrong.

There was one area where he could do some finger-pointing, though.

"We do have some concerns now about the so-called Kennedy Killer letter that was received by a member of the press," Piersall said when someone brought up the topic.

Everyone in the room looked at me. I didn't see Carrie anywhere. She had told me she'd meet me here, but she never showed up. She was smart. Maybe she smelled blood in the water too.

"So you're questioning the authenticity of the letter?" someone asked.

"We are taking a new look at everything about this case at the moment, including the letter."

I stood up. I had to. I had to do something.

"That letter was real," I shouted out to Piersall, but even more to the other reporters in the room.

"Just like Houston was real?" someone yelled out.

"Do you really think I wrote that letter to myself just to get on the story?" I screamed, knowing even as I did it that I was fighting a losing battle.

I walked up to the front of the room and confronted Piersall face-to-face.

"Are you accusing me of manufacturing that letter?"

"I'm saying that given the inconsistencies that have emerged in this case, and given your history in terms of accuracy and integrity as a reporter, it is something that we have to consider."

I should have been mad at Piersall, I guess. And I suppose I was. But mostly I just felt sorry for him. He was like a drowning man desperately trying to grab for a lifeline to save himself.

I was the easiest way for him to do that.

And you want to know the worst part?

If I'd been him—if I'd been any of the other reporters in the room, instead of myself—I would have been thinking the same thing.

That I just made up the damn letter.

CHAPTER 38

T HE REPERCUSSIONS CAME quickly after that.

The attorney for Kevin Gallagher filed a motion for dismissal of the charges of killing Shawn Kennedy. The attorney pointed out all the flaws in the police investigation that had preceded his client's questioning and subsequent arrest. He cited the confusion and inconsistencies in the case admitted by the police commissioner himself at the press conference. He brought up the Kennedy half-dollar connection to the murders, saying this was evidence these were not just individual crimes of passion or money as the authorities claimed.

On the advice of their attorneys, both Gallagher and Tyrone Greene, arrested in connection with the Marjorie Balzano killing, now said they wanted to recant their confessions, claiming they'd been coerced into making them by illegal police tactics and without the benefit of legal counsel. No one really questioned for a second that they had done the murders they were accused of. But there was some doubt about their convictions because of all the unanswered questions about the case.

Meanwhile, the media was calling for Commissioner Piersall's scalp.

Someone had to pay for all this, and he was the most likely target.

The mayor put out a statement of support for the commissioner that was at best tepid and—according to some analysts—a clear signal that his time as commissioner was limited. There was already intense speculation going on about a successor. A half dozen or so names were thrown out in the papers, some of them probably leaked deliberately from the mayor's office to help him gauge the reaction to each candidate to replace Piersall. I noticed that one of the names was Brad Lawton, the deputy commissioner I'd met earlier. Good for him. I liked Lawton. He seemed like a decent, honorable cop. Maybe something good could come out of this for someone, anyway.

As for me, well . . . there was good news and bad news.

———

The day after Piersall's news conference, police showed up at the door of my apartment. They had a search warrant. The warrant said that a Manhattan Supreme Court judge had given them the authority to "search my premises and my possessions for evidence of a crime" that might have been committed by me. The alleged crime was supplying false evidence to law enforcement authorities. And that evidence, of course, was the Kennedy letter I'd told everyone I received in the mail.

It got worse when they discovered all the Kennedy assassination material I had in my place. A complete copy of the Warren Commission Report. Books on the assassination by everyone from Mark Lane to Jim Garrison to Norman Mailer. TV documentaries and videos about various conspiracy theories. And, of course, all the Kennedy/Lee Harvey Oswald stuff I'd taken from Eric Mathis's home in Dallas.

They hauled a lot of these things out with them under the terms of the search warrant.

They also took me down to police headquarters, where they tried to make the case that I had this obsession with the Kennedy assassination and knowledge of all the conspiracy theories, which resulted in my creating the phony letter in an effort to resuscitate my own journalistic career.

They questioned me at some length about this. The *Daily News* offered to provide me with legal counsel before I answered the questions (undoubtedly more for their protection than mine), but I refused. I said I had nothing to hide. I just wanted to tell the truth.

I explained to the police over and over again that most of the Kennedy conspiracy material had come from my father. He'd been fascinated by the topic, and I'd kept it all in memory of him.

I maintained that the Kennedy letter had arrived unannounced at my desk just the way I had told everyone from the very beginning.

"I didn't write the letter," I told the detectives, repeating the mantra of denials that I'd been doing ever since they picked me up.

"So then who did?"

"I have no idea."

"Okay, here's a question for you, then: Why would someone else send that letter to you?"

"I'm a reporter."

"They could have sent it to any reporter. But they didn't, Malloy. The letter was addressed to you. And that really doesn't add up, does it? Think about it. It was the Bratten woman's byline on the original Kennedy story, not yours. So why not write the letter to her? Hell, your byline was hardly anywhere in the paper from what I understand. So, out of all the reporters at the paper or in the rest of the media, why would someone pick you as the person to get this letter? Unless, of course, you wrote it yourself."

The question bothered me. Because it actually made a lot of sense, when I stepped back and looked at it objectively. I'd been so happy to get on the story that I'd never questioned why the Kennedy letter came to me and not to Carrie or someone else. Maybe if I'd asked myself that question back at the start I wouldn't have jumped to so many wrong conclusions so quickly. The damn cop was right. It didn't make sense that I was the only reporter in New York City who got the letter.

The next day I was front-page news. REPORTER QUIZZED BY COPS ON "KENNEDY LETTER," one headline proclaimed. POLICE EYE DISGRACED NEWSMAN IN KENNEDY MESS, another announced. The rival *New York Post* made a point of making clear to everyone my past transgressions too by saying simply HOUSTON, WE HAVE <u>ANOTHER</u> PROBLEM!

The good news was that, in the end, the police let me go and conceded they couldn't prove any involvement on my part in writing the letter or any apparent discrepancies in my account of how the anonymous letter wound up on my desk.

The question of who sent that letter remained unsolved in the case file.

Just like the question of how the Kennedy half-dollars wound up at each of the crime scenes.

———

The bad news came shortly afterward from Marilyn Staley.

"Gil, we're going to let you go," she said.

"You're firing me?"

"There are serious questions about your integrity. Which means there are serious questions about the integrity of this newspaper. No newspaper can survive like that. So we've made the difficult decision that we have no choice but to part ways with you."

I sat there stunned. Trying to take it all in. I'd known this was a possibility, of course. Just like I'd known it was a possibility back when Houston was happening. But because I'd somehow survived that crisis, I guess I assumed I would survive this one too. That I'd somehow get another chance to redeem myself. But now it was over. There were going to be no more chances for me.

I wanted to be mad at someone over how this had all wound up, but I didn't know whom to be mad at. Except maybe myself. The thing is, she was right. I was damaged goods. I was a reporter whose integrity was in serious doubt. Which means I couldn't be a reporter at all.

On the way out of Staley's office, I turned around and asked her one last question.

"Marilyn, do you believe me? Or do you think I made up that letter? I'm not talking about your official position at the paper. I just want to know what you think. It's important to me. Do you think I wrote the letter myself?"

"I don't know, Gil," she said sadly. "I really just don't know."

CHAPTER 39

WHAT WILL YOU do now?" Dr. Landis asked me.

"Look for a job, I guess."

"Maybe this will turn out to be for the best in the long run," she said. "We've talked in the past about your dependence on being a star reporter to validate the other things in your life. Now, for a while, at least, you're going to have to face some of these issues without the defense of your 'I'm a star reporter' persona. This could make you stronger. So that one day, when you do get another job at a newspaper or other media outlet, you'll have grown as a person from what you were before—"

"Don't you get it?" I snapped at her. "It's over. My career as a reporter is over. No one will ever hire me again. I'm finished in journalism. So don't sit there and tell me about how this is all going to work out for the best and it's going to make me a stronger person and I'm going to look back on this one day and laugh. It's over for me."

Landis sat there silently after I finished my outburst, waiting, I guess, to see if I was going to say anything more.

"I'm sorry," I said.

"No need to apologize."

"I'm just confused."

"Understandable."

"And scared, I guess."

I'd returned to Dr. Landis after my last day at the *Daily News*. At first after my firing, I had just sat alone in my apartment and tried to deal with my growing desperation on my own. I never got dressed. Hardly slept or ate. Didn't leave the apartment at all. The TV was always on, but I was barely aware of what was on the screen.

I just kept going over and over in my head all the events of the past several weeks, trying to figure out how things had gone so badly for me again. The panic attacks were back too in a big way. I knew I had to do something. I knew I needed help. And so, like a swimmer desperately battling the current to stay afloat, I grasped for the only lifeline I could find. Dr. Landis.

The *Daily News* wasn't paying for the sessions anymore, of course. But she said that was okay. I could pay her once I got back on my feet. Or we'd work out some sort of other financial arrangement when I was in better shape.

I realized now I'd been way off the mark when I thought of her as a cold, unfeeling professional who didn't care about her patients as real people. Out of all the people in my life, she seemed to be the only one right now who actually cared about me and was concerned enough to help me try to pull my life together. And so I opened up to her about everything in these sessions once I left the *Daily News*.

"Do you know when I think you were the closest to putting it all together?" Landis said to me at one point. "It's when you first came to me and talked about that case you were trying to solve for your dead friend, the Bronx kid who got shot fifteen years ago on the street."

"Victor Reyes," I said.

"The way you talked about it at the time, about how it was important for you to do this one story right, even if it was just a poor guy no one else cared about . . . well, it was very noble. It seemed like it was crucial at the time for you to do that story. Crucial for you to demonstrate that you really did have integrity as a reporter, and this story would prove that. To the world. And, maybe most important, it would prove it to yourself. It seemed very important to the integrity you always talk about as a reporter."

I thought about Victor Reyes. About his mother in that little Bronx apartment grieving for her son. About Roberto Santiago's plea to me for help and my promise to his widow that day at her house. About how important it had seemed then to do the right thing by that story.

Of course, in the end, I'd let them all down.

That's what Gil Malloy does.

Lets down the people who believe in him.

"If you think about it," Landis said now, "it's kind of a shame that the Kennedy story came along when it did. If you hadn't gotten pulled away from the Reyes story, maybe things would have turned out a lot differently for you. The timing couldn't have been worse. If you hadn't been told about the person writing the Kennedy book by the agent, if you hadn't put that together with the Kennedy half-dollars, if that letter had gone to some other reporter instead of you . . . well, it was just the perfect storm for you that everything happened the way it did to put you in this position."

And that's when it hit me.

Just like that.

Sitting there in that office with Dr. Barbara Landis.

Until then, I'd simply accepted everything that happened to me as being an accident. Just assumed it was a random juxtaposition of events that I found out about the Kennedy book at the same time as the murders and the Kennedy half-dollars and all the rest of it while I was in the middle of working on the Victor Reyes shooting story.

"What did you say?" I blurted out.

"I simply said that it turned out to be an unfortunate coincidence, the timing of that lunch with the agent just before all these other things happened that convinced you to get involved in the Kennedy business and change directions from the Victor Reyes story to that one. . . ."

Jesus!

Why hadn't I thought of that before?

The Lee Mathis book about being Lee Harvey Oswald's son. The three New York City killings with the Kennedy half-dollars. The Kennedy letter to me. And the Victor Reyes story. There was no reason for any of those things to be connected to the others. There shouldn't have been. But there was. There had to be. It was the only way everything made sense.

"Thank you, Doctor," I said. "You've been more help to me than you can ever imagine."

I stood up now.

"Wait a minute, our session isn't over."

But I wasn't listening anymore.

"Where are you going?" she shouted out at me.

I headed for the door.

"Back to work," I told her.

CHAPTER **40**

F OR MY ENTIRE journalistic career, I had heard about, been lec-
tured about, and been warned about the dangers of accepting
events at face value as simply fate or happenstance or—the most
dreaded word of all—coincidence.

"There are no coincidences," that old newspaperman had
taught me. "Go after the facts if you want to find out the truth."

I had followed that advice for most of my career. But now, at
the most critical time of my journalistic life, I had ignored that les-
son and written off my lunch with Nikki Reynolds where she told
me about Lee Harvey Oswald Jr. and set everything else in motion
as simply a "coincidence."

But what if it wasn't a coincidence?

What if there was something else going on?

What if there were some facts about that lunch with Nikki
Reynolds that I was missing?

———

Nikki still didn't return any of my calls.

I tried her office repeatedly, but everything went to voice mail.
I knew she was there because someone in the office told me she
was at her desk. But for whatever reason she didn't seem to want

to talk to me anymore. I finally decided the best thing to do was just confront her. Stake out Nikki Reynolds until I found her. Sooner or later, she'd have to talk to me. I contemplated staking her out at her office, but that was on the seventeenth floor of a large building with several entrances. I figured I'd have a better shot at her apartment house. I knew where that was from the time she'd invited me back there for a night of romance a long time ago. Of course, she could have moved since then. But I decided to give it a try.

I confronted her the next morning on the sidewalk in front of her apartment building as she came out the door. She looked surprised—and definitely not happy—to see me.

"What are you doing here?" she snapped.

"I wanted to talk to you about the intriguing series of events that occurred since the last time I saw you."

"I don't have time for this now."

"Why did you call me out of the blue to tell me about Lee Harvey Oswald Jr. and his book? There's something going on here, and you're right in the middle of it, Nikki. I think you know the answers I want. Or at least you know some of the answers."

"I have no idea what you're talking about."

"Sure you do. That's why you won't return any of my calls."

"No one returns your calls anymore," she said with a small smile.

"That's true. But you weren't returning my calls this time even before other people stopped doing it. Ever since that lunch we had and then people started dying and I got a letter linking the victims to the Kennedy assassination and I wrote about your author and his Oswald book."

"He's not my author anymore."

"Yes, why is that?"

"I didn't feel I was the right agent for him."

"Right agent for him? Jesus, Nikki, you took him on when he seemed like just another kook. You represent anyone who can make money for you. You used to always say that there was no such thing as bad publicity in the book-publishing business. Then, when all the publicity came out, you suddenly drop him. That's not like you at all."

She started to say something, but stopped. She looked around nervously on the sidewalk in front of her building. Despite her bravado, she looked scared. I'd never seen Nikki Reynolds scared of anything.

"What are you afraid of?" I asked.

"I'm not afraid."

"You look like you're afraid."

"Look," she said, "just let this drop. Walk away from it. That's what I'm doing. You might not have anything more to lose, but I sure do. So that's what I'm doing right now. Just walking away."

Instead of leaving her building, she turned around and headed back through the lobby toward the elevator. On the way, she said something to a doorman standing in the middle of the lobby. I started to go after her, but the doorman stopped me.

He was a big, burly guy of about forty. He looked like he might have been an athlete once, but he'd put on some pounds since then. He still looked pretty formidable, though. I remembered him from when I'd been here with Nikki before, back in the time when I was welcomed into her apartment and into her bed. I think we talked about the Knicks for a while that day while I waited for her.

He took my arm now and began walking me toward the front door and out onto the street.

"You'll have to leave, son," he said, sounding almost apologetic about it—but still firm.

"I need to talk to her some more," I said.

"The lady doesn't want to talk to you."

When we got to the door, he held it open for me politely—but also made sure to block the entrance so I had no way to get back inside.

"For chrissakes," I said. "I've been here before. I've talked to you before. I've been up in her apartment. I spent the night here. I slept with the damn woman."

"I don't know nothing about that," he said with a smile that said he knew everything about it. "But she just said that if you come back here again, she wants me to call the police and have you arrested."

"Why would she do something like that?"

"Maybe she's fickle," the doorman shrugged. "I don't know, lover boy, but I think this romance is over."

———

Since Nikki wouldn't talk to me, I needed to look for information about her from somewhere else. I went online and Googled her name. At first, I just got a lot of hits about her work as an agent and the books and the authors she represented. None of it seemed to have much significance for me.

Then I Googled Nikki Reynolds along with Lee Harvey Oswald. I got a number of hits about the JFK book including, of course, my own article. Next I tried her name along with Lee Mathis. Same results. I just kept entering more names into the search box next to Nikki Reynolds to see what happened. Shawn Kennedy, Harold Daniels, and Marjorie Balzano. Kevin Gallagher, the bartender who confessed to the first Kennedy killing. Tyrone Greene, the guy arrested in connection with the Marjorie Balzano murder. Franklin Jackson, the person he claimed actually killed

Balzano. Anthony Davis, the kid busted for trying to use the Balzano woman's stolen ATM card. Police Commissioner Ray Piersall, who was now trying to blame me for the way the JFK story had torpedoed his own career.

None of it led me anywhere. So maybe I was going at this from the wrong direction. Nikki's connection with the Kennedy book— and the events that transpired from my article about it—was already known. What I couldn't figure out was what possible connection there might be between her and Victor Reyes.

So I started Googling Nikki Reynolds along with the people I knew from that case. Her name with Victor Reyes turned up nothing. Neither did Camille Reyes or Roberto Santiago or even Santiago's wife. No connections whatsoever with any of them. I kept entering more names. Bobby Ortiz, the prime suspect. Gary Nowak, the first cop to arrive on the scene. Finally, I got to Jimmy Garcetti and Brad Lawton, the two detectives who investigated the Reyes shooting.

And that's when I found something.

A connection.

The connection I'd been looking for.

It was right there in front of me.

Hell, it practically jumped right off the computer screen at me.

There was an item on a website called the New York Social Directory with a picture of Nikki Reynolds and Brad Lawton arm in arm at a fund-raising dinner for the Museum of Modern Art that had been held in Central Park. There was an item from Page Six of the *New York Post* about how "high-profile literary agent Nikki Reynolds had been seen around town with high-profile Deputy Police Commissioner Brad Lawton, who was rumored to be in the running to maybe be the next police commissioner. Wow, talk about a power couple!" the *Post* gushed.

As I stared at the picture of the two of them smiling and arm in arm, I felt the adrenaline building in me. I felt the excitement of a big story again. Just the way I always did when I was on the trail of a big *Daily News* exclusive. I didn't work for a newspaper anymore. I wasn't even a reporter now. But all my reporting instincts were still there. I was still operating like a reporter.

I'd gone to see Brad Lawton to do what I thought was just a routine interview for a story about a fifteen-year-old murder case he'd been involved in as a young police officer. Shortly after that, Nikki Reynolds calls me up and drops a much bigger story in my lap, which sends me off in a completely different direction from the old murder case. And now it turns out that Nikki Reynolds and Brad Lawton have been sharing pillow talk.

Nikki Reynolds and Brad Lawton.

Together.

Damn.

PART FOUR

THE
KENNEDY
CONNECTION

CHAPTER **41**

I HAD TAKEN ALL my notes and records and newspaper clippings from my files at the *Daily News* before I walked out of there for the last time. Every story I had ever worked on. Including the Kennedy and the Victor Reyes stories. When I got home, I took out the folders I'd accumulated on both stories and spread them out in front of me.

I started with the Kennedy stuff.

I wrote down all of the events that had happened over the past several weeks, along with the dates in chronological order, on the JFK story.

My lunch with Nikki Reynolds. The first murder in Union Square Park. The connection to the second murder with the discovery of the Kennedy half-dollars. The letter that came to me warning of new murders and talking about the connection to the JFK assassination anniversary date. My visit with Lee Mathis, the man who called himself Lee Harvey Oswald Jr. The trip to Dallas, the third murder, and all the rest of it.

Then I wrote down the dates of the Victor Reyes story I was working on until the day I had my lunch with Nikki Reynolds, when she told me about the Kennedy book.

When I was finished, I read through it all from top to bottom:

*MAY 16—Victor Reyes dies. Detective Roberto Santiago
asks me at the hospital to write about the story.*
MAY 30—Santiago is killed in a traffic accident.
*JUNE 20—I interview Reyes's mother and promise her I
will get some answers about what happened to her son.*
*JUNE 21—I visit Santiago's widow and go through the
material on Reyes in his files.*
*JUNE 23—I interview Jimmy Garcetti, one of the two cops
who investigated the Reyes shooting 15 years ago.*
*JUNE 24—I interview Brad Lawton, Garcetti's partner at
the time on the case and now a deputy police
commissioner in the department.*
JUNE 27—Nikki Reynolds invites me to lunch.
JUNE 30—Shawn Kennedy is murdered.
JULY 1—Harold Daniels is found dead on the Bowery.
*JULY 2—I receive the anonymous letter tying the deaths to
the JFK assassination.*

Looking at it all in front of me like that now, it seemed so obvious that I couldn't believe I hadn't seen it all when it was happening. The timing. The damn timing. That lunch with Nikki Reynolds—and the subsequent events it set in motion—had been what stopped me from pursuing the Victor Reyes story.

———

Next I went through all the material I had on the Reyes case. Much of it was the stuff I'd taken from Santiago's house when I visited his wife on Staten Island. Plus notes from the interview with Reyes's mother and the other interviews and research I did before I abandoned the story. A couple of newspaper clippings were there too. One was a short metro brief that the *Daily News* had run at the time of the Reyes shooting, about a young male being shot and wounded outside his apartment house on a night of violent crime around the city. Another was an obituary in the *Daily News* at the time of Reyes's death a few months ago. It was a paid obituary item, and I realized Mrs. Reyes must have gotten together enough money to buy it in memory of her son.

There was also a clipping I'd saved about the traffic accident that had killed Roberto Santiago. I shook my head sadly as I read it again and thought about Santiago, our time together at Ground Zero, and the strange conflux of events that had gotten us to where we were today. Him dead and me with no career. We'd survived 9/11, but fate has its own agenda for all of us, I guess.

After I had gone through Santiago's files, I reread the original police report from fifteen years ago on the Reyes shooting. I was looking for something—anything—I might have missed that would give me a clue to what really happened on that hot long-ago summer night in the Bronx.

The details were pretty much the way I remembered them the first time:

Nineteen-year-old Victor Reyes had left his home in the Bronx that night. Shortly afterward, his mother, Camille Reyes, heard gunshots and ran outside. Mrs. Reyes found her son shot and bleeding on the sidewalk in front of the residence. She ran back inside, phoned 911 for help, and then rushed back to her son's side.

Police Officer Gary Nowak was the first to respond. He secured the crime scene, waited until an ambulance arrived to transport Reyes to Lincoln Hospital, and then interviewed people in the area in a search for possible witnesses. Detectives Brad Lawton and James Garcetti arrived after that to continue the investigation.

The victim had been shot once in the back. Because the bullet lodged in his spine and could not be recovered, the exact make of the weapon was not determined at the time. But based on forensic evidence obtained, it was believed to have been fired from a .38 revolver. That was confirmed when the bullet was recovered from Reyes's body and entered as evidence by Santiago before his death. The weapon was never found. But that bullet was presumably still in an evidence room somewhere. If I could somehow match the bullet to the gun that fired it, that could lead me to whoever shot Reyes. All I had to do was find the damn gun after fifteen years.

Reyes himself said that he did not know who had shot him. He was disoriented and in shock after the shooting. And even later, when he had recovered enough to leave the hospital as a paraplegic, he seemed to have trouble remembering much about the incident. Doctors pointed out that this was not uncommon in patients who suffered traumatic injuries like this. From the position of the wound, it appeared he was headed back toward the house, not going away from it, when he was shot. At first, police believed he had turned and was running away from his attacker. But then, when he made clear he had never seen the attacker or been aware of any danger until the gunshot, that idea didn't hold up. But for some reason he had turned back toward his house and was headed in that direction when he was shot in the back.

The bullet, as I already knew, did devastating damage to him. Shattering several ribs, smashing into his spleen, and then lodging itself in his spinal cord, leaving him paralyzed for the rest of his life.

There followed a fairly detailed account from Nowak of his attempts to interview witnesses, neighbors, or anyone else on the street who might have seen what happened. From the report, it appeared that Nowak had done a more than diligent job of trying to obtain this information. But he came up empty. No witnesses were ever found, according to Nowak's summary in the report.

But then, at some point later in the evening, an all points bulletin went out for Bobby Ortiz, who was described as a member of the Latin Kings street gang, driving a light green car and wanted for questioning about the Reyes shooting.

When I read that, I went back to the previous section to see if I had missed something, but I hadn't. At first there were no witnesses and the victim didn't know who shot him. Then suddenly there was a search for a suspect.

Still, everything seemed so simple at that point. Ortiz and Reyes were in rival gangs, they got into some sort of gang dispute, Ortiz shot Reyes from the car and then fled. The next step should have been the apprehension of Ortiz, probably with the weapon that he'd used in the shooting. All by the book, all very straightforward.

Except it didn't happen that way.

The file showed the trail of police mistakes and seeming indifference that led to Ortiz slipping through the cracks of justice. Including his subsequent arrest and release by Poughkeepsie police who didn't know he was wanted for a shooting. No, it didn't seem like anyone had looked too hard for Ortiz or was concerned about putting him behind bars for what he had allegedly done to Reyes.

———

I read through the report several times. One thing that jumped out at me was the name Gary Nowak. I'd wanted to talk to him the first time I looked into the Reyes story, but he'd left the force not long after the shooting and I was never able to locate him. I wrote his name down now. I needed to try to find him. I'd tracked down the two detectives who handled the case, but not Nowak. He was the first person there that night. Maybe he wouldn't be able to add anything to the account of what happened that night; probably he wouldn't. In all likelihood, he'd say it was just another shooting. But I'd learned a long time ago to leave no stone unturned on a story. I always talked to everyone. And Nowak was a missing element.

I also went through all of my own notes from the people I'd questioned before bailing on the story for the Kennedy stuff.

Particularly poignant was the interview with Reyes's mother, which made me feel guilty all over again about the phone conversation where I'd been forced to admit to her that I really hadn't done anything more about looking for answers to her son's shooting.

"His life was over at nineteen," Camille Reyes had said to me that first day in her Bronx apartment. "He couldn't work; he couldn't have a relationship with a woman; he couldn't have a normal life anymore. That heart attack he had wasn't what killed him. It was that bullet fifteen years ago. It just took him a long time to die."

Then there was the part about how her son had been trying to turn his life around at the time he was shot.

"He was taking night courses to get a high school diploma," Mrs. Reyes said. "He got a job. He promised me he was going to quit the gang life. The job was especially important to him. It was the first real job he ever had. He was working as a busboy at Fernando's. He seemed so happy. And I was so proud of him."

Fernando's. I remembered interviewing Miguel Pascal, who used to work at Fernando's with Reyes and now owned his own restaurant in the Bronx. I found my notes for that interview and read through them again. Pascal had said that Reyes also told him that he quit the gang life. But Pascal had added one other detail—that Reyes wanted to join the police force. "He had a friend or a brother or somebody who had gone to the Police Academy and changed his life around," Pascal told me. "Victor wanted to do the same thing." I'd assumed the friend on the police force was Santiago. But now the police force angle took on more significance.

————

Pascal was a busy guy, but he seemed willing—even eager—to talk more about Reyes when I called him at the restaurant. Maybe because he really liked Reyes when they worked together. Maybe because it helped him deal with the news of Reyes's death. Or maybe because he realized that could have been him in that wheelchair, if things had worked out in a different way.

"You know, I thought a lot about Victor after the shooting," Pascal said to me on the phone. "I thought about going to see him in the hospital and afterward when he got out. But things got busy at the restaurant and my life in general and . . . well, I guess I just never could find time. I pretty much forgot about Victor until you came by and told me about him dying that day. I'm sorry about that. It must have been a terrible ordeal he went through after the shooting and for all those years. I wish I could go back in time now and be there for him a little more. But we get busy, we have our own lives, and we never get around to doing that kind of thing until it's too late."

I thought about me and Santiago and said that I understood exactly what he was saying.

I told Pascal I was interested in finding out more about what kind of plans Reyes might have had back then for joining the NYPD.

"Do you know if he was ever actually accepted as a police recruit?" I asked.

"Not that I know of," Pascal said.

"How about filling out any kind of application or other paperwork?"

"Not sure."

I made a note to check later to see if I could turn up any kind of record of Reyes actually applying to the NYPD in the period before the shooting.

"But I did see him talking to a cop one day," Pascal said. "Right around that time he told me about wanting to join the force. I wondered what they were talking about. Maybe that was it. Maybe the cop was helping him."

"Where did their conversation take place?"

"In the alley behind the kitchen of the restaurant where we worked. I went out there to dump some stuff. He and the cop were out of sight behind a Dumpster. They didn't see me. I don't think they wanted anyone to see them. But I did. Saw him and the cop talking. Seemed pretty animated."

I described Santiago to him.

"Does that sound like the cop he was with?"

"Nah, not him."

"I don't suppose you'd have any idea who the police officer was after all this time?"

"Sure, I do."

"You do?"

"Kind of hard not to know about him these days. He's in all the papers. The guy they say is probably going to be the next police commissioner."

"Brad Lawton?"

"That was him," Pascal said.

"You're sure it was Brad Lawton you saw in the alley with Reyes that day?"

"Absolutely."

"What do you think they were talking about?"

"You'll have to ask Brad Lawton that," Pascal said.

CHAPTER 42

I WASN'T READY TO ask Brad Lawton anything. Not yet. At the moment, Lawton was still unaware I'd put any of this—whatever the hell it was that he was doing—together and made any connection between the Kennedy and Reyes stories. I wanted to keep it that way for the time being. I would confront him for some answers when I was ready. But first I needed to gather more facts about Lawton himself.

The Internet was filled with stuff about Lawton. Not just his rise from patrolman to deputy commissioner either. There was quite a bit about his personal life. Nikki Reynolds hadn't been the first notable person he dated. There'd been actresses, models, and even a princess or something from someplace I'd never heard of. He was a regular on radio call-in shows, made numerous guest TV appearances, and supposedly was also in demand as a speaker to law enforcement groups. I thought about Jimmy Garcetti, his old partner, drinking in a dingy Bronx bar and counting the time left until his retirement. Garcetti had sure been right when he said that he and Lawton had gone in different directions after their time together in the Bronx.

He'd first made a name for himself in the Bronx when he and Garcetti were there. The Bronx precinct was not a plum assignment for a cop who wanted to advance; it was considered a dead-end career location. But Lawton turned it into a career maker. He began making arrest after arrest, many of them drug busts. One of the articles pointed out that he'd somehow managed to zero in on the gangs that dominated the drug distribution in the area. "It was almost like he knew what the gangs were going to do—who they were going to sell to and where—before the gang members made their deals," said one ADA who racked up prosecution after prosecution thanks to Lawton's street busts. "I've never seen anyone with better cop instincts." The ADA wasn't the only one thinking like that. He'd caught the eye of people in the department with his spectacular record of arrests. They eventually transferred him to a much bigger and higher-profile detective post in Manhattan. There was no stopping him after that. He would be promoted to lieutenant, captain, borough commander, and eventually deputy commissioner in the years after he left the Bronx.

There was speculation that he could wind up as police commissioner, even before the current commissioner Piersall's troubles. Or possibly even something higher. Political leaders had put out feelers to him about running for public office at some point. Councilman. State senator. Maybe even mayor one day. Lawton continued to insist that he was happy to be in law enforcement, but a lot of people saw him as a very attractive future political candidate.

It wasn't just his record. Everything I read described him as a charming and impressive personality who could win over whatever room he was in. Just like I remembered him from that day in his office. He was colorful too, always coming up with good sound bites or quotes for the news media. In a world of wooden, cliché-ridden political leaders, Lawton was a welcome breath of fresh air.

Then there was his personal life. He had been married once,

when he was just starting out on the force. But his wife, Debra, had died, the victim of a street mugging. In a book he had written about crime fighting, *Clean Up the Streets: Crime Fighting in the Twenty-first Century*, Lawton talked at length about the pain of losing someone so close to him to crime and how that had made him even more determined to get criminals like the one who killed his wife off the streets. "There isn't a day goes by that I don't think about Debra," he said with moving passion. "Especially whenever I take someone bad off the streets. Wherever Debra is when that happens, I think she's smiling."

That didn't stop him from being a big man around town on the social front. There were countless pictures of him showing up at police banquets and other high-profile events with beautiful women—some of them famous, or at least semifamous—on his arm. Nikki Reynolds was just the latest in a long line of women Lawton had dated. I also found numerous pictures of him with other celebrities. One shaking hands with Bruce Springsteen at a concert. Another with Bono. And one with Michael Jordan at some sports dinner. No question about it, Brad Lawton moved in some pretty star-studded company.

He had an apartment in the city and a house in Sag Harbor. He was known for throwing parties at both places, with many of the boldfaced names in New York City. One of the topics of conversation at all of these parties was always the awards and plaques and trophies he had accumulated. At the house on Long Island, there was a full trophy case that contained many of these honors, and also such memorabilia as the first patrolman's hat he wore on the street, his original detective's badge, and even a collection of all the weapons he'd carried during his years on the force.

I sat back from my computer and rubbed my eyes. I'd been reading about Brad Lawton for a couple of hours. But it all pretty much came back to the same message wherever I looked: He was a great cop. A great leader. A great guy.

But I knew there was more. There had to be more. Except I wasn't going to find it reading Lawton's glowing press clips. Everyone there loved him. I needed to find someone who didn't love him, someone who might be able to tell me the truth about him.

There'd been three cops at the Reyes shooting that first day: Lawton, Garcetti, and the rookie cop named Gary Nowak. Garcetti and Lawton split up as partners not long after that. And Nowak left the NYPD after less than a year on the force.

Maybe Nowak could give me some answers.

CHAPTER **43**

ACCORDING TO POLICE department records, Gary Nowak had graduated at the top of his class in the Police Academy several months before the Reyes shooting. His assignment to a Bronx street beat was his first as an actual NYPD officer. He had scored in the upper 5 percent of all recruits on his exams and won awards for physical prowess, hand-to-hand combat skills, and marksmanship. As a member of the force, he had already received a citation for bravery after subduing an armed robber during a bodega holdup and another departmental honor for helping to get a family out of a burning house before firefighters were able to arrive on the scene. Gary Nowak seemed like a guy with a bright future in the NYPD. But then he abruptly resigned, about six months after the Reyes shooting. After that, he pretty much disappeared off the official radar.

I had put in a request with the NYPD Public Information Office to try to track down a current address or contact information for him when I first started working on the story after Santiago's death. They'd gotten back to me with some details a while later. But by that time I was deep into the JFK story and never bothered to follow up. I dug out the information I'd gotten from Public Information and read through it.

Gary Allen Nowak currently lived in Sarasota, Florida. He was a schoolteacher there. Taught history and civics at a junior high school. There was a home address for him too. A telephone number. And an email address.

I could have just called him or emailed him, of course. But I wasn't sure if he'd respond or talk to me. Why should he? Besides, I always preferred talking to someone face-to-face rather than over the phone or via email. Of course, it could all be a waste of time. Nowak might know very little. He might have been an insignificant part of the events that happened the night Reyes was shot.

But I had a feeling he was more than that. Why did he quit the police force so soon after that? Why did he turn his back on a career in law enforcement to move a thousand miles away and become a schoolteacher instead? And why did all these big changes in his life happen six months after he responded to the Reyes shooting? I was going to have to talk to Gary Nowak in person to find out the answers.

———

I took an early morning flight out of New York and landed at the Sarasota airport shortly after nine. The sun was already blazing hot by the time I got in my rental car. Even with the air conditioner on full blast, it took me a long time to stop sweating. I turned on the radio. The temperature was 88°, headed for a high of 96°. I made a mental note that if I ever got another job I could someday retire from, Florida would not be my retirement destination of choice. The summer heat in New York was bad and Dallas was worse, but Florida was off-the-charts brutal.

The school where Nowak taught was about a twenty-minute drive from the airport. I'd checked beforehand to make sure he'd be there since it was still summer. They told me that the teaching staff was already getting ready for the fall school term. I pulled out a MapQuest printout of the directions, laid it on the seat beside me, and followed the directions as I drove. I went past strip malls, discount stores, and signs advertising retirement communities until I pulled up in front of the school where Nowak was now living a new life as a teacher.

On the plane and on the drive from the airport, I'd thought about the best way to approach Nowak. I wasn't sure he'd want to talk to me. His days as a beat patrolman were a long time ago and presumably ended unhappily. If he'd come all this way to get away from that life, there was no reason to think he'd want to revisit his past with a newspaper reporter now. So I didn't want to identify myself up front.

In the end, I decided to just wing it and hope I got lucky. I walked casually into the school and tried my best to look like a teacher or a parent or someone else who might belong there. I didn't see any security, which was good. There were a few students milling around, but none of them paid me much attention. I saw a bulletin board on a wall and walked over to read it. It was filled with names and class assignments for the fall. One of them was for Gary Nowak. The listing said he was in Homeroom 321.

As I tried to make my way through the hall to find Room 321, I saw a security checkpoint ahead of me. People were flashing IDs to get through. Trying to do my best not to look too obvious about it, I backed away—like I'd gone the wrong way or forgotten something—and made my way back toward the bulletin board where I'd come in. I needed to confront Nowak face-to-face before he knew I was coming or why I was there. I didn't want to alert him ahead of time and scare him off.

Along the way, I had seen a sign that said PRINCIPAL'S/ADMINIS-TRATION OFFICE. I went back to the bulletin board, studied the list of names under Nowak's homeroom assignment, and then went up to the reception desk in the principal's office. One of the students' names on the list was Patrick McKenna.

"I'd like to talk to Mr. Nowak," I told the gray-haired woman behind the desk. "Gary Nowak. My son is in one of his classes. And there's a question I wanted to discuss with him if he's free."

"What's your son's name?" the woman asked in a bored monotone that sounded as if she'd had this conversation with a lot of other parents before.

"Patrick McKenna," I said. "My name is Thomas McKenna."

She picked up a phone, dialed a number, and told Nowak who I was and what I wanted to see him about. She listened for a few seconds, then hung up and smiled at me.

"Mr. Nowak says he is free to meet with you now."

She wrote me out a visitor's pass, which I pinned to the front of my shirt, and then I followed her directions up to the third floor to Nowak's classroom.

Gary Nowak was sitting behind a desk. He stood up to greet me. He was a relatively big, very fit-looking man of about forty, which fitted with the history of him on the force. He had curly red hair and he was wearing a pale green pullover shirt, loose-fitting khaki pants, and boat shoes.

"You're Mr. McKenna?" he asked, greeting me with a big smile.

"Yes. Thank you so much for taking time see me on such short notice."

"Nothing's more important than my students."

"This shouldn't take too long. I just have a few questions about Patrick's schoolwork for the fall."

He stuck out his hand now as he approached me. I shook hands with him.

"Sure." He smiled, holding on to to my hand. "I just have one question for you before we get to Patrick's schoolwork."

"What's that?"

He suddenly pulled on my hand, whirled me around, and pinned my arm behind my back so I couldn't move. Then he shoved me headfirst into the blackboard behind his desk. I saw stars from the force of the blow. He tightened the grip on my arm behind my back and then grabbed me around the neck at the same time in what I recognized as a classic police choke hold to immobilize a suspect.

"Here's my question," Nowak said, as I tried without success to squirm away from him. "Who the hell are you and what are you doing here?"

I gave up struggling. It was no use. He was too strong, too good.

"I told you . . . I'm Patrick McKenna's father."

He twisted my arm even harder now. "I don't think so," he said.

"Why would you say that?"

"Well, for one thing, Patrick McKenna is black."

Damn. I'd picked an Irish-sounding name to avoid something like that. But you can never be sure about a name.

"Not Irish, huh?" I said, grunting through the choke hold.

"His parents adopted him. I've met them. Mrs. McKenna supervises the PTA committee in charge of the school bake sale. Mr. McKenna—whose name is Donald, by the way—plays golf at the same course here as me. I was in a foursome with Mr. McKenna a few weeks ago. And you ain't him."

He twisted my arm again and smashed me one more time into the blackboard to show he meant business.

"My name is Gil Malloy. I'm a newspaper reporter. I'm here to talk to you about a shooting you dealt with as a police officer a long time back in New York. A kid in the Bronx named Victor Reyes."

I wasn't sure how he'd react to that. I braced myself, waiting for another twist to my arm or collision with the blackboard. But he loosened his grip, then let me go entirely. I stood there wincing in pain and trying to get some kind of feeling back in my almost paralyzed right arm.

"A newspaper reporter from New York," he said.

"That's right. I don't know how much you remember about the case. But Victor Reyes was a nineteen-year-old kid who got shot fifteen years ago in front of his house in the Bronx. You were the first cop on the scene . . ."

"Victor Reyes," he said. "I've always wondered when someone would finally get around to asking me about him."

CHAPTER 44

NOWAK TOOK ME down to the school cafeteria to talk. We got coffees along with an English muffin for him and a toasted roll with butter for me. It had been a long time since I'd been in a school cafeteria. This one was still pretty empty, just some teachers and a few students getting ready for the fall semester to begin in a few weeks.

My arm was still sore from where Nowak had twisted it behind my back. I winced when I reached to pick up my coffee.

"Are all the teachers here as tough as you?" I asked.

"Sometimes it helps in the classroom." He smiled.

"I saw in your records that you had bench-pressed more than anyone else in your class at the Police Academy."

"I was a lot younger then."

"Do you still work out?"

"I try to keep in shape. You never know when it might come in handy." He smiled again. "Like when someone walks into your classroom pretending to be someone he's not."

I took a sip of my coffee and a bite of the roll. I'd eaten something on the plane, but I was still hungry. I realized I'd been up for hours.

"Bad luck my picking that McKenna name as my cover, I guess."

"It wouldn't have mattered." Nowak shrugged. "I had you pegged for a phony the minute you walked into my classroom, even without the McKenna thing working against you."

"How?"

"The ticket in your pocket. It was sticking out. I couldn't read it all, but I did see the words 'New York—LaGuardia Airport.' I didn't figure it was too likely that a parent of one of my students had flown here from New York City and then driven directly to discuss school curriculum. No, I figured instead that it was more likely you'd come from New York simply to see me for some reason."

I let loose a whistle of admiration.

"You would have made a good cop," I said.

"I was a good cop."

"Until you quit."

"Which is why you're here, right?"

"Tell me what happened."

"You tell me first why this is so important to you."

I did. I told him everything. About Roberto Santiago. About the Reyes story. About the JFK story too and how I'd screwed up my career at the *Daily News*. And now I was trying to make things right by finding out the truth about what happened to Reyes on that long-ago Bronx summer night. I didn't hold anything back. I'm not sure why. Maybe because I thought it would help convince Nowak to open up to me in the same way. Or maybe because I just needed to unburden myself by telling the story to someone, and Nowak seemed to be as good a person as any (at least in the absence of Dr. Landis) to be the audience.

At some point, a young teen boy came over to speak to Nowak. He asked him some questions about the civics curriculum and also about the baseball team, which he wanted to try out for. Nowak talked with him patiently about both, reassuring him about the civics course and encouraging him to try out as a pitcher. They discussed both civics and baseball until finally the kid thanked him and left.

"You like teaching, huh?" I said to Nowak.

"It's the kind of job where you feel you can really make a difference, contribute something to make the world a better place."

"And police work?"

"I used to feel that way about being on the force too."

"So why did you quit?"

"Ah, right, that's what you're here for, isn't it?"

"Yes."

"Okay, you told me your story, so I guess it's time for me to tell you mine."

———

"The first thing you have to understand is that I really meant that stuff I was saying before about wanting to make a difference, to change the world for the better," Nowak said. "That's why I joined the NYPD. I thought I could do that as a police officer. All those things they taught us in the academy, to serve and protect and all, I completely bought in with the program. I thought being a police officer was a noble profession, like being a doctor or a minister or something. I saw everything in black and white back then. I believed that good would always triumph over evil. That the good guys always won. I guess I was pretty young and pretty naïve. But that's what I believed."

"Until Victor Reyes?" I asked.

"Until Victor Reyes."

"So what happened that night?"

Nowak sighed and took another sip of his coffee. He looked around the cafeteria. At a woman laying out dishes of Jell-O behind the counter. At a table of students laughing at a joke one of them had made. But he had a strange, faraway look on his face now. Like he wasn't in a junior high school cafeteria in Florida anymore but back in the Bronx on a hot summer night walking his beat.

"I'd only been on the street for a few months," he said. "I'd seen some stuff. But nothing as bad as the Reyes shooting. When I got to the scene, the Reyes kid was screaming in horrible pain. He kept saying, 'I can't move! I can't move! Why can't I move?' The paramedics were trying to sedate him or something, but they were having trouble getting close to him because the mother kept holding on to to her son. Finally, I came along to pull the mother to the side so they could get Reyes into the ambulance. She was hysterical with grief. She just kept crying and praying for her son and calling out to him. I still have nightmares about that scene. Even now, fifteen years later."

I nodded. I'd covered stories like that. So horrible that I would still think about them weeks, months, even years later. It could have been something as simple as that that convinced Nowak to quit the force, I supposed. He could have been so freaked out by what he saw that night that he decided he didn't want to spend the rest of his life as a policeman dealing with tragedy like that. But I knew there was more to his story.

"I was there for about fifteen minutes or so by myself, I guess," Nowak said. "Until the detectives showed up to handle the investigation."

"Lawton and Garcetti?"

"Right. Garcetti was technically the senior member of the team and the lead investigator, but it was pretty clear Lawton was the guy calling the shots. He was smooth, he was cool, he was completely in charge. He asked me what I'd done, and I went through everything with him. How I'd tried to find passersby or witnesses who might have seen something. How I'd talked to Mrs. Reyes—as best I could—about what she remembered. Lawton took down everything I said in these detailed notes. Like I said, he was completely in charge."

"So what happened then?"

"Lawton asked me to control the crowd scene for a little while, then said he was wrapping up the investigation and I could go back to my beat. I'd only been there maybe thirty minutes tops. Didn't seem like much of an investigation to me. But then I was just a rookie cop."

I remembered what Camille Reyes had said to me about the cops: "They asked a couple of questions and then I barely heard from them again."

Nowak continued. "Anyway, after I left, I heard a description had just gone out for a green car and a shooting suspect in the car. Later, they broadcast another bulletin, which included the suspect's name. Bobby Ortiz. That didn't make much sense to me."

"Ortiz was in a rival gang from Reyes. They speculated that the shooting was some sort of gang feud."

"I found that out later."

"So what didn't make sense?"

"How did Lawton and Garcetti know this? I interviewed everyone there. The mother, neighbors, people on the street who might have seen something. But no one saw or knew anything. Not a damn thing. So—and look, I know this wasn't my place—I went to Lawton and Garcetti and asked them how they got the description. They said someone at the scene told them that. Someone I must have missed."

Nowak pushed away what was left of his English muffin. His coffee was cold now. He looked down at it. I think he was deciding how much more of the story he wanted to tell me. But I knew he would tell me all of it. He'd been holding this inside himself for too long. Just like me. Gary Nowak had his own demons to deal with from the past and the choices he had made in his life.

"I bought that explanation," he said. "I bought it then, anyway. I mean, these were experienced detectives, and I was a kid fresh out of the academy. Besides, why would they make up a story like that? And so I believed that I was the one who'd messed up the investigation by not getting the description and the name of the suspect. I felt bad about that. But Lawton and Garcetti had caught it in time, so no real harm was done."

"Except they never caught Bobby Ortiz."

"I did."

I stared at him. "You caught Ortiz? When?"

"A few days after the shooting. The whole thing was on my mind because I thought I'd screwed up at the crime scene. So I studied the wanted bulletin and information and a picture of Ortiz just in case I found out something about him on the street. I did better than that. I saw him. Standing there on the street, a few blocks away from his house as if he didn't have a care in the world."

"And you arrested him?"

"Sure. What else was I going to do? I took him back to the precinct, turned him over to the booking desk, and went home that night feeling damn good about myself as a police officer."

I was confused.

"There's nothing in the records about Ortiz being arrested and booked at that precinct."

"Yes, so I found out later."

"Why not?"

"When I got to work the next day, I learned that the suspect I'd picked up had been released without bail. No charges were ever filed. And no one could explain to me why. So I did the only thing I could think of to do. I went back to the investigating officers on the case, Lawton and Garcetti. But Lawton, really. Like I said, I'd been impressed with him on the street at the crime scene, and I figured he'd help me get to the bottom of this. I thought he'd be as furious as I was that Ortiz was gone. But he wasn't."

"What did Lawton say?"

"He told me that I'd gotten the wrong man. That the person I picked up wasn't Bobby Ortiz, just someone who bore a resemblance to him."

"Okay, you could have gotten the wrong man, I suppose."

"It was Ortiz."

"How can you be sure?"

"He told me that was who he was. Like I said, he didn't seem too worried until I slapped the handcuffs on him. Then he was just confused."

"And you told Lawton and Garcetti that you were certain you hadn't make a mistake on Ortiz?"

"Right. At first, Lawton—he did most of the talking—was very nice and solicitous with me. But then when I kept pressing my point and insisting that I had picked up the right man and that a mistake had let a shooting suspect go free, he became more confrontational. Finally, he barked at me that I'd screwed up the investigation at the crime scene and now I'd screwed up this too."

"What did you say?"

"I told him that I knew what I knew, and that if he didn't want to listen to me I'd take it to someone higher up in the chain of command and let them sort it out. Lawton got really mad at me then. It got very ugly."

"Did you do that? Go to someone higher up?"

"I never got the chance. There'd been a big drug robbery from the evidence room in the precinct several months earlier. Hundreds of thousands of dollars in drug evidence seized from crime scenes had disappeared. Out of nowhere, I was informed that I was a suspect. That an informant had fingered me as selling the drugs on the street of my beat. It didn't make sense. I'd barely been at the precinct when the drugs were stolen out of the evidence room. And, in the end, I was never charged with anything. But the damage was done. I was smeared with the stench of corruption. They transferred me off my beat to a desk job in the property room. Some irony, huh? I'm accused of stealing evidence, and my job is now watching it at the station. Well, that was one of the real dead-end jobs at the precinct, and I was pretty sure I would never get back on the street again. I didn't want to spend the rest of my career cataloging police property. So gave I gave up my dream of being a police officer."

"And you think Brad Lawton was the one who fingered you, who short-circuited your career?"

"I could never prove that."

"But you believe it."

"Yes."

"Why would he do it?"

"I was never sure. But you have to understand something. Lawton was a golden boy at the precinct—on the force—even back then. He'd already made a big name for himself by making a lot of drug and gang arrests on the street. He was an up-and-comer in the department, everyone knew that. Maybe we didn't know he would rise as high as he has—practically the next police commissioner—but everyone knew back then that Lawton had a big future. My guess—and it's only speculation—is that something about the Reyes case scared him. Something that might have messed up that bright future. And when I started asking too many questions about Reyes, he pretty much destroyed my career so that no one would ever listen to anything I said. I was damaged goods after that. I had no more credibility."

Just like me, I thought. Seemed to happen a lot to people who got in the way of Brad Lawton.

"There were a couple of other things that happened I didn't understand," Nowak said. "First, Lawton and Garcetti, they weren't really together at the crime scene. Not at first. Lawton showed up by himself. Garcetti didn't get there until just before I left."

"Don't homicide detectives usually work in pairs?"

"That's what I thought. But they weren't that night. It was Lawton on his own until Garcetti finally made an appearance. I know the official police record doesn't show it that way—I went back and read the records later—but that's the way it was."

"Like Lawton was around nearby and could show up quickly, and Garcetti wasn't?"

Nowak shrugged.

"It didn't mean much to me at the time. But later, when things began to fall apart, I started thinking about it and wondering what was going on with the two of them that night. I asked them at one point, I think, why they showed up separately, but never got an answer. A rookie cop's not supposed to ask questions like that. I guess I never knew my place.

"I tried to think about a possible reason that Lawton showed up earlier than Garcetti. The most obvious one was that he was close to the crime scene. But why would he have been in that neighborhood and why without his partner?"

"You said there were two things that bothered you," I said to Nowak. "What was the second?"

"After I picked up Ortiz only to see him released, I was talking to the desk sergeant about it. He mentioned something about it being the second time in a couple of days that he saw that guy in the station house. I asked him what he meant. He said he'd seen him there in one of the interrogation rooms a few nights earlier. Turned out to be the same night Reyes was shot. Based on the timing he gave me, Ortiz was being held in the station house already for questioning on some other crime at the time Reyes was shot."

"The perfect alibi," I said. "That means someone else must have shot Reyes."

"So I thought, but it didn't work out that way."

"Let me guess," I said. "When you told someone about it, the desk sergeant changed his story. Said Ortiz wasn't there that night, that he'd confused him with some other suspect on some other night."

Nowak smiled sadly. "Better than that. He said he didn't even remember talking to me. Everything I did, every time I tried to dig myself out of the hole I was in . . . well, it just got me in deeper. Like I said, I was damaged goods. When you're damaged goods, no one wants to be associated with you."

"Tell me about it," I said.

Nowak looked down at the cold coffee in front of him.

"So I put in my resignation from the force a few months later. I didn't know what else to do. I went back to school after that and got my teacher's certificate. Then I left New York City and started a new life as a teacher here."

"You look like you've been pretty successful at it, Gary. That your life has turned out pretty well."

"More or less."

"What's the less?"

"I wanted to be a cop. I wanted to be a good cop. I should have been a good cop. I still don't understand what happened back there. And I guess in some ways I'm still a cop at heart. I don't like to leave cases open with unanswered questions. And I don't like to see people get away with crimes, no matter who they are. The bottom line here, Malloy, is that I want to know who shot Victor Reyes just as much as you do."

CHAPTER 45

ON THE WAY back to the airport, I took out my cell phone and checked for messages. There had been three of them that morning while I was talking to Nowak. All from Nikki Reynolds. That surprised me. No explanation, just three successive messages asking me to get back to her. I dialed the call-back number, but it went to her voice mail. I left her my cell phone number again, said I was getting on a plane soon but would try to reach her when I landed back in New York.

I dialed another number. A number I hadn't called in a while.

"Hello, Susan," I said to my ex-wife when she picked up the phone in her office. "How's the wedding planning going with Dennis?"

"Dale."

"Whatever."

"I thought we weren't going to do this again." She sighed.

"Sorry, but this isn't a personal call."

"What kind of call is it?"

"Professional."

"I find that hard to believe."

"Why?"

"Well, for one thing, you don't have a profession anymore."

"Technically, no."

"I really don't have time for this, Gil . . ."

"I'm working on a story."

"Even though you don't have a job."

"I can still do a story."

"You mean like freelance?"

"Something like that."

"So what do you want from me?"

"In the late '90s, there was a big drug theft from the evidence room of a police precinct in the South Bronx. Lots of heroin and crack and cocaine and pills and other stuff that had been seized off the street suddenly disappeared. As far as I know, none of the drugs were ever recovered or anyone charged with the theft. I just need you to check into it, see what you can find out."

"Why do you care about a drug theft from back then?"

"I have a thirst for knowledge."

"C'mon, Gil, give me something if you really want me to help you."

"Okay. Here it is. I need you to find out if there's ever been any connection made between the drug theft and someone who worked in the precinct back then. Brad Lawton."

"Brad Lawton? The deputy commissioner?"

"That's the one."

"The Brad Lawton who probably will be the next police commissioner."

"That's the one."

"The Brad Lawton who's the golden boy of the department right now."

"That's the—"

"Don't say it."

"Will you help me?"

"What are you telling me? That Brad Lawton stole a bunch of drugs? That he's a drug addict? Because, I gotta tell you, this doesn't make a whole lot of sense."

"I don't know. And I know it doesn't make sense. That's why I need more information. I need help. I don't have a lot of people to turn to for help these days. Will you help me?"

There was a long pause on the other end.

"Okay," she finally said. "I'll nose around a little and see what I can find out. Tell me what you know . . ."

———

Next I called Carrie Bratten at the *Daily News*. She picked up after the first ring. Probably hoping it was someone with a big story for her. Her mood changed as soon as she heard it was me.

"I don't want to talk to you ever again," she said.

"I'm doing fine, Carrie. Thanks for asking."

"Just stay away from me."

"Gee, I wonder if Bernstein ever said that to Woodward."

"Look, Malloy, you've screwed up your career. And you came close to screwing up my career too. I survived this only because everyone blamed you for what happened, as they should have. But the damn stench of all your mistakes and sloppiness and overall lack of integrity is on me still too. I have to do my best to make sure people forget I was ever with you if I want to get back to the top again. I'm going to do that. I have to do that. So just stay away from me."

"I just have one question, Carrie."

"I told you, I don't want to talk to you."

"Who was your source?"

"What source?"

"The source in the police department who told you about the Kennedy half-dollars at the crime scenes?"

"I'm not telling you my confidential source."

"Was the source Brad Lawton?"

She didn't answer. She didn't have to. I knew I was right from her stunned silence.

"He's the one that set this all in motion, right?"

Carrie hung up the phone. Damn, I thought as I stared at the silent cell phone, Brad Lawton just kept turning up everywhere I looked in this story.

———

As soon as I was off the flight and in a cab headed to Manhattan, the phone rang. It was Nikki Reynolds. She sounded very upset.

"You've got to stop," she said to me.

"Stop what?"

"Stop what you're doing."

"You mean asking questions?"

"Don't even try talking to me again. I mean it. You have to stay away from me. Don't ever show up at my apartment or try to contact me again."

"What's the matter? Your boyfriend Brad Lawton is upset over that?"

"He's not my boyfriend."

"I thought you two were really tight."

"Oh, we're tight," she said. "He's in love with me. He told me so. He's going to marry me. He told me that too. He thinks he's going to be mayor one day, and he said I'd be the first lady of New York. I believed that too. I believed everything he told me. That's the thing about old Brad. He'll tell you anything to get you to do what he wants. And he always gets what he wants in the end."

"Was he the one who told you to take me out to lunch that day and get me excited about the book?"

"It was supposed to be a joke. That's what I thought, anyway. I'd told him about the crazy guy who'd sent me the manuscript claiming to be Lee Harvey Oswald's secret son. He got all excited, and he convinced me to push the idea to you. Brad could be very convincing. Back then, well . . . I'd do anything he wanted."

"And now?"

"Now I know what kind of person Brad really is."

I heard some kind of noise in the background. Like a PA system. Someone was saying something about a doctor being summoned to a floor.

"Where are you, Nikki?"

"In a hospital."

"What happened?"

"I fell."

"You fell?"

"It's not serious. I've got a black eye and some bruising on the side of my face. They put in a few stitches, but they say I'll be okay."

"Did Lawton do that to you?"

She didn't say anything.

"Why did he hit you?"

"This is the last time I will ever talk to you," she said. "Just stay away from me. Stay away from him. For my sake. And for your sake too."

"I'm not afraid of him," I said. "I don't have a career to ruin."

"It's not my career I'm worried about."

"What else is there?"

"I'm worried about my goddamned life!"

"Because he hit you?"

"Did you hear anything I just told you about Lawton? He'll do anything to get what he wants. Anything. Everyone says how everything always seems to work out so great for him. Everything just falls into place for ol' Brad. He's one lucky guy. Well, what if it isn't luck? Maybe Brad makes sure that things happen the way they do for him. Like your friend Santiago."

"What are you saying, Nikki?"

"Don't you find it just a little bit odd that Santiago got killed by a hit-and-run driver right at the same time he's looking into the Victor Reyes case?"

"Are you telling me that Lawton had something to do with Santiago's death?"

"Look, you saw what happened to Santiago. He starts digging into a case from Brad's past, and then he winds up dead. Lucky break for Brad that your Santiago died, huh? But then, like I said, Brad Lawton always gets what he wants. One way or another. Think about it. Think about that before you make things even worse."

CHAPTER 46

T HE IDEA WAS so shocking, so mind-boggling, so preposterous on the face of it that I hung up the phone with Nikki still telling myself that it was simply the paranoid delusions of a woman who was going through some kind of nervous breakdown.

I mean, Lawton was a deputy police commissioner. A highly decorated and awarded member of the force. He might be a dirty cop, he might be guilty of a lot of things—but there was no way he could have played a role in the death of a fellow officer. Was there?

The minute I asked myself that question, I knew the answer.

It depended on what Lawton stood to gain from Santiago's death.

———

On the face of it, the Santiago hit-and-run case seemed open and shut.

After his evening duty shift ended, Santiago had been crossing the street to get to his car that was parked on the other side. Witnesses said a blue Buick—later determined to have been traveling at more than 75 mph—blew through a red light and hit him in the middle of the crosswalk. The car never stopped, just kept barreling down the street. But it was a nice spring night, and the street was crowded with people who saw the incident. At least three of them got the license plate number of the speeding car.

The plate was registered to George Sledzec, a forty-four-year-old unemployed mechanic with a history of vehicular and alcohol violations. He was already on probation for a DUI that left a young boy seriously injured after he plowed into the kid on his bicycle outside a schoolyard. Three weeks before Santiago's death, he'd had his license suspended for crashing his car while drunk into his neighbor's front porch at four in the morning. So Sledzec shouldn't even have been behind the wheel of a car the night that Santiago died.

The cops found him passed out at a bar. When he woke up, he claimed he'd blacked out and had no idea what happened. His car, with the same license plate that had been identified by the three individual witnesses, was parked nearby. The left front headlight and the front end of the car were smashed in, where the car hit Santiago as it sped down the street. There were also blood and DNA samples found on the front end of the car that matched Santiago. There was no question that Sledzec's car was the vehicle that struck and killed Santiago.

Sledzec continued to claim that he couldn't remember anything about what happened that night after he passed out.

He also insisted he was innocent.

But since he was already on record as admitting that he had no idea what he did or didn't do during his blackout, no one believed for a second that he wasn't the person who killed Santiago.

He was charged with vehicular manslaughter, and the prosecutor threw the book at him—hitting him with the most severe count, which could send him to jail twenty-five years to life. The prosecutor also delivered a blistering attack in court, saying he wished he could have sought even more time and he hoped Sledzec never tasted freedom again. Sledzec was remanded without bail to Rikers Island until his trial, where a speedy conviction seemed a foregone conclusion at that point.

———

I met with George Sledzec in the visitors' room at Rikers the next day. He was a balding, overweight man who looked particularly slovenly and dumpy in his prison uniform. I've interviewed a lot of prisoners. Some of them are threatening and potentially violent. Some are belligerent and angry. Some are scared. Almost all proclaim their innocence. But Sledzec was different. He just seemed . . . well, bewildered by where he was and what had happened to him.

"I still don't understand," he told me. "I know I've got a drinking problem. I know I forget things when I drink. But I just can't believe I would do something like this—something so horrible— and not remember any of it. Even me. I think about that night all the time in here, go back and try to reconstruct the events all over again. But I don't remember anything until I was arrested."

"Tell me what you do remember."

"I spent that day looking for work. I'd been unemployed for six months. The accident with the boy on the bike, and the subsequent court action and all, cost me my last job. And, as you can probably imagine, it didn't make looking for a new job very easy. Not when prospective employers found out I had a police record. I was depressed. I didn't want to go home and tell my wife and my family I'd failed again. So I did what I always do when I want to feel better. I drank."

"At the bar where they found you?"

"Yes."

"What time did you get there?"

"About five or so."

"What's the last thing you remember?"

"Asking for another drink," he said sadly. "That's usually the last thing I remember before a blackout."

"What time was that?"

He shrugged. "After nine maybe. Or maybe closer to ten. I'm not sure."

"And had you gone to this bar before?"

"Yes, it's been a favorite place for a while."

"The people there knew you?"

"The bartender did."

"Why didn't he stop serving you when he saw how drunk you were?"

"They never do. As long as I can pay. That's why it was my favorite bar. They never told me I'd had too much to drink."

"Then the bartender knew you pretty well."

"I was one of his best customers."

"Does he remember what time you left?"

"The cops asked him that. He said no. He said he doesn't pay much attention to the customers. He just pours drinks. It's that kind of place."

"So you have no idea what time you left the bar or what time you wound up passed out in that parking lot?"

He shrugged again. "Not much of an alibi, is it?"

I talked to Sledzec for a long time. Asking him about that night over and over again. Trying to find something—anything—to explain how Santiago's tragic death might have been anything more than an accident caused by a drunk behind the wheel.

"The worst part of this is that none of it would have happened if I'd just kept my promise to myself that night," Sledzec said at one point.

"You promised yourself you'd quit drinking?"

"Nah, I knew I could never keep that promise."

"Then what was the promise?"

"That I wouldn't drive drunk."

"Except you did."

"I guess . . . only, I'm still not sure how that happened."

"What do you mean?"

"I didn't have my car keys that night."

"Where were your keys?"

"I'd lost them a few nights earlier. At the same bar, probably. Doing the same thing. I didn't try to get a replacement set, though, because I figured that it would be better if I couldn't get behind the wheel the next time I got drunk. At least I wouldn't get in trouble with the car again."

"What happened?"

"The police said they found the keys in the ignition."

"So maybe you left them there. You found the keys while you were drunk, then left them there again when you passed out in the parking lot. That makes sense, doesn't it? Do you remember doing that at all? Finding the keys, then getting behind the wheel of the car before you blacked out?"

"I don't remember anything at all," Sledzec said sadly.

———

On the ride back to Manhattan, I went over and over my conversation with Sledzec in my head, trying to put together the strands of information he'd given me into some kind of coherent chain of evidence that made sense to me. I didn't get all the answers I was looking for from Sledzec, but I got some of them.

Here's what I knew for a fact:

Sledzec was a hopeless drunk, a wasted life of a human being who had nearly killed a little kid and eventually might have—probably would have—killed again driving drunk if he hadn't been caught and sent to jail.

It was Sledzec's car that had killed Santiago. Three witnesses saw it. They all got the license plate number. And Santiago's blood and DNA on the front of the car confirmed Sledzec's blue Buick as the car that had killed Santiago.

I also knew that the world was undoubtedly a better place without Sledzec walking around—and more important, driving around in it. I had no real sympathy for the man. I had interviewed a number of family members and grieving friends of drunk-driving victims over the years. That left me little compassion for a man like Sledzec who could run over a kid on his bike and blame it on an alcoholic haze.

Those are the things I knew for sure.

But here's what I still did not know for sure.

I did not know for sure that George Sledzec killed Roberto Santiago.

The story about the lost keys bothered me. Sure, he could have made it up. Maybe even made up the story about blacking out and not remembering anything. Except I had checked the records before the interview, and Sledzec had told the same story from the moment he was arrested. Repeated it again in subsequent interviews with the cops and prosecutors. And stuck to it even when I talked to him now. Why do that? He's already in jail, and will probably stay there for a long time no matter what he does or doesn't admit to at this point. There was something else too. He acted and looked genuinely confused by what had happened and how his keys had wound up back in the car and how he had somehow managed to drive it.

That left only one other possible explanation, of course.

Someone else drove his car that night.

Someone who stole his keys, waited for him to pass out like he did most nights, and then used his car to run down Santiago.

Someone who had a motive for wanting Santiago dead.

Someone who could manipulate the evidence to make sure Sledzec got blamed for the killing.

Someone who always got what he wanted.

CHAPTER 47

THE BIGGEST MISSING piece to the puzzle of what happened to Victor Reyes was still Bobby Ortiz. Fifteen years ago, Ortiz had been named as a suspect in the Reyes shooting. He'd been detained briefly twice—once in the Bronx a few days after Reyes was shot, then again in Poughkeepsie several months later. After that he disappeared. He might be dead. Probably was dead. But I needed to find out what happened to him.

I started by going to his last known address in the Bronx. The one that had been in police records for him when the first bulletin went out naming him as a suspect in the Reyes shooting. The address was gone, though. I mean literally. There was a vacant lot where his apartment building had once stood.

Some people I spoke to remembered the Ortiz family. They said the father had left a long time ago and the mother died a number of years ago. No one was sure where Bobby Ortiz was or if he was even alive. They said he'd been a regular street presence a long time ago, but no one had seen him recently. There was also a sister who used to work as a clerk at a bodega a few blocks away.

The bodega was still there. So was the original owner, who told me he'd owned the business for nearly half a century. He remembered Erika Ortiz and she'd worked there for a few years after school and on weekends and vacations. He wasn't sure exactly what happened to her. But he'd heard she had a couple of kids and moved to Manhattan. Somewhere around 116th Street, he'd heard, in Spanish Harlem.

There was certainly no shortage of people named Ortiz in Spanish Harlem. I called them all, asking for a Bobby Ortiz. It seemed like a wild-goose chase. Hell, she'd probably gotten married and didn't even use the name Ortiz anymore. Everyone I did reach said, "Who's Bobby Ortiz?" or "I don't know any Bobby Ortiz." Except one. She said, "I have no idea where Bobby is."

The address was listed in the phone book. I wrote it down, took a subway uptown and, an hour or so later, knocked at the door. A middle-aged, dark-haired woman opened it.

"Are you Erika Ortiz?" I asked.

"Who are you?"

"I need urgently to talk to your brother Bobby."

"Are you a cop?"

"I'm a newspaper reporter."

"Doesn't matter. I haven't heard from Bobby in years."

"So you said over the phone."

She looked confused. Then it clicked for her. I was the one who had called her earlier.

"What does a newspaper reporter want with Bobby?"

"I'm doing a story that he figures prominently in. It's about gang life in the Bronx. Growing up in that atmosphere and dealing with the violence on the street each day—"

"Bobby left that life a long time ago. He never talks about that anymore."

"I thought you weren't in contact with him."

She didn't say anything.

"It's not a bad story. I think I can help your brother. I think he got a tough break. I want to make things right again. For him. For a lot of people."

I handed her a plain manila envelope that I'd brought with me. It had Bobby Ortiz's name on it. The envelope was sealed.

"Give this to your brother if you see him," I said.

She shrugged. "I told you, I don't know where he is."

"Just in case you run into him one day."

She looked at the sealed envelope.

"What's inside this?"

"Let's just say I'm trying to pay off an old debt."

———

I waited outside her building all night, but she never came out. Until the next morning. At about nine o'clock, she emerged and walked to a subway. She had the manila envelope under her arm. I figured she would have looked at what was inside. And I hoped she'd want her brother Bobby to see it too.

I followed her, keeping back far enough so that she wouldn't spot me, until she got on a downtown train. I boarded the car behind hers, but picked a spot where I could see her from the window between cars without her seeing me.

She got off at Houston Street, then walked two blocks to a high-rise on Allen Street. There was a doorman on duty there. She spoke to him and handed him the envelope. The doorman opened the envelope and looked at what was inside.

It was a picture.

A picture of Victor Reyes, along with a short article about his death.

On the back of the picture, I had written, "I don't think you shot him. I want to help prove that."

Then they talked some more. Their conversation looked animated. Finally, she reached over and gave him a big hug. Then she left.

I waited until the sister was well out of sight. Then I walked up to the doorman and nodded. At first, he thought I was there to see someone else and started to open the door. But I stood there in-stead and pointed to the envelope and the picture and the article that he was still holding in his hand.

"You're Bobby Ortiz, right?"

He looked flustered but bravely tried to recover. "No, I'm Ramon Martinez," he stammered.

"I mean your real name. You're Bobby Ortiz."

"Who are you?"

"I'm the guy looking to help you."

"Help me how?"

"Technically, Bobby, you're still a suspect in the shooting of Victor Reyes. Which means you're now a suspect for murder."

"Murder?"

"Victor Reyes died."

I gave him a quick version of the events that had happened.

"I didn't shoot Reyes," he said.

"I believe you."

"Then why did you track me down after all this time?"

I nodded toward the picture.

"Like I said, Bobby, I think I can help you. I think we can help each other. All you've got to do is tell me the truth."

———

Bobby Ortiz had gotten out of the gang life. After the near miss with the cops in Poughkeepsie, he got scared and realized how lucky he'd been to escape. He was still wanted for a shooting. And so Bobby Ortiz disappeared. He called himself Ramon Martinez, bought enough phony ID material to back it up, and went straight.

He'd been working as a doorman at various apartment build-ings in Manhattan and Brooklyn for more than a decade now.

He had a wife and a son and a good life, he told me.

Ortiz told me all this matter-of-factly as we sat in the lobby of the building. Maybe he always knew this day would come. That he couldn't run far enough to get away from the life Bobby Ortiz had once lived and the things that he had done when he was running with that Bronx gang.

"Why did the police say you shot Reyes that night?"

"I don't know."

"But you maintain that it wasn't you?"

"I couldn't have done it."

"Why not?"

"I was in jail when it happened."

"Jail?"

"Yes. The perfect alibi. Or so I thought."

A woman carrying a bag of groceries came to the door. Ortiz stood up, opened the door, and helped her with the groceries to the elevator. He gave her a big smile, she thanked him, and he came back to where I was sitting.

"The cops picked me up on the night Reyes was shot," Ortiz said.

I remembered that Nowak had told me something similar. And the desk sergeant had at first said he remembered Ortiz being there.

"They probably picked you up as a suspect in the shooting."

Ortiz shook his head.

"Before the shooting. I was in police custody at the time that Reyes was shot."

"Why did they arrest you?"

"They were always hassling us gang members."

"And you were in a gang?"

"You know I was."

"Victor Reyes was a gang member too."

"Yes."

"What was the relationship at the time between your gang and Reyes's gang?"

"We were pretty much at war with each other."

"Which would have given the police a reason to think you had a real motive to shoot Reyes that night."

"Except I didn't do it."

"Right."

"I was in police custody that night, just like I said."

"Do you remember the name of the police officer who arrested you?"

Ortiz looked uncomfortable now.

"It was a long time ago."

"Anything about the officer you remember that might help us identify him to verify your story?"

"I don't remember."

I took out a picture of Brad Lawton and showed it to him. He looked more uncomfortable now. He didn't say anything.

"I'm looking to help you here, Bobby."

"I'm afraid."

"Afraid of what?"

"You don't understand . . ."

"This is Brad Lawton," I said. "He's a police officer. A very important police officer now. He very well might be the next police commissioner of New York City. So what are you afraid of?"

Ortiz looked again at the picture of Lawton.

"Lawton was the one who arrested me that night," he said.

"You're not confusing that with another police officer—a beat cop named Nowak who picked you a few days after the shooting?"

"No, that was different. Lawton took me in on the night of the murder. Before it happened."

"Well, if Brad Lawton arrested you and had you in custody, why didn't he tell anyone that when you were named as a suspect in the Reyes shooting?"

"He didn't want anyone to find out about our relationship."

"What relationship?"

"I was his snitch."

"You provided Lawton with information?"

"Yes. He'd pick me up from time to time on some trumped-up charge. It was a cover to pump me for information about what was going on in my gang."

"And what did you get in return for this information?"

"Drugs."

Ortiz said that when Lawton wanted information, he would pick him up and take him somewhere to interrogate him. Sometimes he acted like he was taking him into custody or questioning about some crime in order to avoid suspicion from any other gang members. He said that's what happened the night Reyes was shot. Lawton had picked him up and taken him to an interview room at the precinct for "questioning." That was the way it worked, he said. Lawton would find out what he knew and then release him, and everyone would assume it was just a normal roust by the cops.

"What time did Lawton pick you up that night?" I asked.

"About seven thirty."

"And how long were you there?"

"Until close to nine, I guess."

"Reyes was shot a little after eight."

"That's why I couldn't have done it."

I was pretty sure he was telling me the truth. It matched the account Nowak had given me earlier. And the desk sergeant told him he saw Ortiz in the station house too—or at least he said he did until someone, presumably Lawton, got him to change his story.

"And then you got arrested again a few days later?"

"Yeah, some street cop pulled me in. Said I was wanted for shooting Reyes. That's the first I ever heard about it. I didn't understand what was going on. But then Lawton showed up and straightened everything out."

"He let you go?"

"That's right. But I was scared. I decided to get the hell out of there. I had a cousin who lived in Westchester County who gave me a place to stay. I hung around there for a while, pulled a few jobs, and scored some drugs. Until I got picked up by the Poughkeepsie police on a DUI charge. After I got out of there, I decided not to press my luck anymore. So I became Ramon Martinez."

I had been writing everything he said down in my notebook as he talked. I scanned through the notes now, trying to put it all together in my head, trying to connect all the dots.

"Where did Lawton get the drugs that he paid you with for the information?" I asked Ortiz.

"I don't know."

"He never mentioned anything about that to you?"

Ortiz shrugged. "I just figured he picked them up off a shipment on the street somewhere. He was a cop. He could do anything he wanted."

"How long did the arrangement go on between the two of you?"

"Close to a year."

"That means he somehow had access to a lot of drugs."

"He gave away a lot of drugs, to a lot of people on the street."

"What do you mean?"

"I wasn't the only one."

"Who else?"

"He was using Victor Reyes the same way."

CHAPTER 48

I HAD ACCUMULATED A lot of facts, a lot of information, a lot of evidence in my investigation into the Victor Reyes shooting. Enough to do a story. Except I had no one to do a story for.

It was an issue that I'd tried to put out of my mind while I worked on the story. I needed to do that. I needed to act like I was still a reporter in order to think like a reporter and act like a reporter to do my job. I'd always disciplined myself that way. Just get the facts, get the information, get the evidence—and the story will take care of itself.

Except now I was forced to confront the harsh reality of my own situation. There was no actual story. Because I didn't work for a newspaper anymore. I wasn't even a reporter. I had the damn story but nowhere to publish it.

I needed someone who could help me make this public. Someone I trusted. Someone I knew well enough to not doubt his or her integrity for a second.

There was only one person I knew like that.

———

I met Susan, my ex-wife, in Foley Square near One Hogan Place where she worked. I didn't want to go up to her office. Maybe I was just being paranoid, but it was the DA's office, and Brad Lawton was a powerful man in law enforcement. I wasn't sure how far his tentacles stretched. I wanted to make sure no one but Susan and I knew what I was doing until it was the right time to go public.

We walked along the streets of lower Manhattan as we talked.

"I looked into the drug robbery at Lawton's old Bronx precinct, like you asked," Susan said. "A huge amount of seized narcotics evidence, mostly street drugs, did indeed go missing back then. It was the biggest theft from a New York City police facility in the history of the department. Internal Affairs and the DA's office were all over it. But no one ever found any answers. There was no viable suspect, no clues, no nothing. Eventually, the whole thing went away. I think they were happy to just sweep it under the rug to avoid any more embarrassment to the department."

"When did Lawton get assigned to that precinct?"

"About a year earlier."

"And when did he leave?"

"A couple years after that."

"Right," I said. "He got a much better gig. Working out of Manhattan as a homicide cop. He was already starting his ascent in the department. And you get a lot of recognition—a lot of media face time too, if you want it—being a Manhattan homicide cop. But it was all because of what happened in the Bronx. He became a star there with all his gang arrests. That got him the big promotion, and he never looked back after that. And I'll bet the number of arrests he made in the Bronx, especially of gang members, went up dramatically following the drug theft at the precinct."

She stopped walking now and looked me directly in the eye.

"What's going on here, Gil?"

I told her everything. From the lunch with Nikki Reynolds all the way through everything I'd found out about Brad Lawton.

"Lawton was an up-and-coming detective in the Bronx," I said. "He was the junior partner to another cop, Jimmy Garcetti. But he clearly had a big future. He was quickly becoming the golden boy of the department, and his star—which would take him all the way to the brink of the commissioner's office where he is now—really started to shine brightly back then.

"One of the ways he made his reputation was with big gang busts. He seemed to know what the gangs in the Bronx were going to do even before they did it. He was always in the right place at the right time back then. He put together an amazingly impressive arrest record, almost single-handedly decimated the violent gangs and their leadership in that section of the Bronx. It set the tone for his entire career. Set him up for his rise to the top. Captain. Commander. Deputy commissioner. Now the police commissioner's job is practically his for the taking. Hell, some people are even talking about him running for mayor.

"I think Lawton took the drugs. I believe he used the drugs to buy information on the street about the gangs so he could be a big man in the department. One of the people he was using as an informant was Bobby Ortiz, the gang member police claimed did the Reyes shooting. Another was Reyes himself. Both of them were double-dealing with their gangs, pretending to be loyal but snitching to the police in return for the drugs that Lawton was providing for them.

"But somewhere along the line Reyes decided he wanted to be a police officer himself, just like his boyhood friend Roberto Santiago had become. He told Lawton about it. He probably thought Lawton would help him. But Lawton couldn't let that happen. Reyes knew too much. If he ever became a cop and told anyone, Lawton's career would be over.

"So Lawton shot him. Tried to make it look like a gang hit.

Made sure Ortiz got blamed for it. He probably wanted to shoot
Ortiz too to make sure he never talked. But he didn't get the
chance. A patrol officer, Gary Nowak, saw Ortiz on the street and
brought him to the precinct for questioning. This was bad news
for Lawton. So he had to cut Ortiz loose, before he told his story.

"Meanwhile, Reyes was still alive. The shot hadn't killed him.
But he was in no condition to be a danger to anyone anymore. He
sure was never going to be a police officer now. He was hooked up
to machines and a wheelchair and was so messed up he could
barely get through the day, much less cause trouble for Lawton.

"And Ortiz had disappeared. As long as Ortiz wasn't around,
he couldn't talk either. Lawton got a lucky break when Ortiz, after
being picked up in Poughkeepsie, somehow slipped through the
cracks of justice and fled again. So he was gone. Reyes was no
threat. And Lawton probably forgot about the whole messy business until Reyes died fifteen years later and Santiago started looking into the old case.

"Santiago died. But then there I was asking questions about
the same case. That's when Lawton came up with the idea to send
me off in a different direction. He knew my background, knew my
whole history of screwing up—of doing anything—to get a big
front-page story. So he lured me with the biggest story he could
think of: the JFK assassination. Probably got the idea with Nikki
Reynolds when they were in bed together and she told him about
the book proposal and manuscript she'd gotten from a man claiming to be Lee Harvey Oswald's secret son. He figured that was
perfect. So he made sure she told me about the book.

"Then he sent me the anonymous letter and somehow planted
Kennedy half-dollars with the murder victims to send me off on a
wild-goose chase. And when it all blew up in my face, I was discredited as a reporter, just in case I ever did go back to Reyes. As

a bonus, he discredited his boss the police commissioner too and opened up the possibility that he could step into the top job. Some of it was just luck, but some of it was ingenuity on Lawton's part to put all these pieces in motion."

Susan hadn't said anything the entire time I was telling the story. She just listened intently. Like she was making mental notes of everything I said. Or maybe she was just trying to figure out how to get away from this conspiracy nut who used to be her husband.

"That's a helluva story," she said finally. "Let me see if I've got everything. You're saying Brad Lawton stole a drug shipment from the police evidence room, then he shot someone on the street in cold blood and fifteen years later lied and planted evidence and sent the entire department after a fictional serial killer just to make sure no one ever found out he took the drug shipment."

"There's more," I said.

"What more could Brad Lawton possibly have done?"

"I don't think Roberto Santiago's death was an accident."

I told her about my conversation with Sledzec and about the missing keys and about him being passed out in front of the bar.

"Jesus," Susan muttered.

"I did some more checking on Lawton's background after that," I told her. "Did you know that back in the late '90s, when he got his first big promotion to homicide cop and was transferred to a high-profile job in Manhattan, he wasn't the first choice for the job? There was another detective with a stellar record named Jack Graynor in Brooklyn who was supposed to get that promotion. Except one day Graynor went into a deli while he was off duty and got gunned down during a holdup.

"A few years later, a city councilman named Ned Colby decided to make a political name for himself by going after corruption in the NYPD. At some point, he started nosing around Lawton's precinct. Until one night when something went wrong with his car—investigators said later it looked like his accelerator pedal got stuck—and he plunged off the West Side Highway into the Hudson River. He died, and his police corruption investigation died with him.

"Then, when the deputy commissioner's spot opened up, there were two leading candidates for it—Lawton and a police captain named Gregory Shore. One day the FBI got a tip that Shore was trafficking in child pornography. They got a search warrant, checked his computer, and found tons of shocking pictures of young children in sexual situations. He quietly left the force soon afterward. And Lawton, of course, got the deputy commissioner's job."

"Are you saying that you think Lawton was responsible for all this?" Susan asked me now.

"Like Nikki Reynolds told me, Brad Lawton always gets what he wants."

"Even if he has to resort to ruining people's careers and maybe even killing them?"

I nodded. "And then there's the story about his wife being killed by a mugger. That doesn't ring true either. No one ever caught the mugger, no one ever saw a mugger. Maybe she knew too much about the man she was married to, and she had to be eliminated too. I can't say that for sure yet. But I believe Brad Lawton is a dangerous man, Susan. An evil man. If even a portion of this is true, then I've never met anyone as cold-blooded and calculating and willing to do anything to get ahead as him. And he does it all in the guise of the charming, likable good cop everyone loves and thinks is wonderful. We've got to stop him."

"Do you have any evidence at all?"

"We have the bullet."

"The bullet that was in Reyes for fifteen years?"

"Yes."

"The bullet is from a thirty-eight revolver, right?"

"Right."

"The police use a nine millimeter."

"Now they do. But in the early '90s, police still used the thirty-eight. I checked. And some of the cops were allowed to keep using them as their official weapon for a number of years afterward."

"Okay, but we still don't have the weapon that fired the Reyes shot. So what good is the bullet if we can't match it up with the weapon that fired it?"

"Lawton has a trophy case at his house on Long Island. I read about it in one of the articles about him. He likes to show it off to guests and at parties he throws for the beautiful people. Keeps all sorts of mementos and stuff from his days on the force in this trophy case. Supposedly it includes guns he used day to day on the street and as a homicide detective. Maybe the weapon he used to shoot Reyes is in there."

"Why would he keep it and then leave it in a display case for the world to see?"

"Because he's arrogant. Because he thinks he can do anything he wants. Maybe it even gives him a high or a thrill to do stuff like that. I think there's a good chance the weapon that shot Reyes is there. If we could just examine those weapons . . ."

Susan shook her head. "It won't work. No way I can get a search warrant for the deputy commissioner based on all this speculation. I need more. I need some sort of hard evidence that actually connects Lawton to the Reyes shooting."

"I have an idea about that . . ."

CHAPTER 49

BRAD LAWTON WAS just as friendly, just as forthcoming as he'd been in our past conversations when he ushered me into his office at NYPD headquarters.

"Good to see you again, Malloy," he said, shaking my hand enthusiastically. "Although I wish it were under better circumstances. I was really sorry to hear about you leaving the *Daily News*. That's a damn shame. What happened?"

"My story fell apart."

"Well, that's not your fault."

"The people at the *News* thought it was. They blamed me."

"Doesn't seem fair."

"Of course, I do have a history."

"Oh, right, that Houston business."

"I'm a little accuracy-challenged is the way they put it."

Lawton chuckled. A friendly chuckle. I remembered how much I liked him the first time I was here. He'd seemed like a good cop.

"I still have a few questions about the story," I said. "Questions about the case. That's why I came to see you today."

"I thought you weren't working as a reporter anymore."

"I'm not."

"But you're still asking questions?"

"The questions are just for me. As you might imagine, this has all been pretty devastating. It's turned my whole life upside down and probably ended my career as a journalist. I'm just trying to figure out what went wrong, what I might have missed and what I screwed up. I know this is my problem, and you don't have to talk to me about any of this. I'm not carrying a press card anymore. But I appreciate any time and insight you could give me."

Lawton nodded sympathetically.

"Of course," he said. "This case has been devastating to the department too. We looked pretty bad ourselves. There's a lot of scrutiny of us now because of how this all turned out. A lot of blame being passed around. No one comes out of it looking good when a case goes wrong like this one did."

"Actually, that's not true," I said.

"What do you mean?"

"Well, you're looking pretty good. The police commissioner is taking all the heat for this. He's the guy up there in front of the TV cameras and the rest of the media looking like a jerk. Just like I look like a jerk. But you . . . there's a lot of talk that the commissioner could wind up losing his job over this. And that you're at the top of the list of candidates to replace him. So, you see, you do come out of this looking pretty good, Deputy Commissioner. Damn lucky for you. I mean it couldn't have worked out better for you if you'd planned it that way."

Lawton stared at me impassively across the desk.

"What was your question about the case?" he asked.

"There're two things that bother me the most," I said. "First, how did the Kennedy half-dollars get to each of the crime scenes? And second, who sent me that letter connecting the murders to the Kennedy stuff? Neither of those two things makes sense any-

more, given what we know now. I mean, if there were three separate crimes committed by three different people for three different
reasons . . . then how did the Kennedy half-dollars get there and
how did the letter wind up on my desk? A letter that appeared
genuine because the letter writer knew about the Kennedy half-
dollars at the crime scenes. A fact that had not been made public
yet. Ergo, it seemed as if the person who wrote the letter had to be
the killer. Except there was no single killer, as it turns out. Very
confusing, huh?"

"We haven't been able to figure that out either," Lawton said.

"No one in your department can explain the Kennedy half-
dollars or the letter?"

"Unfortunately, no."

"Not a clue?"

"No."

"Not even a viable theory?"

"Not at the moment."

"Funny, because I have one."

"You have one what?"

"I have a theory as to what really happened here."

"I'd be happy to hear it."

"I don't think you will be."

"Why not?"

"Because it all comes back to you. Everything—all the misdi-
rection on this case—was your doing."

"Why would I do something like that?"

"To make sure I didn't keep looking into the death of Victor
Reyes."

I ran through it all with him. Everything I believed even if I
couldn't prove it yet. How he'd used Nikki Reynolds to get me
interested in the Kennedy book after I came to his office asking

questions about Victor Reyes. Sent the anonymous letter to me at the *News*. Left the Kennedy half-dollars to be found. And then leaked that information to Carrie to try to get us—really, me—to chase after the wrong story.

"Maybe Nikki mentioned the book in passing when you were in bed or something, and you had a good laugh about this kooky guy and his book," I said. "But then you realized the potential it might have to interest me as a story. I think I probably talked to Nikki at some point about my lifelong fascination with the Kennedy assassination and all the unanswered questions about it. Even showed her my library of books and videos on the subject. She told you that, which made it even easier to come up with the idea to send me off on a wild-goose chase about the JFK killing instead of writing about the shooting of Vincent Reyes.

"Nikki didn't know why she was doing it, of course. She was just doing you a favor. Then later, when people started dying, she got scared. But when she took me to lunch and tried to convince me to get involved with the Oswald book the way you'd asked, it probably didn't seem like that big a deal to her. The only problem was it didn't work. I wasn't interested in the Oswald book. Not then, anyway.

"So you decided to up the ante. Maybe the fact that the first murder victim was named Kennedy gave you the impetus, maybe it was just a coincidence. But you came up with the idea of connecting a Kennedy half-dollar to each of the crime scenes. How did you pull that off? Well, you're a top cop. It wouldn't be too hard. I checked. No one ever found a Kennedy half-dollar at the actual crimes scenes when they first arrived. They always turned up later. You probably showed up at Union Square and dropped it there for the CSI guys to find with Shawn Kennedy. In fact, I'll bet if I check the records you were at the Balzano crime scene at some point too. The Kennedy half-dollar in the Daniels case was found afterward when the body was already in the morgue. I think you planted it there. It's the only thing that makes sense. Somehow someone put the coins there to be found with all three bodies. If not the killer, then it had to be a cop.

"Anyway, after you came up with the plan, you leaked the information to Carrie Bratten. She was writing the story about the Shawn Kennedy murder, and she used you as a source for the Kennedy half-dollar connection with the Daniels case. Except you also needed me to get involved in this, not just Carrie. So you sent me that anonymous letter pretending to be a Kennedy killer. Again, the only person who could have known about the Kennedy half-dollars at that point outside the police—they hadn't been made public yet—was the person who put them there. That would be you on both counts. So I put that together with the Kennedy book stuff on Lee Harvey Oswald Jr. and presto . . . your plan is up and running in high gear. I forget all about poor Victor Reyes. I'm on the trail of a Kennedy killer, running around the country and chasing Kennedy leads instead of worrying about what really happened to Reyes.

"And in addition to diverting me from the Reyes story you didn't want me doing, you got a bonus out of it. I wound up uncovering a whole other story about Eric Mathis, the son of the man who wrote the book. And when that story fell apart, when the whole Kennedy angle and the case against Eric Mathis collapsed, it made your boss, Police Commissioner Ray Piersall, look foolish and incompetent. This likely will cost him his job. Which is a career boost for you. Because your name wasn't connected to any of this, you weren't the one out front taking the blame like he was. I don't think that's why you did it. I think you did it because you were so desperate to keep me away from the Reyes story. But what the hell, it all turned out perfectly for you on every level. You're going to be the next police commissioner. It was win-win for you all around, Deputy Commissioner. You got everything you wanted. But that's the way it always works out for you, isn't it? You always get what you want."

Lawton sat there impassively. If I'd shaken him up, he sure didn't show it. I might have been discussing the weather or the stock market or the chances for the Yankees to win another championship for all the concern he showed in his face.

"The funny thing is, I think the Kennedy book is real," I said. "I think Oswald really did come up with new evidence on the JFK assassination.

"I figure you and Nikki assumed he was some kind of a nut and you were just using him to get what you wanted from me. But the guy nailed it. He really did prove that Oswald couldn't have killed Kennedy. That he wasn't even in Dallas when the assassination occurred. After fifty years, we now have the proof that the Warren Commission and everyone else we believed about the JFK assassination were wrong. The killer is still out there somewhere, or at least never got apprehended.

"We could start all over again and maybe find out this time what actually happened in Dallas on November 22, 1963. I wanted to do that. I wanted to solve the biggest crime story of our times. I wanted to rewrite history. But not anymore. No one would ever listen to me now even if I did nail the damn assassination story.

"And you know what? No one else will believe Oswald's book either because he's been caught up in all this mess too. Even though he had nothing to do with it. He just got caught up in all the lies. His son Eric too, and that cost Eric his life.

"So now we will never know any of the answers about Kennedy. But the basic premise—that Oswald's father couldn't have killed Kennedy because he wasn't even in Dallas that day—is still true. Except no one will pay attention to that either. That might be the biggest tragedy out of all this."

Lawton didn't say anything for a long time.

"Have you talked to anyone else about these ridiculous ideas of your?" he asked finally.

"No."

"Will you?"

"It wouldn't do any good, would it?"

"Because nobody believes anything you say anymore."

"That's right."

"You're damaged goods, Malloy. Accuracy challenged, as you put it."

"Just another aspect of your little plan that worked. No one will believe something as far-fetched as this. But you and I know it's true, don't we? C'mon, admit it. Just the two of us sitting here . . ."

Lawton snorted contemptuously.

"Are you wearing a wire or something, Malloy?"

"I'm not wearing a wire."

"Trying to get me on tape saying something you can use to back up these crazy ideas of yours?"

I stood up and unbuttoned my shirt to show him that there was no wire, no recording equipment of any kind.

"Want me to drop my pants too?"

"Doesn't matter. Whether you're trying to record me or not, I couldn't care less. You're the one doing all the talking. Not me."

Lawton smiled now. Not a friendly smile anymore. A scary smile.

"Hypothetically speaking, though, let's say that everything you just told me is true. It's not, of course. I deny everything. Quite frankly, I think you're delusional and probably need some sort of professional help. But even if it were true, there's no way for you to ever prove it. No evidence whatsoever to back up any of your preposterous claims about me doing any of these things. The Kennedy half-dollars. The letter to you. Nothing to prove I had anything to do with them."

"You're right about that."

"So then why are we wasting time here talking about Nikki Reynolds and Lee Harvey Oswald Jr. and Kennedy half-dollars and fake letters and all the rest of this nonsense? Without evidence, you have nothing. If you try to make these absurd accusations against me, all I have to do is point out your stunning and appalling lack of credibility in the past."

"That's right too."

"So I think we're done here."

"Not exactly."

"What else do you and I have to talk about?"

"Victor Reyes."

"Victor Reyes?"

"Yes. The story I started on. A story I should have been doing all along. The real story here. I might not have any evidence connecting you with the Kennedy story, but I think there's something still out there on Victor Reyes you don't want me to know. That's the story I'm going to find out the answers to. Victor Reyes."

"I have no idea what you're talking about."

"Sure, you do. That's why you killed Roberto Santiago."

For the first time, Lawton looked worried. I let that last statement hang out there for a few seconds.

Then finally I stood up and started walking toward the door.

But, before I left, I turned around and said to Lawton:

"You got rid of Santiago, but you didn't get rid of his files. I've got those files now, the files with everything Santiago found out about you in connection with the Reyes shooting before you killed Santiago. And those files are what I'm going to use to bring you down. First, for the Reyes shooting. And then the whole house of cards will come tumbling down for you. Santiago was a good cop. He would have nailed you for this, if he'd lived. And now I'm going to finish the job. All the evidence I need to put you behind bars for Reyes is in that file. And once I release the information in Santiago's files, there's nothing that can save you. You'll find that out soon enough."

CHAPTER 50

I WASN'T SURE LAWTON would come after me. He might really believe that I was no threat to him anymore. That I was so discredited at this point that no one would believe anything I said, even if it were true. But Lawton had come after Reyes when he perceived him as a threat. He'd come after Santiago too fifteen years later to make sure his secrets never came out. And, I now believed, he would come after anyone else who ever stood in his way on his rise up the police department hierarchy. I was betting that Lawton would come after me now after my little performance in his office.

There was no evidence that could nail Lawton in Santiago's files, of course.

But Lawton didn't know that.

And if he thought there was something in those files that could hurt him, he'd need to get his hands on them before I could make them public.

I wasn't sure how he might do it. He'd used a gun on Reyes. A speeding car on Santiago. Which meant he might shoot me or run me over in the street, or maybe both. Or maybe something else entirely.

So after that day in his office, I started looking over my shoulder everywhere I went. And I made a point of getting out a lot to make myself visible to Lawton if he was somewhere waiting for me. I went to the store. I went to the bank. I took long walks on the streets of Manhattan, giving him plenty of chances to make his move.

But then, when he did, it wasn't what I expected.

Or where I expected.

I let myself into my apartment, carrying a collection of the day's newspapers. The *Post*, *New York Times*, even the *Daily News*. Hell, old habits die hard. I'd been planning on making a few other stops too, but I remembered I needed to drop my laundry off at the cleaner on the corner. I went back to my apartment to get it.

In my apartment, the first thing I noticed was that lights were on. I didn't leave them on. The next thing I knew I was shoved against the wall of the living room by someone who emerged from behind a piece of furniture. I screamed in pain and fell to the floor. He was standing there now. Looking down at me. With a gun in his hand. It took me a few seconds to clear my head and actually see who it was. But of course I already knew that.

"Where are the files, asshole?" Brad Lawton asked.

"I don't know what you're talking about."

"Santiago's files."

"I lied about that."

He smashed me across the face with the gun. I started to black out but somehow held onto consciousness by a thread.

"I can do this all day, smart guy," Lawton said. "In fact, I'd love to do it all day. Is that what you want? So let's try this one more time, Malloy. Where are Santiago's files on Reyes?"

I pointed toward the bedroom. He marched me in there ahead of him and the gun.

"You know, I figured you'd be out of the house longer," Lawton said as we walked. "I was watching you. When you left, I assumed you'd be gone long enough for me to get in here and be gone before you even knew it. I wasn't ready for you to show up back here so quickly."

"The best laid plans sometimes go awry," I said, trying to fight off the nausea and pain running through me. "Just like your plan to cover up the shooting of Victor Reyes. You're screwing up all over the place, Lawton."

He hit me again with the gun, on the back of the head this time. A glancing blow. There wasn't any intention to hit me as hard as the first time. Just to remind me who was in charge here. Not that I needed any reminder of that at the moment.

"Gimme the damn file, everything you've collected," he growled.

I had a desk in the bedroom with a file cabinet next to it. I took some papers off the top of the desk and handed them to him.

"This is it?" he asked.

"That's everything."

He walked to the filing cabinet and opened the drawers. He grabbed a handful of files, smiling as he looked at the name Reyes on the covers, and put them under his arm. Then he went through the rest of the drawers to make sure there was nothing else on Reyes. There wasn't. He had it all.

"This is all about your ambition, isn't it?" I said. "Always has been."

Lawton smiled. Cool. Calm. Completely in control. Just like he'd been back in his office when I talked to him.

"You don't care if a few people get hurt along the way. Like Victor Reyes."

I needed to shake him up. Get him to lose his cool somehow. I wanted to hear the truth from Lawton, no matter what happened next.

"You were afraid Reyes might screw up your big career plan if he got into the Police Academy."

"Can you believe that? A guy like him actually thought he could be on the police force."

"So you shot him because you were afraid he might spill the beans about what you were doing with the gangs in the Bronx."

"I didn't shoot Reyes," he said calmly. "I just didn't want anyone looking into his death because I was afraid they might stumble onto the drug thing after all these years. But I didn't shoot Reyes. No matter what you think you know . . ."

I shrugged.

"The bottom line is that you built your whole damn career on stealing those drugs from the evidence room back in the Bronx. How does that make you feel about yourself, Lawton?"

His face showed some emotion for the first time. Somehow, he still thought he was a good cop at heart. He didn't like it when anyone questioned that.

"I saved hundreds of lives in the Bronx by what I did, using those drugs to get information off the street and make big drug busts."

I decided to keep pushing.

"The great Brad Lawton," I sneered. "Nothing but a corrupt cop."

"I am not a corrupt cop!" he shouted at me.

"You're a disgrace to the uniform," I said.

"Don't call me a corrupt cop . . ."

"Fuck you!" I said.

Lawton's face contorted in rage.

"I am not a corrupt cop," he bellowed. "You have no idea what it's like on the street. You can't always follow the rules. Play it by the book. Not if you want to win. And I always win. Goddamn it, Reyes was one lousy kid. I was saving an entire city. I made that judgment then, and I'd make it again. And there's still so much more that I can accomplish. So many things I can do for the department, for the city."

It sounded like a campaign speech. I remembered Susan telling me that people were talking about Lawton as a future mayor, and I could see that right now. I could also see how completely delusional and self-justifying he was about himself—and anything he did—somehow convincing himself that the ends justified the means no matter what if they helped to put Brad Lawton in power.

"The only place you're going is to jail," I said defiantly.

Lawton stormed over to where I was standing and smashed me across the side of the head with the gun butt. Hard this time. Even harder than the first blow, which had knocked me silly. I lost consciousness briefly, I think, the blackness enveloping me as I lay there on my bedroom floor trying desperately to fight it. Finally, my head cleared a bit and I looked up to see him grinning down at me. I wanted to hurt him back. I wanted to kill him for what he'd done to Reyes and Santiago. But I could barely move. So I just lay there, resigned to my fate.

"So what happens now?" I asked finally.

"What happens now is that I'm going to wind up on the front page of your old newspaper. When I'm announced as the new police commissioner. I plan to be on the front page of the *Daily News* a lot."

"You'll never get away with it," I said. "No matter what you do to me, someone will put everything together. Santiago figured it out. I did too. Nikki Reynolds knows—or at least suspects you of something—based on the Kennedy stuff. There's no way you're ever gonna be able to pull this off without getting caught."

"Well, Santiago's not going to tell anyone," he laughed.

"Because you killed him."

"Santiago was killed by a drunk driver."

"You set up that guy to take the fall."

Lawton shrugged. "Like George Sledzec is going to be any loss to society."

"Well, Nikki . . ."

"Nikki? You didn't hear about Nikki? Poor woman took too many sleeping pills. They found her dead in bed. Or at least they will in the morning."

"Jesus . . ."

Brad Lawton was getting rid of all the possible links between himself and the Reyes and Kennedy cases.

"So what about me?" I asked him.

He walked over to the open window in my living room and looked down at the street below. He kept the gun pointed at me.

"What are we here?" he asked. "About a dozen floors up?"

"Eleven."

"Good enough."

"Good enough for what?" I asked, even though I already knew the answer.

"You've been depressed. You lost your job. Your career is over. You have nothing to live for. So you commit suicide right here in your apartment. You jump out a window because you can't stand the pain of your failure anymore. I don't think I'll have much trouble selling that story to anyone, including your old paper, Malloy."

I had left the window open that day like I usually did. I could hear the sounds of the street below. A few minutes ago, I'd been down on that street safe and sound. Now I was cornered by a psychopathic killer with a gun. I tried to keep him talking. For a lot of reasons, but one of them was I didn't much care for the alternatives.

"Two suicides? Me and Nikki? Don't you think someone will get suspicious?"

"There's no real link between you and Nikki."

"So I'm the last person you need to get rid of?"

"Just one more."

I knew who he meant. "Carrie Bratten."

"That's right."

"You were the one who told her about the Kennedy half-dollars. You were her secret source. Sooner or later, she'll put it all together like I did. She'll go public with that information and then—"

"No, she won't. Because she's going to have a little accident too. Poor girl likes to drink a lot. People who drink a lot sometimes have accidents."

"And once we're all gone—Nikki, Carrie, and me—you figure that no one will ever find out what you did on the Reyes and the Kennedy cases?"

"Uh-huh."

"There's only one problem with that theory of yours."

"What's that?"

"They've been following me," I said to him now.

"Who?"

"The police."

"Right."

"I'm serious. I figured you'd make a move like this. That's why I went to your office again. You can kill me if you want, but that's another murder they'll hang on you as soon as you walk out that door. And unlike Reyes and Santiago, this one will stick."

If I was trying to scare him, it didn't work.

"Oh, the place is surrounded, huh?" Lawton laughed. "You've been watching too many crime shows. It doesn't work that way in real life. And, like I told you, I didn't shoot Reyes. Jesus, that kid turned out to be a pain in the ass, though, huh? Took him fifteen years to die and he causes me all this trouble. All over some lousy spic kid in the Bronx. But it all ends here. Now."

"It won't work, Lawton."

"Why not?"

"Because this time I am wearing a wire."

For the first time, I saw a look of fear on Lawton's face.

"You're bluffing."

I pulled up my shirt and showed him the wire that Susan had outfitted me with after I left her office that day.

———

I've thought a lot since then about everything that happened. About how things could have worked out differently if Lawton hadn't done what he did in those next few seconds.

Of course, Lawton probably figured he didn't have lot of options left at that point. But maybe he did. He'd pretty much confessed to everything on the tape. Except he'd never come right out and flat-out said or admitted that he did any of it. And he specifically said he didn't shoot Reyes, which I thought was weird.

A good defense lawyer might have been able to raise doubts with a jury about what Lawton had actually done or not done, and likely would have gotten some of the evidence thrown out as inadmissible in court. There'd be charges for falsifying evidence with the Kennedy half-dollars, the drug theft in the Bronx, and a lot of other stuff that would in all likelihood send him to jail. But the main charges—the killings of Reyes and Santiago—might never stand.

I could have even envisioned some sort of second act for Brad Lawton after prison. With him making a big deal, like he did to me in my apartment, about how he did all those things with Reyes and the drugs and the rest of it to save the city. How the legal system was broken and didn't work anymore, so he created his own system to keep the streets safe. How he would have been the best, the most effective police commissioner the city ever had if he'd gotten the chance. Hell, people go for all that "second act" crap these days. I could have even seen Brad Lawton on the *The View* or *Dr. Phil* charming people all over again.

But none of that happened, of course.

Instead, the police, who had been waiting outside listening to it all from the wire device they'd planted on me, suddenly smashed through the door of my apartment with guns drawn. Lawton stood frozen for a second, gun in hand. That was all the time he had to make a decision. A second or two. Like I said, if he'd just dropped the gun and surrendered to them at that point . . .

But I guess he knew that he could never do that.

Because he was Brad Lawton.

And Brad Lawton never lost.

Brad Lawton always got what he wanted.

And so Lawton decided to fight. In his mind at that instant, he probably thought he had no other choice. So he backed up to the window and fired on the onrushing cops. I don't think they would have shot him if he hadn't done that. It's hard for a cop to make the decision to use his weapon to shoot at a deputy commissioner, and I'm sure they were briefed to do everything possible to bring Lawton in intact. But when cops are fired on, they fire back.

Which is what happened here, even though I don't think they were shooting to kill. One of the bullets ripped into his shoulder. It shouldn't have been fatal, except the force of the blast knocked him backward toward—and then out—the open window behind him. For a second or two, which seemed like an eternity, he hung there precariously, clinging to a final sliver of hope between life and death. But then he plunged downward and was gone. He landed on top of a taxicab first, then hit the street. That picture of Brad Lawton lying sprawled dead on the street became a classic *Daily News* page one the next day.

Lawton had told me he'd make it onto the front page of the *Daily News*.

And he did.

Just not the way he wanted to be.

CHAPTER 51

I STILL CAN'T BELIEVE Brad Lawton could have done all of those things," Susan said.

"People aren't always what they seem," I said.

We were sitting on a bench in Madison Square Park off of Fifth Avenue at 23rd Street. There's a Shake Shack at the south end of the park. It's supposed to have the best hamburgers in town. The funny thing is that Susan and I had lived a few blocks away from there during our marriage and never once got to the Shake Shack. The problem was it was too popular and the lines were endless, especially in nice weather. But this time we decided to give it a shot.

After we finally made it through the line, she went for a regular hamburger with a Diet Coke and I had a cheeseburger with everything along with a chocolate shake. I always figured that when you went to a place where something on the menu is in the name of the place, you should give that item a shot. So there we were eating our burgers and drinking our drinks. My cheeseburger was good. Maybe not the best cheeseburger I've ever had, but pretty damn close. I wished I'd brought Susan here earlier. I wished I'd done a lot of things with Susan earlier.

"So what are you going to do next?" Susan asked.

———

I had accomplished quite a lot with all my work in the past several weeks, when you looked back on it.

I'd exposed Brad Lawton—the deputy police commissioner who would have otherwise moved on to the NYPD top spot—as a murderer, a drug dealer, and a thief who ruined countless lives before he lost his own.

I'd saved at least a couple of lives—Nikki Reynolds and Carrie Bratten. The cops had gotten to Nikki's apartment in time to rush her to the hospital to save her from the pill overdose. Carrie wrote a first-person story for the *Daily News* about her brush with death at the hands of Lawton in which she mentioned my name somewhere around the twelfth paragraph. Which was her way of saying thank you to me for saving her life. I guess.

George Sledzec was freed on bail while prosecutors investigated his case, and then fairly quickly afterward the charges were dropped. After he was released from prison, he checked into an alcohol rehabilitation program where, from what I heard, he was making good progress. Of course, he still had a long way to go. He could drop out of the program, fall off the wagon, and plow his car into a school bus one day. But all you can do is the right thing and then hope it turns out okay in the end.

Meanwhile, several investigative agencies were looking into the JFK assassination all over again in the light of Lee Mathis's (aka Lee Harvey Oswald Jr.) book claiming he was Oswald's son and laying out a seemingly authentic alibi for Oswald on the day of the murder. No one could be sure anything new would ever come of it all, of course, but it was getting a lot of publicity and attention. One of the networks even ran a special: *Dallas Revisited—Was Lee Harvey Oswald Innocent?* Mathis was quoted extensively in the program. All the publicity made his book a hot commodity too. I talked to Mathis about it. He was happy people were finally listening to his story, even though he was still traumatized by all the tragedy it had brought. I just hoped he lived long enough to enjoy a bit of the fame and fortune and satisfaction from the book. He deserved at least that small happiness after everything he'd been through.

My involvement in the Lawton story had put me in demand too. With newspapers. TV stations. Magazines. Several TV stations reached out to me to offer jobs, and a whole bunch of newspapers were interested in hiring me as a reporter or columnist too. Even Marilyn Staley wanted to meet me for lunch to discuss my future. Now that she cared about my future again.

Funny thing about that. I always thought that once a reporter lost his integrity, once he screwed up like I did, there was no future in the business for him. But we live in a different time. Disgraced politicians get gigs on TV these days. Authors accused of making up facts in their books or plagiarizing get even bigger contracts for the next book. The world is a very forgiving place now. That's what happened to me. I got famous. For the wrong reasons maybe, but I had become a hot property all over again because of what happened.

There was one thing I hadn't accomplished, though. I hadn't found out who killed Victor Reyes. Which is what had set out to do in the first place.

"We still have no evidence Lawton was the one who shot Reyes," Susan said between bites of her hamburger.

"You checked his gun?"

"All his guns. The one at your apartment, plus the guns we found in his home, his office, and his damn trophy case. Yes, we found a lot of guns there. One of them was even a pearl-handled revolver like the kind General George Patton used to carry. I think Lawton thought of himself as some kind of heroic Patton-like fig-ure. But no matches for the guns or bullet that shot Reyes fifteen years ago. Of course, he might have gotten rid of it afterward . . ."

"He never admitted the Reyes shooting to me either," I said. "He talked about the rest of the stuff he did but insisted he didn't shoot Reyes."

She sighed.

"There's something else," I told her. "I've been thinking about this. Ortiz said Lawton picked him up and took him to the station house that night to get information. At the same time Reyes was being shot. That means Lawton had to be there too. I hadn't thought that through before, but now it seems pretty clear. Ortiz couldn't have shot Reyes because he was at the precinct with Law-ton. So that means Lawton has an alibi too. Ortiz's alibi is Law-ton's alibi."

"I think maybe he really was just afraid that if anyone—like Santiago or you—started digging too deeply they'd discover all the drug stuff he was doing back then. He knew that would torpedo his career, and his career was everything to him. He'd do anything to protect that, even murder. That's what this was all about."

"So who shot Reyes?"

"Maybe Reyes was just a gang shooting after all," Susan said. "He messed with the wrong people. He pissed someone off—ei-ther in his own gang or a rival gang—and so they popped him on the street."

"Which means we'll probably never know who did it."

"If it's a gang shooting, the gang member who did it is proba-bly dead or in jail by now. And probably has even forgotten that he shot Reyes or why he did it. Fifteen years is a long time. I know you've tried really hard to find some answers, but I think it's time to just let this one go."

I nodded. She was right. Even I knew there was a time to give up on a story, and this seemed to be as good a time as any on Reyes.

Susan finished her hamburger. She wiped some relish off of her chin with a napkin, then finished her diet soda.

"What are you going to do now, Gil?" Susan asked me again.

"Well, I was thinking about maybe getting in line for another one of those cheeseburgers." I smiled.

She looked at me sadly. I suddenly remembered how Dr. Landis said I always made a joke when I didn't want to answer a question.

"You're going to have to make some decisions," she said. "Sometimes you have to realize that the way you've lived in the past won't work anymore and you need to move on and go in a different direction with your life."

"Just like you did, huh?" I said.

We both realized we weren't talking just about my career anymore.

"Why don't you take one of those big media jobs you've been offered?" Susan asked.

"I'm damaged goods as a journalist," I said.

"They don't seem to care about what you did or didn't do in the past."

"It's not about them. It's about me. Because I know what I did. I used to talk all the big talk about integrity and how it was the most important thing a newspaperman had, blah, blah, blah. I really believed it too. But then, when I had the chance to step up and prove what kind of integrity I had, I screwed up badly. Twice.

That's what I've got to live with. Myself. All those other people—the editors, the TV producers, the talk show hosts—they might have forgiven me for what I did. But I haven't forgiven myself."

"What will you do, then?"

"I was thinking about becoming a teacher," I said. "Not journalism. English maybe. Or history. I was thinking that if I could figure out a way to handle the financial end of it, I could go back to school and get a teacher's certificate. Then I'd try to get a job at a junior high or high school somewhere in the city."

"And you'd be happy doing that instead of being a reporter? Do you think it could fulfill you in the same way?"

I thought about Gary Nowak in that school cafeteria in Florida. Nowak had wanted to be a police officer all his life. He dreamed about it, he believed in it, he worked hard and did everything right to reach his goal. And then, through no fault of his own, that opportunity was taken away from him. And now he had chosen to contribute his skills—to live his life—in a different way. "You do what you have to do," Nowak had said to me.

"I'm not sure about that yet," I told Susan.

"What happened to you on the Kennedy story . . . that really wasn't your fault, you know," she said. "This time it wasn't your fault. It's not like with the hooker."

"You mean I didn't make this one up intentionally?"

"The hooker was different," she said again.

"Her name was Houston, by the way."

"I know. I was with you when you went through all of that, remember? I lived the whole Houston nightmare along with you."

"The thing about the Kennedy scoop," I said slowly, "is that I believe there was a story there. I'm pretty sure that Lee Mathis really is the secret son of Lee Harvey Oswald Jr. And that he did uncover evidence that showed his father was in New Orleans the day of the assassination. That pretty much blows the lid off the Warren Commission Report and any other scenario for what happened that day in Dallas that puts Oswald anywhere near the Book Depository with a gun in his hand. This could have been the biggest story of my career. The biggest ever."

"You really thought you could solve the Kennedy assassination after all these years?"

"I don't know. It has been a long, long time. The trail is very, very cold. But I did have the starting piece: the elimination of Oswald as the prime suspect. All I had to do was start building the case from there, just like I build the pieces—the facts—of any other police case. Because that's what the Kennedy assassination was in the end. A crime story. I'm not sure if I could have come up with all the answers. But I might have. And wouldn't that have been something? It would have been the ultimate triumph for my career. I really believe that could have all happened if things had sorted out differently."

"And now?"

"Even if I did find the answer to who killed Kennedy, no one would probably believe me. People would just call me another conspiracy nut. After everything that's happened, my integrity is gone. I can never get that back. And there's nothing I can do about it."

I got up and dumped our trash in a container. When I came back to the bench, Susan was still sitting there. There was a subway station across the street. She could catch a train there that would take her downtown to Foley Square. To her job at the DA's office and then back to her fiancé. But she didn't seem to be in any hurry to get back there. Me, I had no job to go to these days. So I just waited. We sat in silence for a while.

"As long as I've known you, Gil," she said finally, "all you've ever wanted to be was a newspaper reporter. Do you really think you can just walk away from it that easily? I'm not so sure. And I think you're wrong about something else too. You're not finished as a reporter. You proved that on the Kennedy story at the end with everything you uncovered. Personally, I would like to see you keep going after the true story about the assassination. If anybody could come up with some real answers about what happened in Dallas that day, it would be you. I believe that. I guess I still believe in you."

She stood up now from the bench. "I've got to get back to the office."

She started walking toward the subway station. I walked with her.

"Thanks," I said.

"For the advice?"

"For everything."

She leaned over, softly kissed me on the cheek, and began walking down the steps toward the subway.

"You too," I said. "And best of luck with the marriage to Dale. I really mean that."

She turned around and looked at me with surprise.

"You got his name right."

"Yep, I figured I owed you at least that much."

She started heading back down the steps. Then, turning her head around again, she told me casually, "Oh, by the way, he's not my fiancé anymore."

"You're not engaged?" I practically shouted out, as passersby turned to look at me.

"That's right." She shrugged. "I guess I buried the lead for you, huh?"

"What happened?"

"It's complicated."

"But the bottom line is you and Dale aren't getting married?"

"Not at the moment, no."

"So does that mean that you and I . . . well, that is, you and I could get together from time to time?"

"You never can tell," she laughed and then disappeared down the steps into the subway station.

CHAPTER *52*

THE TOUGHEST PART was telling Camille Reyes that I couldn't find out who shot her son—and that we probably never would have the answer to that question.

I went back to that small apartment in the Bronx, the place where she had taken care of Victor for fifteen years, and explained it all to her. As I sat with her again in the living room, I kept looking over at the picture she kept on the table of Victor as a young, healthy man before the bullet shattered his spine and his life. I thought about how different that life might have been if he hadn't walked outside this house and been shot on that hot summer night. Maybe he would have become a successful businessman like Pascal. Or a police officer like his boyhood friend Santiago. But that gunshot ended his hopes, ended his dreams for a normal, happy life.

"So no one will be able to find out who did that to Victor?" Camille Reyes asked me now.

"I'm sorry, Mrs. Reyes," I said. "It's been too long. The best hope at first was that Ortiz was the shooter, but we know he couldn't have been because he was in police custody. Then I thought it was Brad Lawton, but that doesn't seem to be true now either. That leaves us with the gang thing again and, after all this time, there are just too many possibilities."

336

At that point, all her strength, all her resolve, all her determination fell apart. She began to cry. I walked over, put my arm around her, and tried to comfort her as best I could. At some point, I began to cry along with her. She was crying for her lost dead son. Me, I was crying for something I'd lost too, I guess. The redemption I'd hoped to find for myself by solving the Reyes mystery. I'd done a lot of good things, but I hadn't done that. I hadn't been able to help this woman.

"Maybe if the police had looked harder at the time, they would have caught whoever did this to my son," she said.

"Maybe."

"But they didn't care."

"The police have a lot of cases. They're very busy."

"Not too busy to be drinking."

"What do you mean?"

"One of the cops who talked to me that night. When he asked about my son, he had liquor on his breath. I could smell it on him. All I could think about was how my son was lying there and so badly hurt, and this cop was probably more concerned about getting his next drink."

"What cop are you talking about?" I asked, even though I already knew the answer.

"Not the first one. Not the one in uniform. He was very nice, very solicitous."

That would have been Gary Nowak.

"So it was one of the detectives who showed up afterward?"

"Yes. Not Lawton. The other one. I don't remember his name after all this time. Besides, he barely spoke to me. All I think he cared about that night was getting his next drink."

"Garcetti," I told her. "His name was Jimmy Garcetti."

———

After I left Camille Reyes's place, I kept thinking about what she said. Garcetti was drunk that night. Not a surprise that Garcetti was drinking on the job. At least now it wouldn't be a surprise. But Garcetti told me his drinking started after he stopped working with Lawton, that he'd been a good cop back in those days before turning to the bottle. But it appeared that wasn't true. Of course, drunks say a lot of things that aren't true, and maybe he'd just gotten his time frame messed up from too much booze. But if he'd been wrong about that, what else had he told me that wasn't true?

There was something else bothering me too. Something that had bothered me back at the very beginning of the Reyes story, but I'd never taken the time to pursue.

Why hadn't Santiago tried to talk to Lawton and Garcetti?

Both of them said he never did.

And there was no reference to an interview with either Lawton or Garcetti from the files I'd taken from Santiago's home.

They were the investigating officers on the Reyes case and they were both still on the force, so they should have been the first people Santiago went to for information. Just like I did. Unless . . .

And then, just as quickly as I had posed the question to myself, I suddenly knew the answer.

Lawton and Garcetti were suspects.

And a veteran investigator like Santiago never started on a case by talking to the suspects. He first accumulated as much evidence as he could against them. Then, and only then, did he make his move to approach the suspects with what he had. And if there was more than one suspect, as in this case, he always picked the weakest, the most malleable, the easiest-to-turn suspect.

But Lawton had known about Santiago asking questions about the Reyes case. How did he find out?

I raced home and went through Santiago's file again. There was still nothing there about either Lawton or Garcetti. But on one of the last pages, I found a phone number that he'd scribbled on the side of the page.

It was a 718 number.

The area code for the Bronx.

I dialed the number. It rang twice, and then a man's voice came on the line and identified himself as a detective.

"I'm looking for Jimmy Garcetti," I said. "Do I have the right precinct?"

"This is Jimmy's extension, but he's not here right now."

"Any idea where I could find him?"

"He's . . . uh, out on a case right now."

I had a pretty good idea of where Garcetti was at the moment, and it wasn't investigating any case.

"Can I help you with something?" the detective asked.

I hung up the phone.

———

It wasn't hard to find Garcetti. I just hung out at a couple of bars near his precinct in the Bronx, figuring I'd run into him sooner or later. And that's exactly what happened. I walked into a bar and there he was, holding court with what appeared to be a lot of other regulars. They were talking about everything from the Yankees to sexual exploits to the sad state of law enforcement today.

I nursed a beer, stood next to them for a while, and eventually joined the conversation. I don't think Garcetti recognized me as the reporter who had interviewed him before. He looked pretty far gone at this point. Eventually, some of the others drifted away, and I found myself standing next to him.

"How are things looking for your retirement?" I asked casually.

"Getting close," he muttered, talking more to himself than to me.

"Yep, pretty soon you'll be on that fishing boat and away from all this crap here, huh, Jimmy?"

He gave me a quizzical look.

"Do I know you?"

"We met a few weeks ago."

"Are you on the force?"

"I'm a reporter. Gil Malloy from the *Daily News*. We talked about one of your old cases. The Victor Reyes shooting."

He looked down at the drink in front of him.

"Who would have thought that damn kid would die and all this would happen over him?" he said.

"Helluva bad end for your old partner."

"Yeah, well . . . Brad did a lot of bad things."

"I'll bet you knew about some of them, huh?"

"What do you mean?"

"The drug theft in the Bronx back when you two were together here. The way he was using the stolen drugs to buy information on the street and make high-profile busts. Even if he didn't come right out and tell you, you must have figured it out, Jimmy."

"I never knew anything about any of that stuff Brad was supposed to have done when we were together."

"What about now?"

"Like I told you before, Brad and me lost touch. We were never very close after he left the Bronx."

"But you were still close enough to tell him about Santiago, weren't you?"

I saw a flash of concern in his eyes. Even through the alcohol haze.

"Santiago came to you and told you what he thought happened to Reyes, didn't he, Jimmy?"

Garcetti didn't say anything.

"Santiago figured it out. He figured out about the drug theft in the Bronx, how Lawton was using Reyes, and putting it all together he suspected that Lawton had shot Reyes to shut him up. Then Santiago came to you and told you what he thought. He was probably hoping to pressure you into helping him make a case against Lawton. But instead you called Lawton and told him what Santiago was doing."

Still nothing.

"And then Santiago got killed by a hit-and-run driver."

Garcetti picked up his glass, finished off what was left of his drink, and then signaled the bartender for another.

"How'd that make you feel?"

"How the hell do you think it made me feel?"

"You knew that Lawton was responsible. You knew he had gotten rid of Santiago because Santiago suspected he had shot Reyes that night. And you knew you bore part of the guilt for Santiago's death too because you had gone to Lawton and told him what Santiago was doing."

Garcetti took a big gulp of his drink, downing almost half the glass.

"Except Lawton didn't shoot Reyes, did he?" I said to him.

"No, Brad wasn't there."

"But you were, right, Jimmy?"

Garcetti reached into his pocket now and pulled out a picture. He put it down on the bar in front of us. It was a picture of a boat. A fishing boat.

For just a second, I thought he hadn't heard me or maybe had somehow forgotten I was there.

"Three months, two weeks, one day," he muttered again. "Three months, two weeks, one day—and then I could be on this boat. I bought it a couple of years ago. I figured that with the low cost of living down there in Florida, I could live on my pension and spend all my days fishing and trying to forget I ever worked in this hellhole of a city. That was my dream. That's what kept me going all those years. But it all depended on Brad. Brad and me, we've always needed each other in some strange way. Now Brad is dead, and me . . ."

He stared down at the picture of the boat and finished his drink.

"I know you might find this hard to believe," Garcetti said, "but I was ambitious back then too. Not ambitious like Brad was. But I wanted a future in the department. And Brad, well, he was the perfect partner for me. Everyone could see he was going places. And he was my partner. Me and Brad, we were going to go places together. At least that's the way I figured it then.

"So when Brad came to me and said he had a big problem— that the Reyes kid was talking about joining the force and could spill all sorts of secrets about what Brad was doing—well, that became my problem too. I was linked to Brad's rising star. I needed to make sure no one did anything to dim that star.

"He'd never told me in so many words about the drug theft. But I pretty much figured it out. Hell, he was getting all this information on the street. It didn't come free, I knew that. He had to be giving them something. Money or drugs. He didn't have much money then, so drugs seemed to be the obvious choice.

"Anyway, when I heard about Reyes that day, Brad was all upset. He kept talking about how this could end his career if the Reyes kid ever got on the police force. Brad didn't know what to do. Me, I knew what to do. I drank. I kept drinking all that day and into the evening. By that time, I was pretty far gone.

"All I kept thinking about was how everything Brad and me had been doing was going to go down the drain if Brad got implicated in the drug theft. He was my ticket to the top. Without him, I had nothing. I had had it all in front of me and now it was all going to fall apart. Because of this damn Reyes kid. And the drunker I got, the more angry I got at Reyes.

"Finally, I called his house. I told him to meet me out front. I told him I had some ideas on how to help him pass the police boards and get in the academy, or some crap like that. I think at that point I just wanted to talk to the kid. That's all. At least, that's what I try to tell myself now.

"I don't remember a whole lot else that happened after that. Like I said, I kept putting away the booze pretty hard. But I do remember parking my car on the street down from his house and watching until he came out. But from far away and an angle where he couldn't easily see me. Sure enough, he came out on the street to wait for me. I just sat there and watched him for a long time, the anger building up in me as I thought about the damage he was doing to Brad and me. I had a bottle with me in the car. I kept drinking from it and getter madder and madder as I watched him.

"Finally, I guess he figured I wasn't going to show so he turned around and started back toward the front door of his building. I gunned the car and drove up behind him. He never saw me. Something snapped inside me, I guess. I took out my gun and pointed it out the open window of the car at him. I like to tell myself that I didn't really want to kill the kid. Or mess him up too badly. I just wanted to scare him. But I don't really know what happened at that instant. All I know is that I pulled the trigger and the shot hit him in the back. He went down, and I sped off.

"When I called Brad and told him what I'd done, he made sure he got us assigned to the case. He got there first. He made me go somewhere and drink coffee and splash cold water on my face before I showed up at the crime scene. To try to sober me up, you know. It helped a bit, but I was still in pretty bad shape. And I made a bad mistake. He said we needed to point the finger of suspicion at someone else, one of the gang members in the area. So I put out an arrest bulletin for the Ortiz kid, figuring he was a likely choice. I didn't know Brad had picked him up that night as one of his snitches, and that Brad had been at the precinct questioning him and getting information at the moment I shot Reyes. Brad made sure no one ever got to the Ortiz kid to find out the truth. I was glad he did. But I knew he didn't do it to protect me. He was looking to protect himself. Because if I went down for the shooting, then everything about him and Reyes would come out. So I fingered Ortiz, he made sure Ortiz disappeared, and then everyone forgot about the whole thing."

"Until Roberto Santiago," I said. "And then me. We came around asking questions about it again."

He nodded.

"Not long after Reyes died, Brad put in for a transfer. He didn't want to be my partner anymore. That's when I realized I wasn't going along with him on his rise to the top. But he still looked out for me. A couple of times when I got screwed up with my drinking and got into trouble with the department, he went to bat for me. I would have lost my pension except for him. Brad said he'd make sure I got the pension. He knew how important that was for me. It was a little deal Brad and I made, I guess. I got to keep drinking and not worry about messing up my pension. In return, I kept my mouth shut and Brad got to keep on being the golden boy of the department. We'd been partners once, and being partners on the street . . . well, that's a bond that can never be completely broken."

I thought about that and wondered if Jimmy Garcetti might have actually been a good cop once a long time ago.

"But now you can't live with the secret of the Reyes shooting without him, can you?" I said. "You can't keep quiet about it anymore. Because it's all falling apart now and sooner or later someone besides me will put it together and come looking for you. It's time to do the right thing first, Jimmy. To come clean once and for all."

"They'll send me to jail. A cop doesn't stand much chance in jail, Malloy. Especially an old cop."

"Maybe they won't," I said. "There were extenuating circumstances and it was a long time ago."

"They'll take away my pension."

He took another look at the picture of the fishing boat he'd bought in Florida, where he'd dreamed for so long of retiring and forgetting about the Bronx and the NYPD and Victor Reyes and all the rest of it.

"Are you going to tell everyone about this?" he asked me.

"You could tell them yourself."

"It's too late for that. And yes, you're right, I guess it is time for me to finally do something right."

I still have nightmares about what happened next.

He reached under the jacket he was wearing and came out with his gun.

At first, I thought he might shoot me.

But that wasn't going to be his play.

Instead, he pointed the gun at his own head.

"Damn, I sure would have liked that fishing boat—"

"No!" I shouted.

But it was too late.

Then there was the sound of a gunshot.

Jimmy Garcetti was still holding the picture of the fishing boat in his hand when he dropped to the floor dead.

CHAPTER 53

D**ID YOU TELL** Mrs. Reyes about what happened to her son?"
Dr. Landis asked me.

"Yes."

"That must have given you a sense of accomplishing something out of all this. That was your goal when you set out on this story, wasn't it? To find out for her who shot her son and why. You did that. You did the job that you set out to do."

"Except it wasn't the answer she wanted to hear. I think she hoped—I know I did—that there would be some meaning, some logic behind his death that could explain how a tragedy like this could happen. That his death had some significance, even if his life never did. But there was no meaning, no significance, no reason behind Reyes's death. It was just a stupid accident. I wish Lawton had done it so there was someone that she—and me too—could truly be angry at. Instead, the only person to blame was a drunken old cop who made a mistake one night and lived with the memory of that until it became too much for him to bear."

"You told the truth. That's all that you can do."

"Sometimes the truth doesn't seem like enough."

I thought about Camille Reyes sitting in her little apartment, staring at the picture of her dead son as I left there for the last

348 R. G. Belsky

time. About Roberto Santiago's widow and her three children on Staten Island. And about Lee Mathis in that wheelchair and hooked up to an oxygen machine, waiting to die with the guilt of how his actions contributed to the death of his son.

"There are no happy endings here," I said.

"Didn't you once tell me that happy endings don't sell newspapers?"

"I just wanted a happy ending on this one," I said.

"What will you do now?" Landis asked.

"Everyone keeps asking me that question."

She smiled.

"I guess I have two major goals," I told her. "First, I want to try to win Susan back and make our marriage work this time. I know what I have to do to be with her again. I need to change. I need to become a better person. I keep thinking back on all the things I did—and all the things I didn't too—that doomed our relationship the first time. Do you remember when I told you about sleeping with Nikki Reynolds once when she was trying to get me to do a book deal? Somehow, when I remember that story, I always forget about a big part of it. I like to think that Houston and all the things that happened afterward drove me away from Susan and into Nikki's bed. But that's not the way it happened. I was still on top then. It was before Houston. I had everything, and yet I still wound up in bed with someone like Nikki. Houston didn't break up my marriage to Susan, like I always say. I broke up my marriage. That's the kind of guy I was back then, Dr. Landis. I don't want to be that guy again."

Landis had been writing this all down in her notebook. But when I looked now she had put the pen down and the notebook sat unused on her lap.

"What's the second goal?" she asked.

"I want to solve the Kennedy assassination."

I thought that would startle her. But it didn't seem to. Almost as if she was waiting for me to say it. I guess she had me down pretty well by that point.

"I went to see Lee Mathis before I came here," I said. "He doesn't have much time left. You can see him slipping away quickly now. I think what he uncovered in that book might be the most significant thing we've found out about the assassination in the half century since it happened. Think about it. Lee Harvey Oswald didn't shoot Kennedy. He wasn't even there that day. That means everything we know—or everything we thought we knew—about one of the most important and history-changing events of our time is wrong. And we have to start all over again to try to figure out what really happened. Someone has to keep doing this. It won't be Lee Mathis. But I don't want everything he did—everything he found out about his father Lee Harvey Oswald and the events in Dallas—to die with him. There's something else too. Those threats against me—the phone call in New Orleans—I still don't know for sure who did that."

"Brad Lawton, presumably."

"That's the most logical person. I know he sent me the first letter with the Kennedy half-dollar to get me started on the whole thing. So it makes sense that he did all the rest of it. But maybe it was someone else. Someone besides Lawton who just didn't want the Kennedy case reopened again after all this time for reasons we're not aware of yet. On the other hand, maybe it all means nothing. There are so many questions I still have—"

"And you really think that after all this time you can answer all the questions and finally solve the Kennedy assassination?"

"It would be the greatest story of my life. Maybe the greatest story ever. If I'm really as great a reporter as I like to think I am, maybe I can pull it off. So whatever I do going forward—whether I'm a reporter or a teacher or anything else—that's what I want to do. I want to find out who killed John F. Kennedy."

"And do you plan to do all this by going back to being a newspaper reporter again?" Landis asked.

"You told me once, when we started this, that you thought being a reporter was part of my problem. That I based everything in my life on my worth as a reporter. And that this prevented me from confronting, and dealing with, some of the real issues in my life. I didn't buy that then, but now I think there's something to what you said."

She tapped her pen on her notebook, like she was thinking carefully about what she wanted to say before the words came out of her mouth.

"I believe—and this isn't necessarily me as a psychiatrist talking—that most of us are put on this earth for a purpose. I believe that my purpose is to do what I do in this room. And I believe that you were meant to be a reporter. It's the one thing you do well, the one thing you're passionate about, the one thing that seems to be a part of your inner being as a person. It's almost as if being a reporter is part of your DNA, Malloy. I don't want to see you just throw this all away."

"Weren't you on the other side of this debate before?" I smiled.

"For the record, I think you can find answers to your life at the same time as being a reporter. I didn't think that when you first came to see me. But then you were defensive and unwilling to talk about or confront any of the issues in your life. You've made a lot of progress. We've made a lot of progress together. Because you're willing to open up now and talk to me about everything—even your innermost secrets. That's very important. I'm proud of you."

Except that wasn't really true.

I hadn't told her everything.

There was one secret I was still keeping inside of me.

CHAPTER 54

WHEN I THINK about my life now, I divide it into two parts. Before Houston.

And after Houston.

No matter what happened with the Kennedy and Reyes stories, no matter what I ever do in the future, that story I wrote about a legendary New York City girl named Houston was clearly the defining moment of my career. The story, and the repercussions from it, changed me irrevocably. And so now, if I truly wanted to confront the mistakes of my past and find some sort of closure so that I didn't make them again, I had to confront the truth about Houston too.

Which is why I found myself standing outside a town house on Sutton Place in a ritzy neighborhood on the East Side of Manhattan.

A pleasant-looking blond woman in her thirties answered the door when I rang the bell.

"Mrs. Walter Issacs?"

"Yes."

"Hello, Houston," I said. "I'm glad to finally meet you."

Her face flashed with what I first thought was anger but then realized was sadness. Her shoulders sagged. She dipped her head briefly, and I wondered if she might cry. But then she lifted her head and looked me directly in the eye. She was a tough lady. The street made you tough.

"How did you find me?" she asked.

It wasn't easy. I'd spent much of my free time after leaving the *Daily News* going back on her trail, trying to finally find out what happened to her after all this time and, even more important, if she really existed. I eventually tracked down someone who told me she'd confided to a couple of people that she was getting married. She said she'd fallen in love with a man who was going to take her away from the life of prostitution. She told them he was a lawyer.

I determined the last time she'd been seen on the street or was actually known to be active in the call girl business, then went back through all marriage licenses issued for that year. Then I cross-referenced them against the listings in the American Bar Assocation for lawyers in the New York area.

I started knocking on doors of the addresses of every one of them. I did the same thing each time: said "Hello, Houston" whenever a woman answered the door. None of them knew what I was talking about. Until I knocked on the door of Mrs. Walter Issacs.

Houston.

Her real name, she said, had been Vicki Ellison. We sat in her living room filled with designer furniture and plush carpeting and expensive-looking paintings, and she told me the story of how she had gotten there. About growing up in Minnesota and being shunted around from foster home to foster home after her parents died in a car crash. About the foster father who repeatedly raped her until she finally ran away. About hitchhiking to New York City where she dreamed of becoming an actress or a model. And about how she'd instead wound up turning tricks under the name of Houston.

She was good at what she did. So good that Houston became a legend. But she didn't want to be a legend. She just wanted a life.

And so when she got the opportunity to live a real life, she jumped at it and never looked back.

She met a corporate lawyer named Walter Issacs in a coffee shop one day. They started up a conversation and he asked her out to dinner. She accepted. That night she made love with him, the first time she remembered having sex with a man who wasn't paying her for it or forcing her to do it. He knew nothing about her past. Six months later, they got married. They now had two children—a boy, four, and a girl, two.

It was a perfect life—or at least as close to a perfect life as anyone could live—until I showed up at her door.

"I'm the reporter who wrote a series about you in the *Daily News*," I said.

"I know who you are."

"I looked for you then, but I couldn't find you. If I had, my career—my life—would have been different. People didn't believe you existed. But here you are. It makes all the difference for me."

"And now you're going to walk out of here and tell the whole world the story."

I didn't say anything.

"My husband doesn't know anything about my past. It would destroy him. Destroy our life together. My children, my friends, the people at our country club—they only know me as Victoria Issacs. I walked away from being Houston a long time ago. I left her behind when I married Walter. But now you're going to open all of that up for me again, digging up my past, by writing a story about finding me."

She sighed.

"I guess I always knew that one day someone like you would show up at my door. I used to think about it all the time. Every day I wondered when this would all come to an end. But I just kept taking things one day at a time. Trying to be a good wife. A good mother. The best person I could be.

"I'm an artist now. Did you know that?" She pointed to some of the pictures on the walls I'd noticed when I came in. "I painted those. I've sold a lot of my work at art houses and galleries and shows over the past year or so. I've always liked to draw and paint, and now I've discovered I have the real talent for it. Funny how things work out in life. I guess I'm not exactly what you were expecting, huh?"

She looked at me, waiting to see what I would say. Looked at me with piercing blue eyes. Looked at me like she must have looked at men as Houston to sell herself to them. But she wasn't trying to sell me anything. She was pleading with me. Pleading not to take away her life.

"I'm not going to write a story about you," I said.

"Why not?"

"I don't have any reason to do that."

"Of course you do. You write the story about finding me and it vindicates you. Makes you a big star reporter again. The man who tracked down Houston, the legend of the New York City hookers. I'm your winning lottery ticket."

"I'm not going to write a story about you, Mrs. Issacs. I'm not going to tell anyone. Your secret is safe with me. You have my word on that."

She looked confused.

"But you spent all this time, all this effort to track me down. Why do all that if you weren't going to tell the world that you were right back then when you claimed I existed? If you're not going to do that, why did you look for me now?"

"I needed to find you for myself," I said.

———

It was a beautiful September day with the sun shining brightly on the East River when I left the town house of the woman who was called Houston in another lifetime. She had made mistakes in her life—bad mistakes—but somehow she persevered and battled back and built an entirely new life, a better life, for herself.

"I guess I always knew that one day someone like you would show up at my door. Every day I wondered when all this would all come to an end. But I just keep taking things a day at a time. Trying to be a good wife. A good mother. The best person I could be."

Maybe one day that will happen to her. Someone else will track her down and reveal her secrets and take away this life she has built.

But not me.

And not today.

On this day, Vicki Ellison, who went on to be Houston and now was Victoria Issacs, continued to hold on to the belief that she could somehow make up for all the bad choices she had made, put the past behind her, and become the kind of person she once hoped she could be.

Maybe we do get second chances in life.

Houston did.

So why not me?

ACKNOWLEDGMENTS

This is a work of fiction. There is no Lee Harvey Oswald Jr. No secret grandson. And no history-changing trip to New Orleans on the eve of the assassination. But the questions that remain about the death of President John F. Kennedy more than a half-century later are very real. It is the greatest murder mystery—the biggest crime whodunit—of our time. So I decided to write this book about what might have happened if a newspaper reporter somehow uncovered a link between a series of present-day murders in New York City and the events in Dallas on November 22, 1963. This was more than just an intriguing story line for me. It also gave me a unique opportunity to use my own fascination with the JFK assassination story as a basis for my fictional character's obsession with the same topic.

Thanks to the following for their help:

Nalini Akolekar of Spencerhill Associates, who is the kind of agent every writer dreams of having and did such an amazing job of turning *The Kennedy Connection* from what I thought might be a pretty cool concept for a suspense novel into a reality.

Todd Hunter at Atria Books, whose enthusiasm for Gil Malloy's relentless pursuit of Page One exclusives has made it possible for Gil to come alive in this book, as well as more Gil Malloy books to follow.

Greg Gittrich of *NBC News*; Michael Goodwin and Ed Kosner who ran the New York *Daily News* when I was there; plus Rupert Murdoch and everyone else at the *New York Post* for giving me the opportunity to spend my career working at the best job anyone could ever have—being a journalist in New York City. *The Kennedy Connection* may be fiction, but a lot of the newspaper zaniness in the book is pretty damn authentic. I met a lot of Gil Malloys along the way.

And thank you, most of all, to Laura Morgan. For everything.